THE LAKE HOUSE
AT LENASHEE

SHEILA FORSEY

POOLBEG

Published 2021
by Poolbeg Press Ltd.
123 Grange Hill, Baldoyle,
Dublin 13, Ireland
Email: poolbeg@poolbeg.com

A catalogue record for this book is available from the British Library.

ISBN 978-178199-736-9

www.poolbeg.com

ABOUT THE AUTHOR

Sheila Forsey's childhood was steeped in listening to stories. They were told not from a book but from memory. Stories that gave her a love of words which was the stepping stone into her writing. Ireland's windswept coastline, rugged mountains, valleys and ever-changing sky inspire her writing. A deep interest in Ireland's intricate past has led her to write historical fiction.

She is an honour's graduate from Maynooth in creative writing. She is the recipient of a literature bursary award from Wexford County Council and Artlinks. She facilitates creative writing workshops throughout the country.

She lives with her husband and three children close to the tapestry of the Wexford coast.

ACKNOWLEDGEMENTS

I am indebted to the wonderful Paula Campbell and all her team at Poolbeg Press for bringing my words to publication. A special word of thanks to my incredibly talented editor Gaye Shortland for being so insightful and patient, and for her astounding knowledge of Ireland's history. Thank you, Gaye, for everything.

Thank you to my agent Tracy Brennan across the ocean. I must mention the constant support of a small group of writers who are there to help, guide and have a giggle or even a cry with – I would be so lost without you.

To my family and friends who constantly support me.

Finally, to my husband Shane and my three children Ben, Faye and Matthew. Thank you for all that you do every single day.

Shane, for all that you do

'Oh, *what a tangled web we weave,*
When first we practise to deceive.'
Sir Walter Scott 1808

CHAPTER 1

Paris 2019

It was the balm of the wild orchids that had evoked the memory. A memory of a house that had insisted on coming back – always when she was least expecting it. A house overlooking a silver lake where the events of one night in the summer of 1967 would be replayed like a kaleidoscope in the recesses of her mind for decades – haunting her nights. No amount of sleeping pills or bourbon could ever seem to still it.

Every detail of the lake house was still vivid to her. The gabled lodge at the entrance of the long treelined avenue leading to the house and the shimmering light that shone down the grand staircase through the stained-glass dome. But the strongest memory was of the pewter mist and how it hung like a veil over the house, making it almost dreamlike.

On first sighting the house, she had thought it was like a grand old lady sitting in the shade of the blue mountain behind it. It was more lovely than she had imagined, the image of the sunken lake in the grounds mirrored in the many windows. The façade of the house was of cut sandstone that glittered in the summer sun. Moss-green shutters framed the windows and ivy snaked over a semicircle of blood-red glass over the door. There were many rooms in the lake house but none so elegant as the library with its embellished high ceiling and glass-fronted bookcases filled with books of forgotten stories and forgotten lives. A room filled with the scent of wild orchids that grew abundantly below the library window. Lenashee was a place like no other she had ever encountered.

Strange how she could recall all the details of the house all these years later. One would think with the distance of years that the memory of it would fade like a tattered sepia photograph of long ago, but in ways it had become stronger. So many times she had dreamed of it and awoken to find that it still had the same power over her. But she had managed to hide it. Keep it as an eternal secret. A secret that she had promised to keep.

That night the people in that house had to put their trust in each other and then allow the truth to slip through the cracks of time. Years had passed, and the events of that night had remained as silent as stone. Just as they had promised.

She opened a small wooden jewellery box and took out a brooch of a large spider. She picked it up and opened the pin. Her fingers were aged now, mottled and not as nimble with the onset of mild arthritis, but she still managed to prise the pin open. It was a rose-gold brooch, with a diamond-encrusted body and two red rubies as eyes. She had bought it at a pawn shop on the Rue des Francs-Bourgeois on the day she arrived in Paris fifty-two years before. It had cost her more than she could afford but she was drawn to it. She had bought it as she knew the spider would be a symbol to her of what she had conspired to do before she left Ireland. Her youthful mind had innocently imagined that she would need a symbol to remind her. Her aged mind was more cynical – she had never needed a

2

reminder. A reminder that on that night all those decades ago she had helped to spin a web of truth and untruth as intricate as any spider's web.

Spiders' webs were instilled in her mind from an early age. She often thought of the story of the spider that she had heard as a child from her teacher in that dark schoolroom of long ago that smelled of dust and rancid milk bottles. It was a story from the Bible. But her teacher, Miss Kennedy, had put her own spin on it. In her mind's eye she could still see her, her thin body walking around the classroom asking about compositions and telling of how some famous battle involving Strongbow or Cromwell happened in Druid, or a neighbouring village – Kilkee or Kilrush – centuries before. Ordering them to say prayers on their bended knees to protect their sinful souls against the devil, damnation, purgatory, and the fires of hell. Warning them not to fall from the one true path or they would surely burn for all eternity. Finally reading the day's gospel from her leather-bound missal with its intricate gold edging on each page and a gold ribbon to mark the page.

But Miss Kennedy liked to tell one story most of all. She would take a deep breath and, with her voice poised for dramatic effect, she would tell the story of the Massacre of the Innocents – her version. In her clipped sharp voice she would tell how Joseph and Mary with the Child Jesus were fleeing King Herod. Herod had ordered the execution of all male children under two who lived in Bethlehem. Mary and Joseph were trying to protect the Child Jesus and they hid in a cave. A spider had spun a web over the entrance to the cave to fool Herod and his soldiers into thinking that there was no one in the cave. The soldiers went on by. The web had deceived them. The child was saved.

The brooch that she had bought was a simple reminder

of the web they had spun at Lenashee. She had persuaded herself over the years that, as in the story, they had also spun a web to protect the innocent. But late at night, when sleep evaded her, the enormity of this web was overpowering.

She fixed the brooch now to her cream stole. Her hand lingering on it for a moment, remembering. She then touched her steel-grey hair, once blonde, which was cut into a soft feather-cut that framed her face and glanced into the mirror. Her honey-coloured skin was now lined but her blue eyes were still bright with that hint of hazel flickering in them. Tonight, she – Moira Fitzpatrick born to a labourer in a small town in County Clare in 1945 – was to be the guest of honour at a dinner held at the Embassy of Ireland in Paris, to celebrate her achievements. Her career saw her hailed as a celebrated food writer and teacher living in the heart of Paris, who had championed French cooking and produce for over five decades. She would be celebrated amongst the elite of Parisian society.

But nowadays she preferred the quiet of her apartment in the heart of Paris and her Persian cat George to mixing in society circles. She had company if she wanted. But other than her daily chats with her housekeeper Francoise and her work, life was quiet. Unlike a lot of Parisians who tended to disperse to the countryside for the weekend, Moira liked to stay in her apartment, occasionally venturing out in the early morning for a café au lait and a tartine and a read of *Le Parisien*. She still wrote for various food magazines and was often asked for her opinion nationally on food produce and appeared occasionally on television in France.

Tonight was something that she must do. She would be glad when it was over. For the fortieth anniversary of her first book, *For the Love of French Food*, it was being rereleased and there was a lot of publicity about it. Her publisher was keen that she availed of the publicity that she was being offered. But she was very cagey about it. When the book was first released, she'd had a bad experience when a journalist had begun asking her lots of personal questions about her earlier life in Ireland. She had become very selective after that. But she knew she would have to attend tonight as if she refused it would appear rude. The embassy said it would be a celebration of her Irish and French connection. But privately she had no desire to improve her Irish connections.

Ireland was her birthplace. The place that she was reared in. The place she went to now only in her memory. The place she left with a battered suitcase full of Catholic guilt and a few clothes and her precious cookery books that had been her grandmother's. She had vowed she would never return. She had kept that promise. She was now the last member of her family alive. She had not visited Druid, the small town in Clare where she was born, for over fifty years. Even missing her parents' funerals. She had learned of her brothers' deaths through scrolling through the internet. She had cut all ties when she had stepped on French soil.

When she had arrived in France, she had learned the language. She had embraced everything about France and at times Ireland was but a distant memory. But at other times it was more present. At the most unusual times and when she was least expecting it, she would dream of it and she could almost inhale the scent of the damp bracken that covered the hills and valleys she had grown up in. Or see the yellow of the gorse as it bloomed on every hedgerow and hear the wood pigeons as they called to each other in some secret code. But they were dreams. Dreams buried deep in her soul. But life changed that night in 1967 and she changed too.

She had never married. She often wondered why she was not drawn to marriage. Perhaps it was easier to live with your memories when you lived alone. It would have been much harder if she had a husband to worry about. She'd never had any great desire to have a long-lasting relationship. No, she had lived a life that allowed her to have complete privacy when she wanted it. And the older she got the more she craved it. She would go tonight and when Ireland was mentioned she would sigh wistfully and talk of the beauty of her homeland. Ireland was beautiful so it would not be a lie. She had come from the West of Ireland and it had a raw beauty that was almost mystical. She often thought of that wild beauty that was so present in the Ireland of her childhood. But most often these thoughts turned dark and her demons arrived.

She looked at her image in the mirror. She was afraid that when she grew older she would resemble her mother but thankfully her heart-shaped face was more like her kind father's. How many secrets can one face hide, she wondered? She closed her eyes and pushed the memories away – they always brought her back to that house. It might not even be still standing, she surmised. It might be ghost-like – shimmering there amongst the weeping willows or perhaps it was more like a skeleton with its flesh gone – left like a tomb and fallen into ruin with its secrets and its stories. A sepulchre old and forgotten. Perhaps it was only in her dreams it was full of heavenly light, shimmers of violets, magenta, carmine and rose that filtered through the stained-glass dome down the carved staircase into the grand marbled entrance hall. Only in her dreams was it filled with roses of richest pinks and deepest reds and only in her dreams did the candles flicker in their long golden holders on the dining table that was now forever set for a banquet.

She had built a life, quite an extraordinary one. Far away from the lake house at Lenashee. She reminded herself that Lenashee was only a memory. But, more importantly, a memory that must always remain hidden.

CHAPTER 2

The evening passed as she had expected. She was very much the guest of honour and there were gushing speeches about her career. She had a speech prepared that spoke of the importance of French produce that was sourced locally and how it should be treasured as much as liquid gold. Her voice was light and eloquent. There was no whisper of her Irish brogue. After dinner she was the first to leave. She knew it looked odd, but she really did have a terrible headache and she was very tired. She thanked the ambassador and quietly left with a chaperon from the embassy who took her back to her apartment. She never tired of watching the streets of Paris – it was so far away from what she had come from.

Once back in the quiet of her living room and the company of George who was purring quietly on the velvet couch, she sipped some valerian tea and listened to some Verdi. It had been her ritual for decades. There was a note from Francoise to remind her of her meeting with Rupert Andrews, her English publicist who was over on a flying visit to Paris. She sighed. She loved Rupert dearly, but she did not quite have the energy for his enthusiasm right now.

She knew he would be full of plans. She took herself off to bed, but sleep did not come. She took a drink of water and a sleeping tablet. She closed her eyes, grateful for her chemical-induced sleep.

She woke early and felt quite drowsy from the sleeping pill. She was trying to wean herself off them. She washed and dressed in a cool linen cream trousers and pink twinset. She made a café crème and prepared natural yoghurt with stewed apples and cinnamon and ate it on her veranda, watching her beloved Paris. At ten she went into her office and was sitting at her desk when Francoise arrived in. At seventy-seven she was glad that she could still live alone. She knew that a day might arrive when she would need more help than just Francoise, but she was financially prepared for that. Whatever she needed to do she would do but she intended to stay in her apartment for her lifetime if possible.

Rupert arrived at eleven and he waited for a few minutes in the small opulent living room until Moira was finished on a call. Then she called him into her office which was just off the living room.

Rupert was tall, elegant and mid-thirties with exquisite taste in clothes, food and just about everything. His long slim body was dressed in a dark svelte Givenchy three-piece suit and crisp white shirt. His black mane was sleeked back, and the scent of expensive cologne trailed after him. His blue-black eyes were intense and dancing with excitement.

He held out his arms to Moira and kissed her lightly on both cheeks. 'Moira, my beauty,' he said, his voice light, crisp and very English.

Francoise brought in some freshly brewed coffee on a tray and sat it in front of them. Francoise had worked for

Moira for many years and was well used to Rupert calling.

'Francoise, my darling, how wonderful the aroma of that coffee!' Rupert said in perfect French.

'It's your favourite blend, Monsieur Andrews,' Francoise said, smiling a shy smile.

'Ah, you spoil me, Francoise!' Rupert replied.

He sat down across the desk from Moira, crossing his long slim legs. 'My dear, I was speaking to Javier who works at the embassy and he said you were spectacular last night. And huge news – *For the Love of French Food* is already hitting the number one spot in food and lifestyle books in the US. Quite an achievement! Also number one in Australia, UK, New Zealand, France – and Ireland of course. How exciting is that?'

'Very,' Moira said, trying to summon up some amount of enthusiasm.

'Now before you say no, I think this would be wonderful – there is to be a special evening in Dublin at the President's residence in the Phoenix Park and they want you as guest of honour. Please consider it. I, of course, will escort you. Anything presidential is bound to be luxurious. And you know how I adore luxury.'

'Absolutely not,' Moira said, looking up and slightly frowning.

Rupert uncrossed his legs and sat up.

'Well, maybe give it more than a nanosecond to decide!' he said, his face taking on a pleading look. 'All my other clients would simply die for your invitations and you rarely take up any of them.'

'My decision is made,' Moira replied resolutely.

Rupert looked hard at Moira. 'Please consider it. I have always honoured your request about interviews or anything else in Ireland, but this is the President asking.'

'Rupert, I have given you my answer. Please write and send my deepest apologies. The usual wording. Now what other business needs attending to?'

Rupert poured some coffee and sat back. 'Fine! Message received loud and clear.'

They chatted for a while and planned a small bit of publicity. They had worked together for almost fifteen years and were more than comfortable in each other's company. Rupert had been a constant in her life since he first became her publicist. She had even introduced him to his partner, André.

Francoise knocked on the door to see if Rupert was staying for lunch.

'Dear Francoise, how lovely of you to ask! Thank you, but I have to dash – I have a luncheon arranged with a new client.'

Then he got up to go. He kissed Moira on both cheeks.

'I will leave you, my lovely. Goodness, I almost forgot. I have something for you.' He took a letter from his inner jacket pocket. 'I kept it separate from the normal correspondence as it's marked private and personal,' he remarked, raising an eyebrow.

'Oh?'

'An Irish postmark! I picked it up at the office in London. Probably a fan letter but as it was marked private I brought it.' Rupert handed her the letter. 'I'm taking you to lunch tomorrow before I fly back. No excuse. We need to celebrate how superb your sales are.'

'Oh, I don't know, Rupert. I'm not really up to going out.'

'I'll take you to your favourite – L'Espadon. You know how much of a fuss they make at the Ritz when you dine there and of course as your companion they will make a fuss of me too – you cannot deprive me of that!' He smiled that perfect smile that Moira knew had allowed him to break many hearts. 'Anyway, the reservation is made. I am sure they will think it rude if I cancel.' He raised one groomed eyebrow into a perfect arch.

'Fine,' Moira replied, holding the letter.

'Splendid.' Rupert kissed her on the cheeks again. 'I'll be here at noon to collect you. We can have an aperitif first.'

'Very well, see you tomorrow,' Moira sighed.

She put the letter on the table and walked Rupert out.

Then slowly she walked back into her office and closed the door. She picked up the letter. She opened a drawer and took out a silver letter-opener and slid it through. It was a typed letter. She put on her glasses which hung on a gold chain around her neck.

Dear Miss Fitzpatrick,

As I don't have your address or private email, I am sending this to your publisher. My name is Kate Wilson. I am a history student in Trinity College in Dublin, Ireland, and I am writing my thesis on historical cases about women who took their own lives in Ireland in the last century. One of the women I am researching is Rosemary Purcell. She took her own life and drowned off Howth Pier in 1967. Well, it was assumed she did anyway, but her body was never recovered. Her clothes were found on the pier. I have not managed to find out very much about her. She was a model for a short time and worked for Brown Thomas Department Store in Dublin City. I tracked down a letter that she sent to a convent in Devon. There was a nun there who, it seems, was a sister to her – although this only came to light recently. Rosemary had written the letter the week before her clothes were found on the pier. In the letter she said that she was staying at a beautiful house on a lake in the West of Ireland and that the food was glorious and cooked every night by a young girl called Moira Fitzpatrick.

In the letter she sounds excited about life, so it seems strange that she took her life shortly afterwards. I am afraid the letter was never received by her sister. It arrived but it was put in a drawer and only found when the building was being put up for sale about two years ago. The nun died eighteen years ago but the remaining nuns were unaware that she had a sister. I have contacted the gardaí, but all that the file on Rosemary Purcell says is that she was presumed drowned.

I recently bought your book. I am a huge fan. It states in it that you first fell in love with food during your early years in County Clare when you worked as a cook. I hope you don't mind me asking but I just wondered if the cook Rosemary referred to in her letter could possibly have been you and perhaps you might remember her?

If this was you, I would really appreciate a call or an email. My contact details are at the end of this letter.

Many thanks and congratulations on your incredible success.

Yours sincerely

Kate Wilson

Moira walked into the living room and took a crystal ashtray and a gold cigarette lighter from a drawer. She lit the edge of the letter with the lighter and watched it as it began to burn. She threw it into the ashtray. She never took her eyes off it as it curled into itself. Then she allowed herself to breathe. She closed her eyes on the memories as the letter burnt to ashes.

CHAPTER 3

Dublin 1967

Rosemary Purcell perused the glove department of Brown Thomas, tidying away anything that looked even minutely out of place. She then picked up a small handheld gilded mirror and cleaned it until it shone. Before she put it down, she checked that her dark hair was in place. It was slightly backcombed into a rounded bouffant with a fringe that reached her arched eyebrows. Her perfectly applied lashes had not moved since she applied them earlier that morning. She discreetly took her foot out of her kitten-heeled shoe to rest it for a second. She had not had a break all morning. A new delivery of Mary Quant pastel shift dresses had arrived in and needed to be displayed. A bag with a Niellí Mulcahy wool dress that a customer had just bought in the designer's shop had gone missing in the store as she was trying on shoes. She had caused an uproar, saying that the dress was stolen, until Rosemary found it beside the gloves where the customer had left it down earlier. Another shopper had arrived in looking to add many items to her summer wardrobe and demanded that she was served by Rosemary. Everyone seemed to be looking for her for one thing or another.

Rosemary had an innate gift for finding just the right accessory to go with any outfit, just the right shade of rouge for any complexion, just the right heel to complement any outfit and the perfect coat for that awkward customer. In her five years on the sales floor of Brown Thomas she had become known as the stylist to the elite. Many of the stores high-profile customers demanded that they were always looked after by Rosemary Purcell.

She tidied some full-length cream leather gloves that she had shown to her last customer and was just about to take a much-needed tea break when she spotted Mrs Ida Williams waving at her. Ida Williams was possibly Brown Thomas's most important customer. She came from a wealthy political dynasty in leafy Donnybrook, the Griffith family, and not only spent a huge amount in the store but was a great advocate of Irish designers and Brown Thomas. Rosemary had helped her pick her wedding gown for her much-publicized wedding to the well-known businessman Harry Williams. A very grand affair that had all the heads of state there including the Catholic Primate of Ireland and Archbishop of Dublin John Charles McQuaid. Ida was a socialite of great importance in Dublin society and spent much of her time raising money for various charities through fashion shows and charity balls. Since Rosemary had joined Brown Thomas, Ida relied heavily on Rosemary's opinion about fashion. Ida often rushed in just to ask Rosemary what type of shoes would best complement her outfit. Or purchase the perfect pair of gloves for the races or just casually drop in to pick up a silk scarf on her way to her permanent table reserved in the Lafayette Room in the Hibernian Hotel. Rosemary was always on trend with her advice and, since she had begun advising Ida, the result was that Ida was frequently photographed as the most stylish person in Ireland and was even known for her fashion sense as far away as New York. No one knew that her secret was that Rosemary had such a keen eye for elegance. But over the past few years they had formed a strong bond. Rosemary was as polished as any socialite and spent her money wisely to always look her best. Although Ida was known for being very selective about choosing her social circle, they had found common ground in their love of style.

Ida was instrumental in getting Rosemary involved in modelling. When a model had become ill at a charity fashion show Ida had called on Rosemary to step in. Rosemary had at first refused but eventually relented. Afterwards Sybil Connolly, the Irish designer, had requested her for another show. The money was not enough to allow her to give up her job just yet. But she could see modelling as a gateway to something else. Or even somewhere else. Rosemary was good at recreating herself. She had already done it once. No one would have guessed that the years prior to Rosemary working in sales was far from the polished floors of Brown Thomas.

She smiled in greeting as Ida approached. Ida was tall and fair with high cheekbones. Her green eyes were framed by fashionably thick false lashes and, although her nose was slightly out of synch with the rest of her face, Rosemary thought it gave her a regal quality. Ida walked with her head held high and a waft of expensive perfume about her. She was dressed in a duck-egg linen dress-coat with a cream pillbox hat and cream gloves. An outfit that Rosemary had handpicked for her.

'Rosemary, you were such a hit at the fashion show. I knew you would be. Did you know there is talk of a New York fashion show? I will talk to Sybil and make sure you are on the list of models to go.'

'Would you? Really? I would love to see New York, Ida.'

Ida was known to most as Mrs Williams, or before she married as Miss Griffith, but she had insisted that Rosemary call her by her first name.

'I'm in urgent need of some costume jewellery for my gold-silk evening gown. I am hosting that charity dinner dance tonight that I was telling you about. It will be rather dull, so I need something to lift the air. I need your advice. I feel like something new. I'll wear my elbow-length gold-silk gloves.

'*Hmm*. I am not sure about costume jewellery with that. You mean the Ib Jorgensen gown?'

'Yes.'

'Let's see.' Rosemary walked over to a different counter of jewellery and examined some pieces. The she took out a pair of small diamante earrings from a glass case. The earrings glinted in the light with a gold hue.

'I think these small diamante earrings will be enough. More understated is better. They will also go with your pale-blue Sybil Connolly costume. It has a hint of gold and the earrings would really pick up on it.'

'They are pretty. Not unlike earrings I saw on Jackie Kennedy.'

'That reminds me – you looked so graceful in the photographs at the Castle.'

The whole country had been on alert as the wife of the former American President, Mrs Jackie Kennedy, came to holiday in Ireland with her two children. Part of her stay involved a day at the Curragh and a banquet at Dublin Castle. Of course, Ida and Harry were in attendance. There was a photograph on the front page of the *Irish Press* of Ida and Jackie Kennedy in conversation at Dublin Castle and the caption was: **Mrs Jackie Kennedy was sure to have lots to talk about with Mrs Ida Williams as they are both great ladies of style!**

'Rosemary, you were so right about that hat for the races – it was simply perfect. I was surprised Mrs Kennedy didn't wear a hat. But of course, she looked stunning. That rich hair of hers.'

'Tell me, is she as elegant as she looks?'

'Even more so. It's not just her clothes. Her voice is so light – almost like a whisper.'

'I adored the chiffon gown that she wore with the fur stole at the banquet. I'm not sure the camera did it enough justice?'

'It was the most perfect shade of green and the stole I believe was ermine. I loved her knee-length coat she wore to the races.'

'Yes, I think that's one of her favourite designers – Oleg Cassini.'

'You should be writing a fashion column, Rosemary. Ernestine Carter, the fashion writer for the *Sunday Times*, was at an event that I attended in New York. You could start writing a fashion column here, Rosemary! Now back to why I am here – oh yes, before I forget, I have a shoot next week with *Young Woman Magazine*. It will showcase a couple of items from Sybil's range. My picture will be on the cover and inside an article titled *Mrs Ida Williams Shows Us Lenashee Lake House*.

'I'm not familiar with that name. Lenashee – is it in Dublin?'

'I wish it were. I'm afraid it's in the wilds of County Clare of all places. Sybil is in America, but she is sending someone down to do the styling. Harry bought a dusty old country house down there. I've visited it only once since he bought it and, believe me, that was enough. Full of creaky doors and not a shop in sight. A small town more like a village on a hill is the nearest shopping experience. I'm not exactly a country kind of woman. But Harry has practically begged me to go down for one last visit before his renovations begin. He plans to turn the house into a guesthouse for people who love to shoot and hunt, so the advertising already begins, hence my photo shoot. It will specialise in catering for equestrian holidays. It should do well with the British and the Americans. It's not that large, more a country house than hotel really. It was belonging to a Lord and Lady Harris and was used as a summer residence. Harry has promised me that the plumbing and electricity is working. I suppose it is pretty if you like that sort of thing. It's quite a grand old lake house but much too old-fashioned for my taste! Harry loves the fishing there.'

'I had not put you down as a fishing type of person.'

'Heavens, no! A lavender bath is quite enough water for me unless it is the French Riviera. No, my brother Desmond loves the fishing too and he is coming down with his wife and daughter. His wife is … under the weather, shall we say? A break in the country air will, according to her doctors, do her good! I'd better be off. I still have some arrangements to make for this charity do tonight. My goodness, Rosemary, I have just had a thought! One of the judges for the best-dressed lady at tonight's event has taken ill. You could take her place. You know more about fashion than anyone else I know. Would you, please? There will be dancing and cocktails and there is a terrific band. It should be good fun.'

'Really? I'm not sure.'

'Why not? Please say yes. I can't wait to introduce you to some of my friends. Please come.'

'I don't have an escort.'

'It is in the Shelbourne at eight o clock. No need to be worried about being on your own – just ask at reception for me and I will come personally to escort you into the ballroom. The cream of Irish society will be there. You never know whom you could meet, perhaps even someone to sweep you off your feet!'

CHAPTER 4

Rosemary was not someone who attended dances. She kept herself very much to herself and, other than getting the train out to Bray on her day off, she rarely left her flat other than to do chores and for work. She loved to read and had found some books in a second-hand bookshop on Bachelor's Walk. She was looking forward to relaxing for a little and reading before she headed out so, with time owed to her, she decided to take a couple of hours off and leave work early.

Ida had offered to send a car around to pick her up later, but she had declined the offer. She preferred to keep things like where she lived private. There were very few people who knew anything about Rosemary, except for her sister Ellen who knew everything about her. Her life outside of work was private and she intended on keeping it that way. She was renting the flat now for over five years. It was a fresh start. A place to forget her past.

She unlocked the door and immediately took off her shoes and grabbed the post. She had purchased a bunch of lilac from a flower-seller on Grafton Street and, as she organised a vase, the sweet, heady perfume permeated the air. The flat consisted of a bedroom, a kitchen which also worked as a sitting room and a small washroom. The kitchen was cosy with light-brown linoleum dotted with pink roses, a sink, a cooker and a dresser that she had painted jade and filled with fine pale-pink china cups, saucers, and plates. In the sitting area on a small brown couch were pale-mustard velvet cushions, a lamp, and a brown rug on the floor.

She put the kettle on the gas ring for a pot of tea. She took out a cup and saucer from the dresser and cut a slice of soda bread and spread it with some butter. She wanted to sit down and savour the contents of the letter – she knew it was from Ellen. Ellen was due to take her final vows in a few months. Rosemary had not seen her in almost five years. They had felt it was better that way. At first Rosemary had hardly known how she would cope when Ellen said she was joining a convent, but she knew for Ellen's sanity she had to cope – this was how she had chosen to live her life. Rosemary had no such deep faith as her sister. In fact, she was not sure if she had any. But she was glad for Ellen that she had. They wrote often and each letter was like a treasure to Rosemary. Ellen was the only link to their past. Not that they ever talked about it. It was like a golden rule yet an unvoiced one. If they were ever to move on it was the only way. This letter was all about her sister's upcoming final vows. Rosemary planned to go to Devon to be there. As she read through the letter, she could see that there was no faltering in her sister's faith. She would now be Sister Luke. She folded the letter and put it away in a pink hatbox with all the other precious letters from Ellen.

She tidied up and read a chapter of her book and then she began to prepare for the evening ahead. She had a bath and then began styling her hair in a half-up bouffant that she had seen in a new fashion magazine. She put on a dove-grey chiffon dress with a row of mother of pearl around the sweetheart neckline. She had bought it in the sales at Brown Thomas. She had fallen for the dress and had discreetly made sure that it was hidden so that it was still there when the sales arrived. With seventy-five per cent off it was still expensive but she knew it was worth every penny. She carefully put on her silk stockings so as not to rip them and put a cream stole over her shoulders. She had paid off every week for a year for the fur stole at Barnardo's fur shop. She took her time with her make-up and applied some fresh lashes and a rich brown lipstick. After slipping into elegant slingbacks and grabbing her gloves, she sprayed some perfume and then went out to get a hackney car.

The Shelbourne Hotel was where many of the high society of Dublin gathered and had played host to princesses, presidents and film stars as well as the cream of political society. With its Victorian décor it was the epitome of glamour and sophistication with chandeliers, ornate tapestries, and crystal candle-holders.

A footman helped her out of the car and she walked in. Lots of glamorous couples were arriving and she felt self-conscious as she was on her own. However, she was only in the door when she saw Ida, standing with a group of very well-dressed ladies and gentlemen, holding court in the middle of the grand reception. Ida looked the part of the perfect hostess. She had the gold-silk gown on, and her fair hair was in the perfect beehive, her make-up perfection. She had a cocktail in one hand and a cigarette in a gold cigarette holder in the other. She smiled at Rosemary and beckoned her over with the hand holding the cocktail.

'Do meet this charming lady who has the best advice in style that I have ever met. She is also a model and I think she is just delightful,' Ida said to the group.

Rosemary held her head high and smiled in acknowledgement to them as they introduced themselves to her.

After Rosemary had checked her fur stole into the cloakroom, Ida ushered them all into the ballroom.

The music was playing, and a crooner was singing 'Moon River'. The drinks were flowing and ladies in chiffon and taffeta in candy colours passed by, laughing and chatting, grabbing glasses and lighting cigarettes. The ballroom was literally glittering.

A tall handsome man, dressed impeccably in a dark suit, walked towards them.

'This is my brother, Mr Desmond Griffith.' Ida said. 'I must run and check on something urgently. Desmond, would you be a dear and look after Miss Purcell?' And then she flitted away.

Desmond Griffith smiled and held his hand out to Rosemary.

'Lovely to meet you, Miss Purcell,' he said.

He had the same fine bone structure as his sister and his hair was just as fair. It was sleeked back without a hair out of place. His hands and face were tanned – not from an Irish sun, Rosemary surmised. His voice was elegant and polished. He grabbed two cocktails from a waiter and handed one to Rosemary. She sipped it. It was sweet and cool.

A large woman arrived up and almost knocked the glass from Rosemary's hand. Her face was puce and her bright-lemon dress under a little pressure at the seams. She seemed to be in a huge hurry to talk to Desmond.

'Desmond, how is dear Florence?'

'Mrs Sutton, how lovely to see you,' Desmond replied.

Rosemary sensed his discomfort. She recognised Mrs Sutton. She was one of the most frustrating women to ever shop during Rosemary's time in Brown Thomas. She had made several of the staff cry and had managed to get one of them sacked when she had burst through a dress, ripping the seams, and then blamed the shop girl for giving her the incorrect size.

'I believe you were travelling as usual since I last saw you – and congratulations on the birth of your new son. My goodness, it has been so long since I saw you or Florence.'

'Yes, it must be a few months now,' Desmond said rather cagily.

'How is she? Florence? I believe she is not here. I do hope she is feeling better, I believe she has been quite unwell. Not pneumonia, I hope. I know someone who had that recently and died.'

'No. Thankfully nothing like that,' Desmond said lightly.

'You should bring her to visit us for lunch when she is better. I will call and make the arrangement. I really do miss her at our gardening group. She has quite the green fingers and your daughter is such a joy. They are so alike. I am hosting a dinner for the gardening group – perhaps I will drop in and see if she would like to come? It's next Thursday. You would be most welcome too – I would love to show you my begonias.' Her eyes were almost popping out of her head with enthusiasm.

Desmond drained the last of his cocktail before answering. 'I think she needs a little more time before visitors, but she will be delighted that you thought of her. As soon as she is up and about, she will be in touch, I'm sure.'

'What exactly ... is the matter with her? Not catching, I hope?' Mrs Sutton asked, backing away a little from Desmond, much to Rosemary's amusement.

'No. Nothing contagious. Just a little run-down after the birth of Joseph.'

'But that must be what … three months ago now? Surely she has recovered?' Mrs Sutton was not going to be put off.

'Yes, indeed, she is getting better and stronger every day.'

Rosemary could hear the irritation building in Desmond's voice.

'It was a … traumatic birth and took a lot out of her. But she is gaining strength every day. Allow me to introduce Miss Rosemary Purcell, one of Ida's friends.'

'Miss Purcell, I recognise you from somewhere,' Mrs Sutton said, squinting her small beady eyes. 'I don't have my glasses on. But I think I do know you. Are you related to the Purcells in Howth – they're in the boating club with my boys?'

'No. Lovely to meet you,' Rosemary said, trying to hide a smile.

'*Hmm*, I seem to know you from somewhere, perhaps the Lafayette Room – do you dine there a lot?'

'Very often, yes, it's probably there,' Rosemary said, lifting an eyebrow. She had been only once to the Lafayette Room, but she was not going to tell Mrs Sutton that.

'That must be it. It's almost a second home to most of us. Very well, I need to check that they have my requirements for dinner later. I have a very delicate constitution, I'm afraid. I hope Ida remembers me when she is judging the best-dressed lady tonight, Desmond. My outfit took quite a bit of effort.' She smoothed down her bright costume and looked right up into his face.

'I'm sure she will, you look delightful.'

'Thank you. Goodbye, Miss Purcell, see you in the

26

Lafayette again soon.' She walked off, beaming at Desmond's compliment.

'I think I need a fresh drink after that.' Desmond grinned as he grabbed two cocktails from a passing waiter's tray. He lit another cigarette and offered one to Rosemary. She took it.

'So, Rosemary, how do you know my sister?'

'I work in Brown Thomas.'

'Enough said. I can imagine that you see lots of Ida,' he said with a grin.

'Your sister is a very valued customer and I've come to know her very well,' Rosemary replied, smiling.

'Your accent – you're not from Dublin?'

'No. We moved around Ireland a bit when I was growing up,' Rosemary replied noncommittally.

They chatted casually for a few moments and he told her about his daughter Julia and his baby son Joseph.

'I'm sorry to hear your wife is unwell.'

'Oh, she's recuperating in hospital, but I'm picking her up on Saturday and the doctor in charge of her believes that she'll be fine with some rest and a little break out of the city.'

'I'm glad.'

'It's been a difficult few months.'

Then Ida returned.

'Isn't she a darling, Desmond? Rosemary, I want to introduce you to some others, and we can begin deciding who should win the best-dressed lady.' Ida linked Rosemary's arm. 'We have a much better picking than I had anticipated.'

'Mrs Sutton is expecting to be at least in the running,' Desmond warned her.

'Oh dear! Quickly, Rosemary, before she sees me and

asks me about it. You must meet my husband Harry. I am forever talking about you to him and telling him about all the help that you give me.'

Rosemary had seen pictures of him, but she had never seen him in person.

Harry Williams was standing beside the bar with a group of men and women who seemed to be holding on to every word that he was saying. Rosemary was struck by his strong Dublin accent and his intensely brown eyes that seemed to almost dance as he was talking. He was telling a story and when he finished everyone burst out laughing. He looked up and Rosemary was caught unawares as his eyes seemed to drink her in.

'Here's my lovely wife and whom have we got here?' he said, looking directly at Rosemary.

'Allow me to introduce Miss Rosemary Purcell,' Ida said rather grandly.

Rosemary could feel Harry Williams's eyes bore into her. It felt so intense that she wanted to look away. His eyes crinkled at the edges and he smiled a crooked kind of smile, pushing his hand through his thick wavy brown hair.

'Miss Purcell. Well, how do you do?' he said, holding his hand out.

'Pleased to meet you, Mr Williams.' Rosemary could feel all eyes on her.

'Oh, call me Harry – I insist,' he said, smiling.

'There's Mrs Collins. I have to chat to her for a minute. Harry, will you look after Miss Purcell for a moment?' Ida instructed.

'Be a pleasure,' Harry replied as he grabbed two fresh drinks and handed one to Rosemary. He moved so he was closer to her.

She could feel his arm touching hers and she held her

breath. She couldn't describe it, but it was like he had some sort of magnetism about him. She had read about him. Harry Williams was an affluent businessman. He had gone from being a child of the Liberties to one of the most influential businessmen in Ireland. He was often photographed with politicians. It didn't harm his career to have married into political royalty. When he married Ida Griffith, he had married into one of the most politically influential families in the Republic of Ireland. Rosemary had also read that he was good friends with the Archbishop – John Charles McQuaid. The Archbishop had huge influence in society. Harry was also involved in charities and Ida was constantly in with Rosemary picking out outfits for charity fundraisers that she was organising and were often linked to charities that Harry was a founding member of. But listening to him hold court with these people Rosemary thought the articles had not captured his charisma. She knew she had never met anyone quite like Harry Williams.

'So, Miss Purcell, I believe my wife thinks very highly of you.'

'I think very highly of her too,' she replied.

They chatted casually for a little while and when a waiter was passing by Harry took her near-empty cocktail glass from her and grabbed two more. She could feel the alcohol going to her head. For a moment their hands touched as he was gesturing, telling her a story. It was only a second, but the feeling lingered. Rosemary had no interest in getting involved with anyone, certainly not a married man but she had not anticipated the effect that a man such as Harry Williams could have on her.

The rest of the night passed quickly as Ida introduced her to some of her social circle, including the guest of honour Mrs Lynch – wife of the Taoiseach. There was music and dancing and lots of glamour. The band had the dancefloor full all night. Rosemary read the name of the band on the big drum on the stage: *Earl Gill and The Hoedowners*. She had danced with Harry and felt herself melt into his arms. She danced with others too, but she could not get the feeling she had when she had danced with Harry out of her mind.

Then they picked the best-dressed lady who had worn a taffeta dress in a peacock blue and Mrs Lynch presented the prize. Mrs Sutton did not look happy as the prize-winner walked up to collect her prize of a rich brown fur stole.

All too soon the evening was over, and people were saying their goodbyes.

Ida caught Rosemary's hands. 'Thank you for being here tonight – it was so much fun having you.'

'I had a great time. Thank you for inviting me.'

'I'll have to chat with you about my photo shoot down in Clare. Oh, I wish I didn't have to go. Desmond says that I can't even entertain because his wife is not well enough. I'm just not at all looking forward to it and it's such a long drive. I'd much rather stay in the city for the week. One day of birds and fishing and I am done.' Ida laughed and then paused. 'Oh, my goodness, Rosemary – would you come down with me and help me with the shoot? You could advise me. We could talk fashion and drink gin. My brother's wife and her little girl will be there but, as his wife is very much convalescing, I will have no one to talk to except Vonnie my housekeeper who is coming down to look after the house while we are there. I fear I will be very bored. If I could entertain any of our friends it would be something, but you could come down to keep me company. Please say you will come! There is meant to be a stylist coming down, but I prefer to pick my own clothes. With your help it would be wonderful. I'd make sure you'd be handsomely paid for it. You've given me so much advice it's about time you were paid properly for helping me with all my fashion queries.'

'Well, I'm not sure,' Rosemary replied. There were tons of reasons that came into her mind as to why she shouldn't go.

'Please, Rosemary!'

'Well …' Rosemary knew there and then that she should say no. She had made a point of not getting too friendly with anyone. That was one reason. But Harry Williams would be there and what she had felt dancing with him was dangerous. He was a married man, and she knew she had no right to feel like that. But then she saw Harry Williams looking over at them. Something had passed between them and she knew by the way that he was looking at her that she had not imagined it. Her mind was racing. She certainly would not get involved with a married man. Her work for now was enough and soon she might move to London. She would have gone to New York only for Ellen. Even if she had not seen her in five years, it was good to know that she was not too far away. But men had not featured in her plans. But something was different about Harry Williams. Something that she knew she should stay away from. Ida was still waiting for a response.

'I … really don't think so.'

'Please! I would so love you to come.'

'Well … I suppose I could see if I can arrange to get cover so I can get the time away from work.'

'Tell them that I want you to come to the country to help style the shoot and I will be wearing clothes mostly from Brown Thomas. Free advertising for them! That should get you off and paid for it,' Ida said, smiling and clapping her hands in delight.

'Alright,' Rosemary said, smiling.

'Great! We go Saturday. The shoot is on Wednesday. I'll bring lots of fashion magazines. I'm actually looking forward to it now.'

Harry walked up and put his arm around his wife.

'Harry, I've just asked Rosemary to come down to Clare with me. I know you'll be gone fishing and I'll just be bored. Rosemary will keep me company.'

'That's a great idea. Yes, we plan lots of fishing. I hope you like salmon and trout, Miss Purcell.'

'Yes, I do.'

'Julia is my brother's little girl, and she'll love the company,' Ida said. 'Florence, his wife, will possibly just sit by the lake. She loves to read books about gardening. Gardening bores me. I adore roses but I've no interest in learning how to grow them. I promised Desmond to help keep an eye on her and Julia over the week.'

Somehow the idea of Ida looking after a child or someone convalescing seemed odd to Rosemary.

'I'll see you in Clare then, Miss Purcell,' Harry said.

'Actually, could you come over to the house tomorrow, Rosemary,' Ida said. 'You can help me choose what to take down and ask the store if there is anything specifically that they would like me to showcase. I'm designing a room for my clothes too and I would love your thoughts on the design. Now I must rush and say goodbye to Mrs Sutton – she is not too pleased that she got no mention for the best-dressed lady and from her fashion sense which is quite deplorable I'm afraid she never will. I do have a reputation to keep! But I need to assure her that she was close – she donates hugely to almost all the charities that I'm involved in. I will get our driver to drop you home, Rosemary.'

'No. I can get a hackney car.'

'Nonsense. Harry, will you escort Rosemary to the car, please? Our driver will take you wherever you need to go. I need to talk to the charity organisers before we go – they bore me but they do have a good cause. Goodbye, Rosemary, Harry will see you out.'

'Oh, I don't want to put you to any trouble,' Rosemary said to Harry as Ida walked off.

'Not at all, Miss Purcell.'

They went to retrieve her stole from the assistant in the cloakroom.

'Allow me.' Harry took the stole and placed it around her pale shoulders, his hand lingering on her neck for just a second.

She could feel the heat of his hand.

He offered her his arm and she slid hers through it. As they walked out to the car, she could feel the closeness of him.

At the car he took her hand. 'We'll meet again soon. I look forward to it – immensely,' he whispered.

'Thank you for walking me out,' she said, holding his stare.

He still held her hand and she knew she should take it away. But she couldn't. Again, it was only a moment or two, but she felt a physical loss when he let it go.

She sat into the car and looked up at him. He held her gaze. She wanted to look away. She had to remind herself again that he was a married man and Ida was her friend and patroness. But as he turned around, she knew that she would count the days until she saw Harry Williams again.

CHAPTER 5

Africa 2019

Julia awoke and listened intently to the sounds of the African morning. Through her hotel window she watched the shimmering blue waters of the Nile and the sounds of Baher Dar, the capital city of the Amhara region in Northern Ethiopia. She was here for another two days to soak up the ancient monasteries, the music, and the very sense of the place. She had first visited with her father when she was only sixteen but had returned on many occasions. But it was that first visit that was the most precious, forming a tapestry of images, sights and sounds that would leave her with such a passion for travel.

She was looking at a well-worn photo of her mother. It was taken when her late mother was pregnant with her. She kept it in a leather wallet that was worn now and frayed. It had travelled the world with her. Her mother was looking away from the camera and she was smiling, a large sun hat over her tumbling long red curls. One eye was slightly closed as if the sun was in her face, her skin pale with a scattering of freckles. The image of her mother was always there to look at. She liked to think that her mother had looked over her all these years. It was strange now to be twice the age her mother was when she had died. She had been only three and half years old then. She had tried hard to recall her but somehow the memory was lost except sometimes a certain song or a certain scent reminded her of her. Even the scent of rain reminded her of her – she had no idea why. She could not recall her voice or how she acted or how she laughed. But still these things stirred a memory that she could not really identify, just a feeling that she associated with her mother which had given her comfort over the years.

Her father, her brother and she were a tight unit. Her father had passed his passion for travelling on to her – the new sights of a new country to explore – the intoxicating aromas of India, the rain forests of Malaysia, the ancient temples of Cambodia and Sudan.

How he would marvel at the sights she had visited over the last few days. Lake Tana where the ancient Egyptians had arrived to help discover the source of the great waters that covered their land. She had witnessed where the Blue Nile met with the White Nile. Yes, he would have breathed in the sounds, sights and aromas of this enchanting place.

But now he would no longer be entranced by such things. She had all but lost her beloved father to the ravages of terminal illness. Her kind loving father now lived in a world that seemed as foreign to him as it was to her, his beautiful mind at times regressing into the past.

It was three years since her father had been diagnosed with cancer. His illness was now in the later stages. Early dementia had also decided to join the battle. It was agonising to watch as she and her brother saw the father as they knew him begin to slip away. Joseph had dedicated his life full-time to the care of their father.

She was thankful that her husband David did not expect

her to ring home when she was away working. She liked to immerse herself totally in the place that she was writing about. But she did keep in some contact with Joseph who now lived permanently in her father's house in Howth in Dublin. Nurses and carers looked after his physical needs. But his care was now so demanding that Joseph rarely left the house.

Julia looked at the photo again and then put it back in the leather wallet. She had the same looks as her mother, though her red hair was beginning to grey now and she had no intention of dying it. She quite liked it and had decided to embrace it.

She had a quick wash and changed into a long white linen shirt and loose linen trousers.

She had not checked her email with all the travelling. She checked in now reluctantly. There were a couple from her editor with some feedback on a new travel book that she planned to write.

She scanned through and saw an email from Joseph.

My dear Julia,
I know you're travelling but I know you'll read this when you get a chance, he wrote. **He has faded even more, I'm afraid. But where he was at times content, now he seems to be upset all the time. The doctor was here and believes that the dementia has really progressed. The reason I'm contacting you is he has begun to constantly talk about someone called Rosemary, asking if we can find her. But that's all he says. Perhaps it's some long-lost love from when he was young. It's heart-breaking to see him like this. Perhaps this Rosemary never even existed but I wish I could put his mind at ease and tell him that I'd found her. I wonder if you've ever heard him talk of anyone of**

that name or can shed any light on it?

Take care of yourself,

Joseph x

Rosemary! She had never heard her father mention that name. Certainly, no-one close to him of that name. His poor mind was deteriorating so much. A mind that had made him one of the most interesting men to talk to that she had ever known. But she knew that Joseph was obviously concerned about him for him to email her about it. No, she had no idea what it was about. Her mother was the love of her father's life. He was a very handsome man. She was sure he'd had relationships before he met her mother but there was never any talk of affairs or anything. After she died, he did have a few relationships but never with a woman called Rosemary. Perhaps it was just the disease or the medication playing tricks on his poor mind. She replied, saying this and expressing her concern and promising that she would see them soon.

She adored her father, but she was perhaps not as selfless as Joseph. Life outside her father's care had ceased for now for her brother. Joseph barely left the house except to walk the dogs.

But it sounded like her father was getting much frailer. She would go straight to the house when she returned to Ireland. She only had another day and then she would return.

She set about her day, taking her camera, notebook and a Dictaphone. She liked to record what she saw and try to write about it when she got back to where she was staying. Today she would visit a monastery on one of the nearby islands. Half of the area was Christian and there were ancient monasteries dotted all over the islands surrounding Lake Tana. Most forbade women to visit but one had allowed her. She grabbed some coffee, some yogurt and fruit and took her lithium. She took great care of her health. Being bipolar she was extra careful. But she had been well now for a long time. In the past she had suffered many episodes that had almost destroyed her. But now with regular psychotherapy, medication, and a healthy lifestyle she lived as normal a life as possible. But the fear that it could raise its head was always there. With a scarf for her head for the monastery visit and her backpack, she was off to meet a guide that she had hired.

That night the heat was sweltering. Sleep evaded her. She got back up and took out a book she was reading about ancient Africa, but her mind was too distracted.

It was the email earlier that had unsettled her. Somewhere in the recesses of her mind she had heard the name Rosemary before. Perhaps it was the heat, but it was as if an image of a woman was invading her mind. She had never known anyone of that name and yet there was something strangely familiar about it. But no, it must be the heat and the exhaustion. Yet it was as if there was a memory unearthed. She tried to think back. Had she ever heard her father talk of someone called Rosemary? Like a feather floating and disappearing a flash of a memory jolted her, a woman with shining dark eyes and long lashes flickering. She tried to hold on to the image but then like a bird it was gone. Gone like a whisper. But it had left an unsettling feeling in its wake.

CHAPTER 6

A few days later in Dublin the blast of cool air hit her. She had flown to London from Africa and had a meeting with her editor. Then after trying to recover from the jet lag at a London hotel she flew into Dublin, picked up her car and drove to Howth. Although home was now the cottage she shared with her husband in Wexford, her childhood place still had a huge sense of home for her.

After putting the code into the iron gates, she drove up the avenue where chestnut trees and ash trees were fully leaved. The summer was stretching out in front of them. The house was set in a large mature garden with sweeping views of Ireland's Eye, Howth Harbour, and the north county coastline. The two large wolfhounds, Tom and Jerry, sat sleepily in the sunny doorway and nuzzled her in greeting as she went to the door. It had once been an old rectory and her father had bought it in the early seventies to rear his children.

Joseph opened the door just as she was about to try the handle and grabbed her in a big bear hug.

On her last visit, before she had left for Africa, Joseph had some colour to his face but now it looked almost grey.

A wave of guilt engulfed her. Their father's illness was having a huge effect on her brother. Joseph was tall and slimly built and she could see he had lost some weight. His dark hair was now a blue-grey. His eyes, though, were still the piercing blue that they always had been.

'Come in, coffee is just brewing. You're looking good.'

'Thanks.'

'How was Africa?'

'Africa was … what can I say? Each time I go there I leave knowing there is so much I still need to know about it and so much that I need to discover.'

'That's what makes you such a good travel writer. Your piece in *The Times* about Sudan was excellent. Come on, we can have our coffee in the conservatory. Maggie cooked some muffins especially for you.'

'How is Maggie? I did send some flowers for her daughter's wedding.'

'She's as bossy as always and working far too hard. I tried to tell her, but you know what she's like. So stubborn and believes that anyone else will not be able to do what she does. I have two new carers looking after Dad. They're great. Of course, Maggie believes they are appalling and should be fired. She's so fond of Dad. She's a bit heartbroken really.

'How is he?' She noticed how Joseph looked away from her out towards the window before answering.

'I think we've lost him. It's a fucker. At first he was a little more content, now it seems like he is really suffering.'

'In what way?

'He's not in any pain. But he's fading away before our eyes. The cancer is bad enough but with the dementia now taking hold its chronic to be honest. He's unaware of what is happening then out of the blue he talks about things in

40

the past as if they were the present. Then this whole thing about this Rosemary person seems to be taking him over. It's as if he goes into a trance when he talks about her and then he gets so upset.'

'Oh! He's still talking about her a lot?' Julia asked, surprised.

'Yes, even this morning. Weeping in bed. I asked him what was wrong, and he just said he was crying for Rosemary and could we find her. At first, I tried asking him who she was but all he did was cry in response. So, I stopped asking him and I said she's fine. Sure, what else could I say?'

'Did you find out anything about this Rosemary?'

'Not a clue. Possibly she never even existed.'

'Is he awake?'

'The carer is just dressing him. But, Julia, don't be too shocked if he's not sure who you are at first,' Joseph said gently.

'Really?' If that was the case, he really had deteriorated a lot.

'Yes, I'm afraid so. He wasn't sure who I was earlier,' he added gently.

They chatted for a few minutes more and eventually Alice the new carer came downstairs. A nurse came every day too to check but she would not arrive for a while.

'He's sitting up now,' Alice said. 'I might ask the nurse to check with the doctor to see if she can give him something to relax him. He's very agitated this morning,'

'Thanks, Alice. This is my sister Julia – we are going up to see him now. He does seem agitated. It would be great if the doctor could give him something to ease it. There is coffee brewed and some muffins. Help yourself.'

'Great and nice to meet you.' Alice looked mid-thirties with a thick brown ponytail. She smiled warmly at Julia.

'Nice to meet you too. Joseph tells me you are great at looking after Dad. Thank you.'

'It's a pleasure. He's a lovely man,' Alice replied, helping herself to a mug of coffee.

Julia and Joseph then went up to their father's room.

The coolness of the bedroom was comforting but as Julia came closer the scent of disinfectant was almost overpowering and a stark reminder of the fragility of her father. A Persian rug in russet reds covered the dark-oak wooden bedroom floor. On an ornate dressing table photographs of her and Joseph stood side by side. A photograph of her mother Florence sat in a golden frame on a bedside table. The other bedside table held a lamp and a beaker.

Her father looked so small in the large bed it was as if he had shrunk since she had last seen him. Medical paraphernalia dominated the room. A commode sat in a corner. She could feel the sting of tears. He was skin and bone. She sat gently beside him on the bed and touched his face. He opened his eyes and they looked frightened. She couldn't help it – tears began to flow down her cheeks. Her beautiful father, who prided himself on always looking so dashing. A most interesting and gifted man. Now he looked lost.

Julia tried to smile and hide her tears.

'Daddy, it's me, Julia.'

He tried to lift his hand. She caught it and pushed it towards her cheek.

'Rosemary?' he whimpered.

Julia was taken aback. 'It's me – Julia.'

'Where's Rosemary?' he asked.

He looked at her and then he touched her face, as gently as you would a new kitten. He touched her hair and then her face again.

'Where is she, we must find her!' Then he cried, large tears running down his face.

'Why are you so worried about her, Daddy?' Julia asked.

'Tell me where she is. Do you know where she is? Why will no one tell me?' He covered his face with his hands.

Julia tried to comfort him and eventually he stopped and seemed to calm down.

They watched as he began to stare into space. Slowly he began to softly hum.

Julia sat closer to him to hear. It was a soft tune. Not one she remembered him ever singing. Then suddenly the words of the song came back to her from the recesses of her mind.

'*Where Lagan streams sing lullabies*
There blows a lily fair ...'

Julia seemed to almost lose her balance. Joseph caught her just in time.

'Are you alright? You looked like you were going to faint!' Joseph said, shocked.

Julia had felt she was going to faint. How could she describe what she was feeling? That email about the name Rosemary had unsettled her. Now this song. Like lightning a vision of a woman seemed to appear in her memory.

Her father continued the humming as if in a trance. Joseph leant over his father and slowly the humming began to subside, and he looked at Joseph fearfully as if he had never met him before. Julia could hardly believe how bad he had become.

'You can watch your TV show,' Joseph said as gently as you would to a young child who was frightened. But his father didn't register anything.

Julia noticed that a television was now installed in the room.

'He watches old cartoons. It seems to relax him a little,' Joseph said gently. He switched the TV on – Winnie the Pooh appeared on the screen.

Their father had rarely watched television and then only if it was David Attenborough, westerns, or something political.

Joseph held a beaker of juice to his father's mouth. Then he settled the pillows behind him.

'Alice will be up in a few minutes,' Joseph reassured his father.

'I need some air,' Julia whispered to Joseph.

They walked down the stairs and into the kitchen which led out to a kitchen garden. The scent of jasmine filled the air.

'Christ, he's worsened enormously,' Julia said. 'I can't believe it. You should have rung me.'

'I didn't want to worry you.'

'Why? Did you think I'd fall into some manic fit over in Africa?' she asked tersely.

'No. To be honest his decline has been so rapid. I knew you would be here soon. Are you okay?'

Julia looked at him. 'Just shocked to see how bad he is.'

'You seemed to almost faint in there – it's a shock to see him like this.'

'Yes, it's a shock but to be honest it was the song too.'

'The song?'

'When he was humming that song, I could remember something. It was as if the last decades evaporated. I could see her. A woman, a dark-haired woman. She was singing it to me. I can't explain it, but it was the strangest experience. When you first told me that Daddy was looking for someone called Rosemary, well, that night I couldn't sleep because the name *does* mean something. That song

44

has unearthed something in me. It's like a distant memory yet it seems so personal to me. But it scares me too, the feeling. Like déjà vu but not a particularly good déjà vu. Oh gosh, I must sound all over the place. To be honest, I don't know but the name Rosemary, the song ... it's as if memories are being unearthed deep in my psyche but I'm not sure I want to know them.'

'D'you think there was a person called Rosemary in his life? I just thought he was hallucinating with the meds. That song "My Lagan Love" – he's singing it constantly.'

'Is that what it is? I thought I recognised it. But I've never heard Daddy sing it. Ever.'

'No. Now that you say it. Neither have I. Maybe he used to sing it. Ah, I don't know. This bloody illness! Then this Rosemary person – that is driving me mad. I wish I knew what he was on about or maybe it's all the meds. They're sure to have side effects.'

'If we were to find out who she is, it could help him though?'

'I'm pretty certain it's the meds, Jules. But there's no harm, I suppose, in trying. Not sure how we can. I was thinking of asking Aunt Ida?'

'You know what she's like. She'll only tell us if she wants us to know. She managed to hide enough about Uncle Harry and all his shenanigans. She likes to say that anything that she is not comfortable talking about is nonsense and she certainly won't tell us if our father had an illicit affair or something.'

'Fair enough!' Joseph replied. 'But maybe it's just rubbish.'

'Maybe but something tells me that it's not.'

Julia didn't want to tell Joseph that for some totally unknown reason she was sure it was not nonsense because she was certain now that there was a Rosemary in their lives, and it seemed by their father's reaction she had left quite an impression. She was determined to find out who she was and what she had meant to her father. She just hoped that she would be glad about what she found out. She had a strange ominous feeling about it, but she was certainly not going to tell Joseph this. He looked worried enough as it was.

CHAPTER 7

Saint Margaret's Private Mental Hospital – Dublin 1967

Florence sat down on the chair opposite the doctor, her hands holding on tightly to the armrests. Doctor O'Gorman sat across a fine oak desk with a green leather inlay. He was a tall thin man with receding hair that was sleeked back with some sort of wax or pomade that made it glisten. He was sitting back in his chair smoking a pipe. He took the pipe out of his mouth and held it in the air while looking intently at her. His stare was so intense and scrutinising that she looked away, anywhere but at him. There were framed documents on the wall and photos of him receiving something from the Lord Mayor of Dublin. Another from the Minister for Health – Charlie Haughey. The office had nothing out of place and a hint of wood polish permeated the air, mixed with smoke from the pipe. It was different to the stale cigarette smoke that seemed to Florence to seep from the very walls of Saint Margaret's. They said she had been here twelve weeks. She had no concept of time now. Was it only twelve weeks? She had little memory of arriving in. Her last memory before she arrived was of her husband prising her daughter out of her arms as they tried to hold on to each other. She tried to imagine the scent of her daughter's hair, the scent of her skin, her sprinkling of freckles on her pale alabaster skin.

She watched the sun stream through the window, letting in golden light. She had loved the sunshine. She remembered that. She loved the sunshine and so had Julia. A vision of Julia playing on the beach building a sandcastle invaded her thoughts. If she could go back. Go back to that time, that place. If only she could go back.

'I'd like to talk to you, Mrs Griffith,' the doctor said. His voice was gentle and polished and reminded her of Desmond's.

She looked at him.

'How do you feel about your baby now?' he asked, scrutinising her face.

They said she had a baby. She knew she had. She did remember him. A small boy. A precious boy. But it was too late now. She was sure of that. She didn't want to go back. What if he came to harm? She must protect him. Whatever personal cost it was to her, it didn't matter. She must protect him. The voices were still there. They were biding their time. But she couldn't stay here either. It was not safe. The room was full of them. Hiding in the walls, watching her. She could hear the doctor talking. She wanted him to stop and leave her alone. She wanted everything to stop.

'I know it's difficult to talk, Mrs Griffith, but all we want to do is help you.'

This time it was Sister Bartholomew, a small elderly nun who had accompanied her to the office from her private room, who was speaking to her. Florence looked at the large cross and chain hanging around her neck.

She wanted to talk but she was afraid to. They might hear her if she did. She wanted to tell the doctor to lock her up and throw away the key. She wanted to scream at them that she was too afraid to talk.

'Mrs Griffith, I know you have had a difficult time, but I really feel your place now is with your son and your family. I have suggested to your husband that a few days in the country might help to bring back your appetite. Perhaps then you will be strong enough to deal with your new baby. You were simply exhausted trying to do everything right. Plenty of rest and you should soon be as good as new.'

Florence stared at him but made no reply.

'Mrs Griffith – the doctor is trying to talk to you,' said the nun.

Florence remained silent. She caught a long strand of her hair and began to curl it around her finger. The doctor scribbled something on what looked like a prescription pad and then handed it to Sister Bartholomew. He then touched his fine thin moustache, put his pipe back into his mouth, took a long pull on it and then swirled out smoke from the corner of his mouth. He held the pipe in the air again. He sat nearer to the desk and looked directly at Florence.

It was then that Florence could feel a dark shadow beside her – it seemed to be whispering something. She dared not speak because she knew that when she spoke things got worse. The voices would hear her. If she remained silent, they found it harder. But even if she wanted to speak, she couldn't.

'I know talking is difficult, but you must try. For your own sake as well as your baby's,' the doctor said gently.

'She will need to have her appetite improved too, doctor, very much. She is eating very little,' Sister Bartholomew said in her lilting Galway accent.

'I see. Well, hopefully that will improve as soon as she begins to recuperate. You have been through a very difficult and frightening time, Mrs Griffith. I know it's all very confusing but it is important that you understand that all this talk of seeing things and hearing things are just hallucinations. Nothing more. I know they seem real. But they are not. It's just your mind playing terrible tricks on you. Your hormones are very upset and unsettled from your pregnancy. I have prescribed some strong tranquillisers and sleeping pills. Once you get some country air and then get home to your new baby, I believe things will settle and this will hopefully be the end of it. Sister, talk to her husband and give him the medication that I have prescribed.' He then looked intently at Florence, scrutinising her. 'I understand that your new baby is being looked after by a nanny. But I think that when you feel a little better you will be able to look after your baby again yourself. Get some rest, some fresh air and take your medication and I expect to see a big improvement.'

'A break in the country air will help bring back her appetite,' the nun agreed. 'I'm a firm believer in it.'

'Yes, Sister, fresh air – nothing like it. Mrs Griffith, you must try to remember that nobody is trying to harm you or your baby. The medication that I have prescribed will help these hallucinations to stop and hopefully help you to find your voice again too. I will schedule an appointment for you with me when you return to Dublin after your little break, and we will see how things are then.' He looked away then and began to write something down.

Sister Bartholomew got up and gently helped Florence to stand.

'Good day to you, Mrs Griffith,' said the doctor. 'I am confident that when I see you at your appointment you will be feeling much improved.' He checked his watch and got up to open the door for them.

'Thank you, doctor,' Sister Bartholomew replied.

The nun turned to Florence as they walked slowly down a long dark corridor.

'Come along, dear, and we will get you packed and ready for your husband to collect you. You must remember now to try and eat. You need to build up your strength. '

The nun was walking beside her, gently holding her arm while her long habit gave a soft swishing noise as it touched the floor, her walk sprightly for her advancing years. But Florence was not listening to what she said.

There were statues of saints along the corridor. Florence was not familiar with them. Yet she seemed to have married into a staunch Catholic patriotic family. Florence Griffith. It sounded almost foreign to her. Hers had been a bohemian upbringing, one that her husband and his family had encouraged her to keep quiet about. Perhaps if she had faith now it would help her.

When they reached the room, the nun said, 'I'll go and fetch some soup for you. You really must try to eat it, dear. You heard the doctor.'

Florence made no reply.

'Your husband will be here in about an hour. When I come back with the soup, I will help you pack. Look, I have a small gift for you. It will protect you.' The nun took out a small simple cross and chain. 'See – I'm putting it in your case. Now I will go organise that soup.'

She left and Florence looked around the room that she had occupied for the last twelve weeks. She began staring at the wall.

They told her that she had imagined everything. All of it. She had imagined that someone was going to harm her baby. She had imagined that there was a voice in the radio telling her terrible things that could happen to her baby – the most terrible things that she could imagine. She had imagined the dark shadows that were following her everywhere she went. The doctor had told her that when she saw her dead mother in the room with her she had imagined it. She had told him that her dead mother had been dug up and was sitting there with pieces gone out of her flesh, but she was still alive. Then she screamed and said that they must have buried her mother alive and that she was not dead at all – she heard him say that she needed treatment. It followed. They said it would make her better. But they were wrong. They had said that she had imagined all of it. That it was a hallucination – she was delusional, she was hysterical, she was tired – lack of sleep was making her have crazy thoughts. Was it madness? Was she mad? A madwoman? She was in an asylum after all!

She wanted to believe that she had imagined it, even if that meant that she was mad. It would be easier. She desperately wanted to believe them. But it was hard to think – the voices were quietened but they were still there. But she knew now that no one believed her. That was more terrifying than anything. Desmond didn't believe her. Desmond whom she had shared a bed and a life with didn't believe her. In sickness and in health. She remembered that. She didn't remember him vowing to lock her up. Taken away like a wild animal.

She tried to remember what had happened. She remembered screaming at him, clawing his face. Begging him to believe her. Julia screaming and then it all seemed to go black.

He had arrived at the day room to visit her. Brought her chocolates. She had wanted to pick up the box and throw them in his face. She wanted him to leave but she didn't ask him to. She just turned away. She had prayed he would leave. Had she loved him? She couldn't remember. He said that she did. And he kept telling her that he loved her. He seemed like someone she once knew, someone that had passed into her life, someone that had perhaps been a part of her life but not someone that she had ever loved. He was now someone that she had no feelings for – good or bad. How could he be her husband? She didn't hate him, she just felt nothing for him, nothing at all. She felt so tired all the time. She knew it was the medication that they were giving her. Pills of different colours and sizes.

She had tried to stay awake as much as possible, but the medication was making her drowsy. If she were awake, the voices couldn't reach her so easily. They reached her best in her nightmares. But somehow, they had started to reach her in her waking hours too. At first it sounded like glass beginning to shatter. Repeatedly she could hear it, then through the noise of shattered glass it was like a darkness, a dark black noise with splotches of grey. She knew now that colours had meaning. Black and grey were to be feared the most – orange and red warned her to be fearful, green was unknown, and purple told her to run. *Run, run, run!* Run as far away as possible. How could she get up and get dressed and pretend that she could not hear the voices or see the colours and shadows that warned her? They would follow her. She knew that now. It didn't matter where she went, they found her. There was no point. They would always find her. They had told her so.

CHAPTER 8

Druid, County Clare 1967

'I have your list ready, Moira. Sausages and rashers, shin beef, livers, and a fine leg of lamb.'

'Did you put in the best piece of shin? Are the rashers good and lean? I hope that's your best leg of lamb?'

'Will you look at her and she a slip of a thing and she calling me out?' Billy Murphy guffawed as he wiped his hands on a bloodstained apron that had once been cream but was now the colour of treacle and stretched across his large stomach.

'I know my shin beef, Mr Murphy. I know fatty rashers too and I'll not settle for them. I'll be back on Monday and be sure to have that goose that I ordered. Not a fat one either!'

'Is it the king and queen that are on the way to Lenashee?'

'I'm not sure, but I'm told that they do have fine tastes so make sure that your goose is the best. I'll be back shortly. I have to go to McDaid's. I'll call in on my way back for this lot. Put a few streaky rashers in too and some of your pig's pudding. Is it fresh?'

'Did I ever sell you anything not fresh, Moira? I've a nice bit of tongue too and some fresh sheep's kidneys if you want them?'

'I would not put it past you, Mr Murphy, to try and get something past me. I know my meat.'

'If you were a few years younger I would give you a good slap on the behind. The cheek!' he said, laughing.

'I'll take the tongue and the kidneys and put some good bones in for my stock too. I'll settle with you when I get back. Thanks, Mr Murphy.'

She closed the door and walked down the street and into McDaid's grocery. She had already ordered most of the basics like tea, coffee, cocoa, sugar, currants, flour, cherries, jelly, jam, spices, tomatoes, potatoes, fruits, vegetables and berries.

There was a large brown counter and Mrs McDaid was wiping it down with a wet dishcloth. A large woman with a blue floral wraparound apron over her large bosom, her hair was cut short and put into its regular curlers with a net over her head to secure them. The scent of rashers and onions frying filled the air, making Moira's stomach rumble. Mrs McDaid lived in the back of her shop with her husband who was partial to rashers and onions for his breakfast. He was known not to get out of bed until the smell of them came up the stairs. Mrs McDaid loved the radio but was slightly hard of hearing, so it was normally on extremely high. Luke Kelly the folksinger was belting out 'The Wild Rover' much to Mrs McDaid's delight as she was slightly swaying as she was cleaning.

'HELLO, MRS MCDAID!' Moira shouted over the radio.

Mrs McDaid looked up and then turned down the radio as Luke was singing the last line.

'Good morning, Mrs McDaid,' Moira said cheerily.

A holler came from the back of the shop to know if the breakfast was ready.

'Well, it would be a good morning if that husband of mine ever decides to get out of bed. Too much porter last night. The scoundrel. Do yourself a favour, Moira, and don't bother getting married. It's nothin' only hardship.'

'Ah, go on with you, Mrs McDaid! Sure everyone knows that you and Mr McDaid are cracked about each other.'

'Cracked, my eye! Cracked to have married a boyo!' Mrs McDaid gave the counter one final rub and then put the dishcloth away. 'I have everything on the list for you, Moira, and some lovely little pullets' eggs that I saved for you.'

'Thanks, Mrs McDaid. I'll be back during the week for some more groceries.'

'Your mother is not too happy about you working for people that you don't know. She said you'll miss the mission too! Did you see the priest? He's a fine handsome man. I'm looking forward to his sermons. We'll have something nice to look at on the altar for a change.' She winked. 'Mrs Burke will be there snoring all the way through it as usual in the front seat. It will be hard to hear a word that he says. But, back to your mother, she's not happy, I tell you.'

'It can be hard to keep my mother happy, Mrs McDaid. I'm sure you know that,' Moira said lightly.

'Ah, she's not the easiest woman alright. She's a great woman for praying though. She said she is going to say a special novena as she's worried you might get led astray up with the big fancy ones in Lenashee. She must have a path to heaven with all her prayers though.'

'She must have alright. Could you see if you could get some more of those pullets' eggs for me and a few more duck eggs too for the sponges?

'I'll save the best for you, Moira.'

'I'll be back on Monday. Bye for now, Mrs McDaid, and

there will be no worries about me getting led astray. I'll be far too busy in the kitchen.' She grabbed the groceries and then she went back to the butcher's and collected her meat.

'I'll take a bit of belly bacon with the goose on Monday. Put that with the order, Mr Murphy, please.'

'I'll hang up the goose for you. It'll be good for cooking next week. But sure, they'll probably be fishing. You'll have lots of salmon and a few wild grouse on the menu too.'

'Probably. Thanks, Mr Murphy. See you on Monday.'

With the car heaving she headed for Lenashee. She was excited and nervous. It was quite an undertaking to be cooking for grandeur all by herself and the money she was being paid was better than three weeks in the hotel. Luckily, she had a week off from the Bridge Hotel she worked in. The hotel was situated a few miles outside of Druid. She had jumped at the chance when asked by her boss, Mr Hunt, to cook for the people coming to the lake house at Lenashee for a week. Money had been sent to Mr Hunt and he had given it to Moira to get all the requirements. They were arriving tomorrow, so she was going to the house today to get things set up. Mr Hunt had handed her the money, telling her that she was as fine a cook as ever he had met. Mr Hunt did not offer compliments often. He had taught Moira all he knew but Moira knew that there was so much more that she wanted to learn. She had met a Frenchman who worked in the hotel for a while who was touring Ireland. He was from Burgundy and he told her about the beautiful lavender fields there. He told her about fine French cooking. She was enthralled by it. Ever since then it was all that she could think about. She dreamed of going to France and seeing exactly how the French cooked. He showed her how to cook Crêpes Suzette. Then a French stew with red wine and a consommé. But her dreams of going to France were just that – dreams. It was as likely to happen as going to the moon. Money was not plentiful in her family and the money that she earned was truly little. She was saving whatever she could to go. But she had the dream, and she was not giving it up even if for now she did work in the wilds of Ireland and going to France seemed a fairy tale. She dared not breathe a word of her aspiration to her mother though.

Her mother believed being a good cook was necessary for her to find a suitable husband but, as far as forging out a career, she had laughed and warned her to get any notions like that out of her head. She had reminded her that when she was not working in the hotel she was needed at home and, as she was heading for twenty-two years of age, she should be looking for a suitable husband – preferably one with a bit of money and land. She had pointed out several suitable matches for her in the small town of Druid, much to Moira's disbelief. There was no way she was marrying anyone to suit her mother, but she would not tell her that – her mother could have a cruel tongue and arguing with her was not worth it.

She wished she liked her mother. But Moira's relationship with her mother was not an easy one. Her mother was not one bit happy when she'd told her that she was going to work in the lake house at Lenashee for a week.

'What? On your own? Sure, we've no idea who will be up there! It's not right for a young girl to be up there on her own with total strangers. We don't know anything about them. They could be atheists for all we know or worse they could be Protestants. We have no idea what could be going on up there.'

'I'm almost twenty-two and well able to look after myself. Anyway, Mr Hunt said that he was told that a Miss

Redmond would be there getting the house ready and she will greet me and be there with me, so I am not on my own. Mr and Mrs Berne from the gate lodge will be around too.'

'I saw Mrs Berne this morning at Mass – she will be doing little with that back of hers. Hardly able to kneel she was. Never really liked the woman – she would tell you nothing, keeps herself to herself. But she was crippled-looking this morning. That daughter of hers was a wild one too. I saw her throwing a bottle of porter into her gob like a man at Dickie Doyle's wake. A tramp – that's what she is.'

Moira knew that there was no point in trying to say that drinking a bottle of porter was hardly bad enough to label a girl a tramp – but she knew there was no point.

'Well, Mr Berne is always nice – Daddy and he always got on well.' Truth was her father got on with everyone. He didn't really have a bad word for anyone. A gentle soul.

'Well, be careful and don't be having anything to do with any of them fancy ones up there.'

Moira had bit her lip. Her mother's usual warning was on the way.

'No man will want you and you need not think you can come home here if anything ever happens to you. I warn you, Moira, I want no scandal ever in this house. It's the road for you if you should ever bring scandal to this door.'

'I'm taking a job as a cook for a week. Why do you say such things to me?'

Her mother was quite obsessed about the subject and every time Moira stepped out to go to a dance or to the pictures her mother gave her the same speech.

'I say it because you need to know. It's the most important thing that I can ever teach you. No one would want a girl that is dirty. So, watch yourself, Moira, and don't darken the door of this house if you ever get into trouble.'

Moira had winced and tried to block her ears. She missed her grandmother so much. Her grandmother had taught her a love of food from a big, stained cookery book called *Mrs Beeton's Book of Household Management*. In the evenings and when her mother was busy, she would take down the book and they would read all about stuffed pheasant and quail eggs, tartlets of greengage jam and Empress Pudding. Her grandmother used to bake queen cakes and fairy cakes and they would spend ages icing them with delicate icing. Her own mother would give out about the waste of sugar.

When Mr Hunt had said that he had to close the hotel to fix the roof she had been disappointed, as the thought of spending a whole week at home under the watchful eye of her mother was nothing to look forward to. So, when she heard about the job it was a relief to know she would only have to sleep at home. She gave her mother money for her keep so she would give her something extra to sweeten her a little.

As she was driving out of the village, she saw her best friend Katie Egan. She stopped and pulled down the window.

'So, you're off to Lenashee?' Katie said. She was wearing a shift lemon dress that she had bought in Ennis and some smart tie-up shoes. Her dark-blonde hair cut to the shoulders and styled with a flick, her brown eyes bright as a button.

'Yes, I'm off now. I can't wait to see it. You look nice. I like your hair.'

'I was trying to get it to look like Nancy Sinatra's. Oh god, I would love a pair of white Go Go boots like hers! Not that anyone will ever notice me in this dive. Could wear a bag over my head for all the notice it will get me here. I was afraid that your mother might try to put a stop to you going. She was giving out to Ma about you last night.

You're missing the Mission too. Did you see the priest? He's a looker but I suppose he'll bore the arse off us. Big auld long voice on him. That's according to Naggie Nelligan anyways. She heard him talking to Father Murphy in the priest's yard. I'd say she was hiding behind the fence. But he has eyes a bit like Elvis, big and dreamy. Your mother was giving out yards to Ma. You'd swear you were going to America to sell your body the way she was carrying on.'

'She never stops. Gave me the usual big speech.'

'Sorry, Moira, but your mother is an ould witch. No offence. I know she is fierce religious and all, but she's still an ould witch. She must think you're going to jump in the back of the car and take your knickers off the first chance you get with a lad. My mam gave me the talk but that was it. Your mother never stops about it. Maybe she's obsessed with sex. Always up for it. Jaysis, your poor father facing that! Don't know how you listen to her. Ma says that your mother has fierce notions and she only married to a labourer. No offence like, I think your father is an ould pet and he is a pure saint to put up with her. Ma said that there were lots of girls after your father even if he was just a labourer, but when your mother got her claws into him there was no escape. Hey, maybe she was up the pole and he had to get married. Can't see her as fast though. But then don't they say it's the quiet ones that are the shockers.' She laughed. 'Hey, why don't we leave and get a flat together in Dublin and we can have lots of boys? Your mother would go to the pope. She would say some number of novenas then for her wayward daughter.'

'No fear of her doing that – she would just shut the door to me.'

'She's not a witch. She's an auld bitch.'

'It won't be for long, I hope. I won't always live here …

61

in Druid.'

'Maybe there will be a rich man at this house, and he will sweep you away. Even a big Protestant. Your mother would lock you up'.

'I don't want any fancy man. I want to train as the best chef and have my own restaurant and people will have to book it to get a table.'

'Well, you must be planning on leaving this arsehole of Clare alright. Druid is not exactly renowned for its fine dining. Greasy chips from the chip shop wrapped up in yesterday's newspaper is as fine an experience as you can get. Or maybe some pig's head like Benji Black's the cobbler – he seems to have a pig's head simmering on the hob every single day. Ma says he eats the eyes and ears first and doesn't even take the hair off the ears. Ma says he has a frying pan and every morning he has to put fresh fat in it because the mice have ate the fat from the day before. Sure, nothing could kill poor Benji. I bet you will have the fanciest restaurant where they will serve champagne and all sorts of fancy foods. Caviar maybe – Master O'Driscoll says it's the finest food you can get. Fish guts, I think it is, but sure the master is a bit cracked. But I liked him in school. Head always stuck in a book. He never beat us anyway. Remember Miss Kennedy asking him if he had a ruler to strike us? The whore! He told her that she would be better trying to talk to us than strike us. Heard she is still terrifying the children over there, the bitch! You better have a special table for your friend Katie Egan when you have this fancy place.'

'I always will, Katie.'

'I can't wait to hear all about the goings-on at Lenashee. I wonder will they be very grand? We will probably see them passing through in their fancy cars. Oh god, I would love something fancy – anything – another day in Jefferies

Drapery Store and I will scream. Mrs Owens came in yesterday and bored me to tears picking out three black buttons for her black coat and a roll of black thread. I thought I would stab her with a knitting needle – she was driving me crazy telling me about her piles and her sore arse. I tell you I need to meet someone to sweep me away from here. Maybe these fancy ones will have a walk around Druid for a day and I can feast my eyes on a bit of grandeur. Even grab myself a rich man to rescue me from this dead-end town, where the most exciting thing to happen is Mrs Murphy having if off with Jacksie Brogan when he has too much whiskey in him.'

'Shush. If anyone hears you, we'll be in trouble, Katie.' Moira grinned.

'I don't care one bit. Well, they are in for a treat with your cooking. They will eat like royalty and get as fat as fools.'

'I better go, Katie. See you soon.'

Moira was smiling as she rolled the window back up and drove her little Mini out of Druid. She couldn't help but giggle thinking of what her friend had said. Katie was always there to cheer her up, no matter what happened.

Her mind was full of recipes and what she was going to cook. She had persuaded Mr Hunt to let her experiment with some recipes over the last year after the Frenchman had left. For the first couple of years all they cooked was bacon and cabbage, mutton stew, lamb or as a delicacy a bit of pork brawn. She had persuaded him to buy in some turbot and she had cooked it exactly as Mrs Beeton had instructed in her book and served it with an anchovy sauce. She had also cooked some lobster that she got from the same local fisherman and again she had followed Mrs Beeton's recipe. They had both gone down a treat with the tourists and Mr Hunt charged extra for what he called 'the gourmet dinners'. But it allowed her to try a few more. The Frenchman had given her a good introduction to French recipes to begin with and one of the things she had learned was that good quality butter was essential and lots of it.

Her neighbour milked a few cows and she had taken some of the milk and churned her own butter after paying her neighbour a fair price for it. The first meal she would cook was going to be a light consommé, strawberry sorbet to follow, then shin beef with red wine and dauphinoise potatoes, and a light ginger sponge cake for dessert with vanilla cream. For breakfast she would cook some liver, rashers, and the pullets' eggs with some soda bread that she would bake fresh, with her fresh butter and raspberry jam she had made herself. She would leave after cleaning up each evening and then return for breakfast. This Miss Redmond was to help her with serving. It was a small staff but a small group too and it was just for a week. She had the option of staying at the house, but she knew her mother would never allow it.

She had often passed the entrance to Lenashee, but she had never been further than that. She had asked her old schoolmaster about it as the Master was a bit of a historian. He had told her what he knew.

She learned that it was originally built around the mid-1700s by Lord Herbert Harris. Herbert was a good friend of the British Crown. As Ireland was then under the rule of the Crown, he was granted lands in Lenashee by King George the Second for his service. Hebert built a house on the lands with a hundred-acre expanse of gardens, planting trees that were brought in from as far away as Japan. He had also built a man-made sunken lake lined by woods on either side. The house had a large garden divided by stone steps that led to the lake. But eight decades later a descendant of his, Henry Harris, knocked down the original and built the lavish lake house for his bride Sophia who was, at seventeen, thirty years his junior. Legend was that she was incredibly free-spirited and beautiful and was not happy with the marriage. But the marriage didn't last long. She drowned herself in the lake after only two years. The rose garden that was being built at the time of her death was called after her. The Master said that the legend was that she still walked along the lake. But Moira thought this was codswallop. She had no time for stories like that. She knew the Yanks liked stories of spirits and ghosts though and there were rumours that this new owner of Lenashee planned to turn it into a guesthouse. The Master had told her that the house had seen numerous repairs, but the integrity of the house was always kept. It then transferred down the line through the Harris family from generation to generation but always keeping the Harris name and in 1948 it was inherited by Lord Charles Harris who married Constance Townsend. They sold off most of the land, just keeping around ten acres of the demesne. The Harris couple now resided in France and had sold the house to Harry Williams, a big businessman in Dublin.

Although she had no time for folklore, Moira couldn't get the idea of the poor young bride who had died so young out of her head. She had mentioned it to Mr McDaid in the grocery store whose family had lived there for generations. He confirmed the story and he told her that he had heard that she went mad. Then one night she ran from the house when no one was looking and threw herself into the lake with a rock tied to her neck with a piece of rope. She was buried in a private plot at Lenashee.

John Berne was heading for sixty and was the caretaker of the house and garden. There was a large staff when the Harris family lived there but they were all gone now except for John Berne and his wife. He lived in the gate lodge with his wife Chrissy – his daughter now lived in Ennis. Moira had often met him with her father. She remembered him saying that the lake house was locked up, with sheets put over everything for most of the year. There were stables and a courtyard. John had a couple of the villagers who helped him to look after the maintenance of the house and of the gardens and woods that remained. Her father told her that the new owner had hired Tim Burke, a local lad, to look after a few horses there. It was good, her father had said, to see a bit of life coming to the place again.

The Thompsons, who were a big farming family and Protestant, were said to have been at a few parties there. Her own mother called the family that had owned the house 'the grandeur' and said that when she was little Lord Charles' mother Lady Elizabeth held a summer fair every year for the locals. Her mother remembered going up with all the locals and eating lots of lemonade and iced cakes. The villagers had often seen a few of 'the grandeur' driving through the village in fancy cars, some of them open-topped, and they always knew they must be up in Lenashee.

So, it was with much excitement Moira turned the car into the drive and past the gate lodge. The gates were closed most of the time but today they were opened. She noticed a bit of a mist as she drove along the avenue.

The avenue was lined thick with trees either side. A green moss had begun to take hold in the centre of the drive. She drove slowly to take in every sight and not to spill or knock any of her ingredients about. The party would not arrive until the following afternoon. But she wanted lots of time to get prepared.

Moira hoped that the woman looking after the house would be easy to get on with. Mr Hunt said that the house was to be ready and all she would have to do was the cooking. The mist was getting a little thicker as she drove but there was a gap in the trees that gave her a glimpse of the lake.

It was just as beautiful as the Master had told her. Today there was hardly a ripple and a family of ducks were bathing in the heat. She turned another corner in the drive and got her first sight of the lake house. A pewter haze of mist lay like a blanket over it. She surmised that the mist was from the mountains in the distance as the house was set in a kind of valley. It took her breath away. It looked larger than she had expected. Like something out of a fairy tale set against the backdrop of Slieve Bearnagh.

She drove on and found herself right in front of the house. She panicked then as she knew that there should have been a road leading to a back entrance but somehow she had missed it, she was so taken with the house. She was about to turn around when a young woman dressed in a blue midi dress with a white apron and red pixie hairstyle came out of the house, waving at her. Moira stopped the car, and it gave a blast of smoke and a slight bang which sounded a bit embarrassing and worrying. She wound down the window and the woman came running over and stuck her head in.

'You must be the cook! I'm Vonnie the housekeeper. How young you look! Hope you are able for this shower – they are very picky. If you drive around the back to the staff entrance, I'll give you a hand to bring in that lot.' She pointed back down the avenue. 'There's a narrow turn-off there that leads to the back entrance. I'll meet you around the back.'

Moira warmed to her immediately. She had the biggest smile with a young, freckled face, and with her trendy clothes she was nothing like Moira had expected.

She thanked her and slowly drove back down the avenue, spotting the turn-off almost immediately.

At the back of the house she parked and got out.

Vonnie appeared and they grabbed armfuls of shopping from the car and went inside.

Moira followed Vonnie down a dark hall into a big kitchen with two small rooms attached.

'There is a big fridge installed now so you can just use the dairy over there for storage. There's a pantry and a room to hang any game like ducks, pheasants or rabbits that are caught and believe me they will be caught!' Vonnie laughed.

The kitchen was as big as the one at the hotel. It was very dated, but it was clean and there seemed to be everything there that she would need. They loaded everything onto the big wooden table and then went out to bring the rest of the shopping in.

Just as they were finished John Berne knocked on the window. He was a small man with a wiry body and a pipe in his hand.

Moira opened the window and said hello.

'I'll be in to help with the fires and if you have any bother with the range or anything else let me know. Chrissy gave the kitchen a good clean so it should be in tiptop order.'

'Thanks, Mr Berne,' Vonnie replied. 'This is the cook, Moira.'

'Sure, I know her father well. A good man,' he said as he tipped his peaked cap at Moira and walked off whistling.

'I'm staying with Mr Berne and his wife until the family arrive,' said Vonnie. 'I said there was no way that I was going to sleep here on my own. It's nice and all, but a bit creepy at night. I heard that you're not staying. I might've considered it for tonight if you were. There are some rooms for staff on the top floor, although some of them need work done to them, but there is one really pretty room.'

'I live just outside the town. So, I'll go home to my own house to sleep. I would like to stay but ... well, I'm sorry I can't.'

'Ah, don't worry about it. Come on – a cup of tea is in order,' Vonnie said as she began to organise some cups and saucers.

They had a cup of tea and chatted.

'I work for Mrs Ida Williams in Dublin,' Vonnie said. 'She insisted that I come down here and get things ready for her – she knows that I'll make sure it is just as she likes. They did hire a few locals to help too and get the place in order. Two sleepy sisters called Betsy and Maggie Bunion. Do you know them?'

'Yes, I do. I think they work for the Thompson family. It's a big grand house on the other side of Druid.'

'Yes, that's them. I was glad to see the back of them, but we got the job done. I was a bit wary of coming down, but I thought a change of scene might be good. The house is much bigger than I had thought. No television though. I can't believe though that *Tolka Row* is over. I loved that programme so much. There's a radio and a gramophone. I brought down my Dickie Rock records. Helps kill the quiet. Mr Berne's wife has been a huge help but with her back at her I don't think we will see much of her. So, I had lots of dusting to do. Mrs Williams's husband has come down a few times and he has some horses in the stables. A local lad is looking after them. The Bernes used to work for the family that lived here but now they work for Mr Williams. Do you know Mrs Williams? You must have seen

69

her in the papers at some stage? Mrs Ida Williams?'

'Oh yes, she was photographed recently with Mrs Kennedy. She's so glamorous.'

'Yes, she's always in the social pieces in the paper and she's married to Mr Harry Williams or Handsome Harry as I call him. They say he's loaded! Handsome Harry could be anything I think, it's just the way he is. Her brother will be coming as well. Mr Desmond Griffith. Very handsome and nice if you like that sort of thing. Always perfectly turned out. He travels a lot. His wife has had her second child and is sick so they thought a break away would help. Since she had the second child, she has not been well at all. At first, they said that she was not coming – that she was going to somewhere like a special place to recuperate. But now she's coming here. She's been away in the madhouse with the nerves. She won't eat and barely sleeps.'

'Really?'

'Yes, she started acting funny as soon as the child was born, and I overheard on very good authority that when she went home with the baby she began acting crazy – cleaning one room for hours and hours until her hands would bleed and washing the floor every half hour in case the child would get a mite of dust. Oh, proper mad she is, Lord save us! And, God love her, she was the loveliest person you could meet beforehand. I used to love her visiting. She was full of fun and would always bring some chocolates for me. Not stuck up like the rest of them at all. Never really did put her and Mr Desmond together, to tell the truth. Anyways the poor thing started imagining things and thought there was someone going to take her new baby. Thought there was a person in the radio talking to her. Lord bless us and save us – cracked as a cracked jam jar she is, and the poor baby is with a nanny all the time.

The nanny and the baby are not coming but they are bringing the little daughter. Julia is her name. She's a lovely little thing. Big blue eyes and red curls. Missing the mother terrible, she is. Mrs Williams is bringing some woman from Brown Thomas down too, a fashion advisor no less for the big shoot. Did you know that there's a photo shoot going to happen?'

'No!' Moira replied, excited at the thought.

'Oh yes, a big fancy photographer is coming to take photographs of Mrs Williams in all the finery from Brown Thomas. This one that works there is great friends with Mrs Williams. Oh, I met her the other day. She was over advising Mrs Williams about her wardrobe. Miss Rosemary Purcell is her name and she stuck up her nose at me. Thinks she is better than me and all she does is work as a clerk in a shop. Even if it is a fancy shop, she is still only a shop girl. All posh talk out of her – explaining how pearls and furs go together. Far from furs this one was reared though, I think. Sat there and let me wait on her like the queen, asking me if I had any lemon for her tea. Lemon! Oh, she talks all nice with a fancy voice and her clothes are a match for Mrs Williams but there was something about her that I could not put my finger on and between you and me I thought she lingered a little too long when Mr Williams arrived. He has an eye for the ladies. Now he is ever the gentleman, don't get me wrong, but rumours are never far away when you have a man like Handsome Harry. Not that he is handsome in a popular way – he has his own way of being handsome.'

A strange sound that seemed to come from upstairs began to echo into the kitchen and made Moira jump.

'You'll get used to the noises. That's just the water cracking from the boiler. The noises nearly sent me packing when I arrived. I suppose it's such an old house it is bound to have strange noises but it's still very unsettling. I can't put my hand on it. There's a kind of a sadness to the place.'

'But it's so beautiful!' Moira said. 'That's a strange thing to say. Why would you say that?'

'Ah, I don't know, it's just a feeling, it makes me uneasy. I get feelings about places. I can't explain it. My mother is the same and her mother before her and would you believe her mother before her. A kind of gift or curse, depending on what way you might want to look at it. Ever since I was a little girl, I get a sense of a place – like if the people had been happy when they lived there. I'm not sure everyone was happy who lived here. There's a sadness that seems to sit in the air and something else too, something that I'm not sure of. But the sadness is clear to me.'

Moira was not sure what to make of Vonnie's revelation. What a strange thing to say, she thought. Then the thought of the young bride who was rumoured to have drowned herself crossed her mind.

'Ah, don't mind me – I think it might be the mist,' Vonnie went on. 'It tends to hang over the house and it gives me the shivers. Did you not notice it – it covers the house like a blanket?'

'Yes, I did notice it – when I drove down it was almost hidden with it.'

'It seems to never leave it. It adds to the sad feeling about the place. I suppose it's the mountains behind us. Come on. Enough of that. Follow me and I will show you around.'

Moira guessed that Vonnie didn't know the story of the young bride and she was certainly not going to tell her or indeed she certainly would run for the hills. She had heard of people having cures for shingles and strange gifts. There was a monk who used to live in a hut near Druid and he was supposed to be able to go into houses and rid them of old spirits that didn't want to leave, but again Moira had never paid much heed to this type of talk. The monk had disappeared one evening and was never seen again. But the hut was still there and people were afraid to go near it.

She followed Vonnie up the servants' stairway that on the first floor led both to the main hall and into the most beautiful dining room, with mirrored walls making it look twice the size that it was. It looked out over the lake.

'Very fancy, isn't it?' Vonnie said. 'You can imagine what it was like when all the grand people used to live here – mind you, Mrs Williams, as modern as she looks, likes to hold on to some of the old customs.'

'In what way?'

'Oh well, you know, always dressed for dinner and afternoon tea on the dot of four.'

Vonnie then led her into a library with wall-to-wall glass-doored bookcases, a marble fireplace and a wooden floor covered by a large red rug.

Moira walked to the window and was hit with the most bewitching scent of vanilla and cinnamon. She looked out and could see some small deep purple flowers that were growing close to the ivy at the bottom of the house.

'Wild orchids, their scent is so strong. The scent travels up in the air,' Vonnie said.

'It's such a beautiful scent,' Moira replied.

'They seem to be growing everywhere. I said it to Mr Berne, but he seems to think that there is no harm in allowing wildflowers to grow. I'm not sure if Mrs Williams will agree. She insists on roses and only roses. Luckily, there is a walled rose garden outside, I'll show it to you later – you pass it to get to the stables – just before the archway to the right you get the scent first – anyways there are lots of roses there, so I have them in all the bedrooms. Mrs Williams prefers red and pink ones and thank goodness they are abundant out there. Come on and I will give you a quick peek at the other rooms.'

On the first floor there was also a drawing room that looked out on the lawn which was set with a beautiful big oak tree and interspersed with more rose bushes. Moira could see a sea of red and pink and yellow amongst some stone statues which seemed to form a walkway near the lake. They left the dining room and climbed the main staircase.

Upstairs there were two more floors with twelve bedrooms, each with its own small dressing room and washroom. Six of the rooms were dressed and ready for guests. Each had a four-poster bed dressed in white linens and cream blankets. The furniture was heavy and dark. Floral damask wallpaper in different patterns and hunting pictures adorned the walls. A glass vase with red and pink roses perfumed each room.

Back in the corridor, Vonnie pointed to the end of it and said, 'Now, there is a door to the servants' stairs over there – the one that leads from the kitchen up to the top floor where any household staff sleep. I have that pretty room I mentioned decked out up there. I'll probably try it tomorrow night when the family come. Well, Mrs Williams will insist on it. She can be, let's say, a bit demanding and might need me during the night for god knows what. A cool drink or an aspirin. She's a bit fond of the gin and tends to take to the bed when she has had a few too many cocktails. Hopefully, I'll be alright up there. I checked it for mice and there don't seem to be any.'

'I'm sure you'll be fine,' Moira said as they descended

the main staircase. 'It certainly is a fine house. The light coming through the roof light is kind of magical. I could look at it all day.' She stared up at the dome-shaped roof.

'It is pretty,' Vonnie agreed.

'I'd better get back to the kitchen and get prepared.'

'Mr Berne has brought in lots of stuff for them too. Brandy, gin, wine, port, rum, porter, ale, and whiskey. I'll get him to bring in lots of wood for the stove too.'

Back in the kitchen Moira put everything away and wrote her menu for the next few days, checking to see if she had everything. At last she was satisfied that she was well prepared. She then had a sandwich of cold ham with Vonnie and she heard more stories about Vonnie's life in Dublin. She learned that Vonnie loved Dickie Rock, Joe Dolan and dancing. She thought Gay Byrne, the television presenter, was very handsome, and she was kind of dating a boy called Charlie that she had met at a dance in Dublin. She had just bought a bright pink mini skirt and was planning to wear it on her next date to the pictures. Moira loved listening to her, and she stayed until Mr Berne arrived to lock the house. Vonnie was going back to the Bernes for the night.

'I'll see you early in the morning,' Moira said to Vonnie. She wished she could stay at the house. But she would never hear the end of it with her mother.

'Bright and early,' Vonnie replied.

'I hope you don't mind me saying but you are young to be a housekeeper.'

'Mrs Williams is a good employer. She made me housekeeper when she got married. Although it's not something that I want to stay doing. Sometimes I think of going to London, but poor Ma has nearly everyone gone so I don't like leaving. See you in the morning, Moira.'

'See you – and thanks for showing me round!'

It was almost eleven o'clock when she got home. Her mother was gone to bed so thankfully she would be able to avoid her questions. But then she heard her at her door.

'Moira?'

She rushed to the door and opened it just a crack.

'Yes, Mam? I'm getting undressed.'

'I hope you are saying your prayers in there, Moira. I'm not happy that you are missing the Mission. He gave a great sermon on chastity this evening and told us all about the black babies in Africa. Say a prayer that your brothers return safe from England and no harm comes to them. Only a mother of sons knows the suffering when her sons leave her. Sure, they are everything to me. Pray that they come home soon, Moira.'

'I will, Mam.'

'I had a letter from Michael today. He always writes to me. But it has made me lonesome for him. Read your prayer book and pray for them.'

Moira was used to her mother talking about her brothers. It was quite clear to her from a young age that sons were valued far more highly than daughters. When a neighbour had three daughters in a row, her mother went down and arranged to get a Mass said to try to lift the curse of having only daughters.

'Of course, Mam. Goodnight.'

But Moira had no intention of praying. She had two cookery books opened on her bed. She could not wait until morning when she would be boss of her own kitchen for a whole week. She got into her nightdress and turned the pages of *Mrs Beeton's Book of Household Management*. Vonnie had warned her that the men planned to hunt and fish and would want their catch cooked. This had caused Moira some anxiety and she was eager to read up on cooking roast grouse and roast pheasant. Trout and salmon were plentiful in the river where they would fish, so she looked up recipes for these too. She made a note on her notepad to remember to put some arrowroot in her béchamel sauce. Vonnie had tipped her off that Mr Williams was partial to lobster. She would have to have a word with Mr Murphy and ask him to tell Jacksie Haze, a local fisherman, to get her some lobster. Then her eyes grew heavy and the pencil fell from her fingers as she fell fast asleep, dreaming of cooking a soufflé and praying that it would stay risen.

CHAPTER 9

The next morning, Moira arrived at six and Vonnie was already there as busy as a bee. They had some tea and soda bread and then Vonnie began in earnest.

'Remember now that Mrs Williams likes to keep things very formal regarding dining. It's her upbringing, I suppose. She will expect afternoon tea to be served when they arrive. Mr Williams – Handsome Harry – is happy with a ham sandwich in the kitchen with the rest of us but when his wife is around he will be playing the country squire.'

'Afternoon tea sounds very uppity.'

'Well, Mrs Williams is very uppity.'

The hours flew in and before she knew it Vonnie was shouting to her that they had arrived. Vonnie had set up in the library for their afternoon tea with fine bone china and silver spoons. Moira plated up griddle scones still warm from the oven served with clotted cream and her own gooseberry jam, a light Victoria sponge, and delicate sandwiches of honey-roasted ham and her own chutney in case they were hungry.

Two cars had arrived, one of them open-topped.

'Come on and we'll greet them. Mrs Williams is like a

model and she has that woman with her that I was telling you about. Mr Berne will carry the bags, but we might be needed.'

They stood outside as the new arrivals disembarked from their cars. A very glamorous fair-haired woman got out of the open-top car. She was dressed impeccably in a pale-blue dress with a white collar, white cuffs and white gloves, black pumps and a large pair of dark sunglasses. The passenger was an equally glamorous, younger, dark-haired woman in a lemon pencil skirt and cream blouse with long dark shiny hair and the longest lashes that Moira had ever seen. Then a handsome man got out of the other car, dressed impeccably in a three-piece suit. He helped a very fragile-looking woman out. She was wearing a light dress and over it a camel cashmere coat with mother of pearl on the collar. It was such a warm day Moira wondered at her having to wear a coat. Her red hair was falling about her face and her skin was as white as Moira had ever witnessed on a living person. The woman looked like she could faint.

Then a little girl in a pair of pink pedal pushers and matching top jumped out and ran over to Vonnie, her red curls bouncing around her pretty face.

'Well, look who it is! Julia in the cutest outfit I have ever seen. Meet Moira, your cook for the week. I am sure if you are good, she might make you some jelly and ice cream.'

Julia looked up at Moira and then slipped her hand into hers. Moira was slightly taken aback. But there was something so gentle about this little child with her big blue saucers of eyes.

'Can we go swimming in the lake, Vonnie?' Julia asked. 'It looks so pretty!'

'That it does, pet, but it's a bit deep for swimming.

Don't worry – you will have lots of fun in this big house – lots of rooms to explore. And myself and Moira will have you spoiled rotten.'

Julia looked at Moira as if for reassurance.

'It's a beautiful house – you will have loads of fun,' she said.

Julia moved a little closer to her, smiling.

'Someone has taken a shine to you,' Vonnie remarked, nodding at Julia.

'Vonnie, it's been a dreadful drive,' said Ida. She looked at Moira from top to toe. 'Who is this?'

'Miss Moira Fitzpatrick, your cook for the week.'

'Good afternoon, Mrs Williams,' Moira said.

Ida gave her a nod of acknowledgment.

'We have some afternoon tea set up in the library,' said Vonnie.

'Oh lovely! I am so looking forward to a cup of tea.'

Mr Berne had arrived and had begun to carry in the bags.

'Please do not mark those bags – they are all Louis Vuitton,' said Ida.

'Very well, Mrs Williams, I will be extra careful,' Mr Bernie replied.

Desmond, who had escorted Florence upstairs, arrived back out.

'I'm afraid my wife is quite ill from the car journey from Dublin,' he said to Vonnie. 'Could you make her some light soup? I don't think she will eat anything else.'

Moira could see the concern on the man's handsome features. She noticed his hands were soft and pale, as if they had never seen any type of manual work. His hair was sleeked back with some type of hair oil and it gave his face an almost chiselled effect.

'Of course. I'll make a light broth,' Moira answered for Vonnie.

'Thank you.'

Moira noticed that the other lady politely said hello and walked in after Ida. Moira surmised that she seemed more distant than unfriendly, but she could see Vonnie's face and knew that she was not impressed with her.

When they were both back in the kitchen Vonnie let rip.

'Did you see that one looking down on us? Thinks she is so grand now! I'll give her grand! Barely said thank you when I showed her the room that I had all prepared for her. All spick and span. I said, "Is everything alright for you?" And do you know what she says, the hussy?'

'What?' Moira asked.

'*Fine, thank you!* That was all! As if she was used to grandeur. I know what she needs – a good slap! I am so vexed.'

'Well, I can see that, but I don't think we can have the luxury of being vexed. Will you bring up the scones and the cream?'

'A hussy, that's all she is.'

Moira just wanted to get the afternoon tea sorted so that she could begin on the evening meal. She had lots to do, and she had no time to try to soothe Vonnie's ego.

'A hussy. I know a hussy when I see one and mark my words, she's a fine example of a hussy. But she has disguised herself in fine clothes and fancy smells.'

Whatever she was, Moira knew that it was certainly going to be a memorable week.

CHAPTER 10

Moira had been taken aback at just how weak the lady who had retired upstairs had appeared to be. Her skin was so white, her eyes hollow in her face and her body was so thin that she looked like she could keel over. She looked like she hardly knew what was going on and her husband had to almost carry her.

Vonnie arrived in for some fresh tea.

'That lady is so unwell – at least, she looks very unwell,' Moira whispered to her.

'I overheard them saying that they are very worried about her. Mr Griffith said that she was sick on the way down and that the journey was terrible. Seemingly it was doctor's orders that she get some country air, but maybe they should have found somewhere a bit closer to Dublin. Did you think she looked mad? I was wondering what she would look like after being in the madhouse. Of course, the fact that she was there is all hush-hush. But sure, she must be better now. They would hardly bring her here if she's not cured.'

'Maybe she was just a bit broken down in the mind though – like, not actually mad,' said Moira. 'There's a woman in our town like that – broken in the mind and she goes away to the mental hospital for a while and when she comes out she's not as broken down. Some fella let her down seemingly. Maybe Mrs Williams is the same – just needed a little spell. They are hardly going to bring her here if she is actually mad.'

'Mr Williams is meant to be off on his travels. He travels a lot. But he was afraid to leave her. I overheard him saying to Madam that he's hoping to get her to sit outside a little to get a bit of colour into her cheeks but by the looks of her they have no hope.'

'Madam – is that what you call Mrs Williams?'

'Yes, she insists that staff call her that. Oh, believe me, you will know all her ways by the end of the week. My friend Annie who cleans the house in Dublin calls her The Queen. Behind her back, mind you. Don't worry, you will get used to her.'

'But I'm just here to cook. I don't expect I will actually see much of them.'

'Ha! You have not worked for the likes of Madam before. If the Pope was in the house she would have him running after her. She has several little bells. She gets them especially from Italy. I am wondering though if they will be heard through the thickness of the walls. We'll see because mark my words it won't be long until she starts ringing them.'

'What for?'

'Goodness knows what – she might need an extra pillow or a fresh glass of water. Something like that she deems an emergency, and she will keep ringing it until it's attended to. I will answer it but if I can't there's no one else but you. Poor Mrs Berne can hardly walk with her back, so she won't be up here like she was supposed to be. But don't worry, I'm really hoping that we can use the excuse of not hearing it because of how solid the walls are.'

Moira was not impressed to hear this. She was employed to cook and there was no mention of being at anyone's beck and call. But she didn't say anything to Vonnie. She would see how things played out.

'Madam's husband, Mr Williams – Handsome Harry – is coming later tomorrow. He will be here for Sunday lunch if not before. I want to go to Mass in the town in the morning. If I go to seven Mass I will be back to serve the breakfast and I can let you go to a later one. Mr Berne said he would drop me there.'

'That's perfect. Will the family go?'

'No. My mother says they are like Protestants – they only go when it suits them.'

'I see.'

'I don't know what this Rosemary one will do. Doesn't look deeply religious to me,' Vonnie said sourly.

'Right, I'd better get back to this dinner,' Moira said hurriedly. At least she would be able to get to Mass. She would never hear the end of it with her mother if she didn't. Her mother always went to the three Masses on Sunday so she would notice if she didn't go.

'So, you will have Madam and that one Rosemary, Mr Griffith and the little one for dinner tonight. Can't see Mrs Griffith having many dinners. Can you get me some of that broth and I'll take it up to her? She's in bed.'

'It will be ready in a few minutes. It just needs another simmer.' Moira went back to preparing her meal. She had the shin beef and red-wine dish simmering to be ready for later.

Rosemary knocked on the kitchen door and asked if she could have some lemonade for Julia. Vonnie told her that she would bring it up in a while. Moira noted that she was very offhand with Rosemary.

'Miss Prim and Proper, acting like the gentry,' Vonnie

muttered after Rosemary left. 'Acting like she is used to being waited on!'

Moira tried to ignore Vonnie's irritation about this Rosemary lady. She had enough to worry about and she thought that Vonnie was overreacting. Miss Rosemary Purcell did not seem rude and Moira had not seen any problem with her.

The evening was ticking by and the aroma of thyme, wine and rosemary filled the kitchen. Molly had all the serving dishes ready and warmed. While Vonnie served the light consommé with freshly made bread, Moira got the sorbet ready and then the main course. Once that was served, she had the desserts ready. Once they were served, she waited anxiously for the verdict.

Vonnie came in, smiling.

'Well, you're a big hit. They all ate like there was no tomorrow and I can tell you Madam is very fussy.'

'Really! Thank goodness. Is there anything else that they need?'

'I will set up glasses and the brandy decanter in the library and you can make the special tea.'

'What's that?'

'Easy. Elderflower water, ice, mint and lots of gin served in a china teapot with china cups.' Vonnie grinned.

'What about Mrs Griffith?'

'I brought down the broth you made – I doubt it was even touched. I will bring up some hot milk with a bit of cinnamon in it. She might drink that.'

'God love her. All the food and she not having a bite.'

'I'd better go. They are going out to walk along the lake for a little while before it's too dark. It will give me time to get the brandy and gin-tea prepared in the library,' Vonnie said as she went back to the dining room.

Moira could not help smiling. So her food had gone down a treat. She could not be happier. She was already looking forward to serving lunch the following day – her special roast lamb.

Just before she was about to leave the little girl came into the kitchen. Moira admired her tumbling red curls, alabaster skin with a just a smidgen of freckles and big blue eyes. She was dressed in a simple blue-and-white polka-dot dress with red ankle socks and red ankle boots. She really was a strikingly pretty little girl. But then she noticed that she was crying big silent glass tears.

'Goodness, what has you so sad?' Moira asked as she knelt beside her.

'My mummy is sick … I am not allowed … to go up to her,' she cried in a soft whisper.

Moira was not sure what to say. Her mother did look sick.

'Well, I'm sure she will be better soon and then you can see her. She probably just needs some rest after that big journey. Would you like some lovely hot cocoa with some of my special biscuits?'

'Why are they special?' Julia whispered.

'They are special because I only give them to special people.'

'Am I … special?' she asked, her bottom lip trembling.

'Very special,' Moira reassured her. 'You can help me to make the cocoa if you like?'

'Yes, please,' Julia said and the tears of a few minutes ago vanished for now.

It was late by the time Moira eventually finished up and said goodbye to Vonnie.

'I'm off to bed. I'll see you in the morning.'

'I'll be here bright and early,' Moira replied.

It was chilly when she went out and although heading for ten o'clock it was still light. The heady scent of night stock filled her senses, and the distinctive call of the corncrake broke the stillness.

She started up the car and drove down the avenue. Seeing Mr Berne, she stopped to say hello.

'Good evening!' he said, tipping his hat and taking his pipe from his mouth.

'Good evening, Mr Berne.'

'Everything alright for you in the kitchen tonight?'

'Everything is fine, Mr Berne, see you tomorrow.'

She drove off the few miles to her house just on the edge of Druid.

The town had thirteen pubs, two grocery shops, a draper's, a tailor, a cobbler, a post office, a butcher's, a chip shop, a chemist's, a doctor, a Garda barracks, a church for the staunch Catholic community that filled the pews every Sunday and a small Protestant church.

An austere priest's house was built beside the church where Father Murphy and the curate Father O'Toole lived. They had a housekeeper who kept the house spick and span and was rumoured to have a liking for the holy wine. Then the Protestant community of about thirty went to the small old Protestant church, which had mottled walls and seemed to Moira to be always filled with organ music and singing.

A fair was held in the town every month and then the streets would teem with livestock and men drinking and bartering.

When she got home her mother was sitting at the fire reading her prayer book, a gold-embossed book with each page delicate as silk. It was sent from a nun relative who was in a convent in Dublin. After seeing the library at

Lenashee it struck Moira that the only books in her house were bibles and prayer books, some of them ornate with parchment paper and leather bindings. But other than her grandmother's cookbooks there were no other books.

'Well, what kind of people are they?'

'They seem nice.'

'Are they Catholic?'

'I don't know.'

'Is there holy water and is there a Sacred Heart lamp burning?' her mother asked sharply. Her face was in a permanent frown and, although it was once youthful and pretty, any semblance of it now had disappeared.

'I didn't see one.'

'Who are they? These people?'

'Important people from Dublin.' She had no intention of telling her mother that it was Mrs Ida Williams. Her mother would know her from the newspapers. She would probably find out anyway as nothing like that could be kept secret in a town as small as Druid. But she was not going to be the one to tell. She was warned by Vonnie that they liked to keep themselves very private – especially now that Mrs Griffith was there to recuperate – and Madam would not exactly be walking around the town of Druid talking to the locals.

'Prods probably,' her mother said, scowling.

'Maybe.'

'I hope you're going to Mass in the morning?'

'Of course. I'm very tired, though, so I might go to bed now.'

'Don't forget Confession. You missed it today. You can go on Wednesday.'

'Yes, I'll go then.

'Remember to look after yourself up there with them

lot. I don't want to hear of you having anything to do with them. Watch yourself, Moira.'

'I will.'

Moira sighed as she washed and then crawled into bed. One day, she promised herself, she would not have to listen to her mother and hopefully it was not too far away. She was always worried about going to Confession. Especially if she was unlucky enough to get the parish priest. He would always ask her if she had any bad thoughts about young men. She would squirm in the dark confessional box and try not to gag as his breath smelled of liquor and the scent of it regurgitating in his mouth filled the small box. She would always reply no. She would say that she was quick with the tongue to her mother, or she had forgotten to say a night prayer the evening before. Eventually the priest would give absolution and she could go and walk up the aisle and find her pew and kneel and say the Act of Contrition and any prayers the priest had given her for penance. Her mother believed in penance and prayed night and day.

Moira's father liked to go down to the pub every night. He wasn't a big drinker, but Moira knew that he went to get a break from her mother. Her mother didn't complain if he brought back some piece of news. Her father was far from a gossip, but it was a small price to pay for a few hours' peace in the evening over a pint or two of porter.

The next morning, after the breakfast was cleared at Lenashee, Moira drove to ten o'clock Mass. Her mother was already there, kneeling in her usual pew at the front. Her father stood at the back with the other men. The priest came out and began Mass. After the Gospel reading, he talked about sin and how the world was losing its purity. He said 'this uncivilised new music' was the cause of it.

There was a parish dance, but he assured the parishioners that he would preside over it and make sure that no one got too close. Moira had seen him at the parish dances as he went around the couples with a large stick, making sure the couples were well apart.

'Promiscuity and filth will not enter this parish. Be careful of the Devil's music poisoning the minds of the young with talk of drink and jezebels!' he said with venom from the pulpit. He reminded everyone that no one could escape the black fires of hell if they fell from the true path of the most Holy Catholic Church.

As Moira bent her head in prayer she wondered if it was a sin to be thinking about how best to roast a pheasant when she was meant to be saying her prayer before Holy Communion. But the priest had a lot on his mind this morning and was in no rush to get the Mass over quickly. She reckoned he wanted to impress the missionary priest who talked for half an hour on his work for the poor people in Africa – a country so hot that the soles of your shoes would melt. 'Poor pagans' he called the people who lived there. He was handsome but she decided that Naggie Nelligan was right – he did have a drawly voice and she found herself itching for him to be finished. She had lots to do for lunch. She had left some seed cake and some warm gingerbread for Vonnie to serve tea at eleven. She could not wait to get back to the house and to the kitchen where for once she was the boss.

The lake looked beautiful as she stopped at the curve in the avenue to get a glimpse on the drive back. She took the narrow turn-off that led her to the back of the house. She reckoned that the family had possibly all retired to their rooms. She breathed in the heavy scent of roses that came from the rose garden and was about to go in when she heard the faint sound of singing. She sneaked around to the side of the house to where she had a view of the lake, to see where the singing was coming from.

Miss Purcell and Julia were sitting on a blanket on the lawn. Miss Purcell was singing to Julia, a beautiful song. She really had a lovely voice, with a kind of haunting sound to it.

Moira turned to go back, knowing it would not be appropriate for her to be out there. But Julia had spotted her and called her over.

'Moira, Moira! Come here quickly!' she called excitedly.

Moira walked over, feeling awkward.

'Sorry, I didn't mean to intrude,' she said.

'Oh, lovely to see you – you're not intruding at all,' Rosemary said. 'Julia wanted to come outside. It's such a beautiful morning.'

'Did you hear Rosemary sing?' Julia asked excitedly.

'I certainly did, Julia. You've such a lovely voice, Miss Purcell.'

'Oh, thanks. It's a long time since I sang, to be honest.'

'What's the name of the song? I think I have heard it before,' Moira asked.

'"My Lagan Love".'

'Please sing it again, Rosemary,' Julia pleaded, her blue eyes wide in anticipation.

Rosemary laughed and began. She emphasised one line: *'Like a lovesick Lenashee.'*

As she sang, Desmond arrived out. He was dressed in tweed trousers and a shirt and tie. Moira noticed he had long blond lashes that framed his blue eyes. He seemed almost too good-looking to be a man to her, too pretty.

'Rosemary, I do love that song,' he said as she finished.

'And how beautifully you sing it! You remind me of Nana Mouskouri.'

'What does it mean – Lenashee?' Julia asked Rosemary.

'I'm not sure to be honest, Julia,' Rosemary replied.

'It means a type of fairy, Julia,' said Desmond.

'Oh, maybe there are fairies here in the garden and that's why it's called Lenashee,' Julia whispered, as if the fairies could hear her.

'Yes, there very well may be.' Demond grinned, glancing at Moira.

'Good morning,' Moira said awkwardly. She felt she ought to go. It would not look good for the cook to be out in the garden like this. She could feel her face redden with embarrassment.

'How lucky we are that we found you, Moira!' he said. 'You're a wonderful cook. Although I fear that last night's sumptuous meal and that breakfast, which was certainly fit for a king, has done nothing for my waistline!'

'Thank you.' Moira liked his voice. It was not unlike the missionary's voice. Except without the long drawl. He sounded educated and precise. 'I'd better go.'

'Actually, could I have a word, Moira?' he asked as she began to walk away.

She could feel her heart beat. Why would he want a word? It was hardly to complain – he had just said he loved the food. Her mind was racing.

'It's about my wife – is there anything at all you could prepare that might help her to recuperate? I was just up with her, trying to get her to sit outside, but she seems very tired. I need to try to build her up a little but her appetite seems to have vanished.'

'I could make some chicken soup perhaps. Maybe some homemade lemonade and some rice-milk? They are particularly good for anyone trying to recover.'

'That sounds excellent. Oh, by the way, Mr Williams phoned earlier to say he will be here for lunch. So, you'll have another mouth to feed.'

'Thank you for telling me. I'd better get back to the kitchen. Bye, Julia.'

She noticed as she walked away that Mr Griffith's wife was looking out from her bedroom window. Moira looked back at the group. Rosemary was singing another song and Desmond was sitting on the blanket beside her with Julia on his knee. Vonnie didn't like Rosemary much but from what Moira could see of her she seemed a nice enough person.

There was something lonely about the sick woman looking out of the window – she hoped that they were right and somehow this little break would help her. She would make the chicken soup straight away and hopefully it would help to build her up.

She set about her day. She wanted to cook the leg of lamb with her French recipe for dinner. She longed to visit a proper French restaurant. There was such a one in Dublin called Jammet Restaurant. She had heard that it was everything in sophistication, serving grouse and sole, French wines and a drink called a Peppermint Frappé and even an oyster bar. She had no idea why she was so in love with everything French but the more she learned about it the more she wanted to learn.

She could hear Mrs Williams ringing her little golden bell and thought she'd better go to her. Vonnie was nowhere around. She followed the noise and it seemed to be coming from the library. It mesmerised her how the bell could be heard all over the house. It was such a small bell, yet the sound carried like a church bell.

'Where's Vonnie?' Mrs Williams asked crossly.

'I'm not sure, to be honest. I'm just back from Mass.'

'Well, when she comes back, kindly tell her to come find me. I need her assistance with the ironing of my clothes.'

'I will tell her as soon as I see her.'

'By the way, Moira. Breakfast was exceptionally good. It's a hotel you work in now, isn't it? Where is it?'

'It's just a few miles outside of Druid. It's called the Bridge Hotel. It's quite small.'

'Never heard of it. You would do well in Dublin in the right house.'

'I want to someday go to France to learn from great French chefs. That's my plan.'

'Very good,' Ida said as she looked away, Moira's plans clearly of no interest to her.

Moira walked back into the dining room and down the servants' stairs that led to the kitchen. She had no interest in working in a domestic kitchen all her life no matter how grand it was.

Vonnie arrived in with her arms full of roses.

'Gosh, they're so pretty,' Moira said.

'I know. Mr Berne offered to get them from me, but I just love going into the garden. You should see it before your week is up. Go down through the back lawn and take the turn through the hedge that has an archway and that leads you into it. It's full of blooms now.'

'Mrs Williams is looking for you to iron some clothes.'

'Oh no! I hate ironing her clothes. She's so particular, and they are all so expensive. I have enough to be getting on with! And what about Mrs Griffith? I need to take her something to eat – she ate no breakfast.'

'I'll look after her. Her husband asked me to make some invalid food to build her up.'

'Thanks, Moira. I'd better go see Madam before she

94

starts ringing her bell again. I'll just leave these roses in the pantry in a bucket of water.'

Moira decided to take up some rice-milk with a little nutmeg to Mrs Griffith and then serve her the chicken soup for lunch. She walked up the grand staircase, carrying the rice milk on a small tray. It was hard not to admire the light through the stained-glass dome. With the sun streaming through Moira thought the light was like a rainbow. She put the tray down on a small table and knocked gently on Mrs Griffith's bedroom door. But there was no answer. She opened it and very quietly walked in with the tray. Mrs Griffith was sitting in a chair, dressed in a nightgown with a blanket over her. She was staring at the wall in front as if in a trance. Moira wasn't sure what to do. She tiptoed over, pulled a small table beside her and put down the rice milk.

'Here is some rice milk – in case you're hungry,' Moira said ever so gently. 'It's light and easy to digest.'

The vacant stare on the woman's pale face rooted Moira to the spot. It seemed to her that Florence Griffith was not aware that she was there.

'Sorry to disturb you, but I thought you might like some,' Moira said a little more loudly.

But Florence remained in a trance-like state. Moira thought she had never seen someone look so lost before. This woman needed more than rice milk and rest to make her better, but it was not her place to say it. She knew that the woman had no intention of trying the milk.

Moira left and closed the door.

She waited for half an hour and then went up with a fresh jug of water and a fresh glass. Florence was now sleeping in the bed. The milk sat there untouched.

CHAPTER 11

Florence tried to get herself out of bed. She shivered and put on a robe that was beside the bed on a chair. Thankfully, someone had taken away the milk from earlier. The smell of it had made her feel nauseous. She remembered sitting in the chair at the window earlier, but she had no recollection of when she had returned to the bed. She had sat at the window earlier and watched Julia on the lawn. The lake looked blue with a tinge of silver. The reeds growing to the side swishing gently in the breeze. The sky was pale, and a sense of floating clouds had broken the perfect day. Florence knew that Desmond had brought her away, hoping things would be different – in other words, that she would be different. If anything, she already felt worse. She closed her eyes and tried to think of a different time, a time that she had not felt like this. A time that she had felt like a mother, a time that she felt like a wife and a time that she had not felt that she could be losing her mind. But it was like her memories were disappearing and new ones were being replayed. She wanted to hold on to the ones that mattered so much to her, the ones of Julia. The little girl that meant the world to her and the baby that she

96

so wanted to protect. She tried to think of the best memories that were stored away. She tried to recall when Julia was born. Perhaps if she recalled these precious memories, she could somehow store them away in a secret vault in her mind that nothing could tear apart.

She recalled how she had marvelled at how she had given birth to such a perfect little human being. How happy they were! Her precious little girl. Then she remembered Desmond pestering her to have another child. Her instinct told her that their little bubble was perfect as it was. But she went ahead and soon she was pregnant again. But within the first week she was sick. It continued right throughout the pregnancy until eventually her son came into the world. Unlike Julia's birth which was quick, her son's birth was long and traumatic. She thought she would die, and she prayed that she would. The pain was crucifying. She could still almost feel how she felt ripped to shreds.

She remembered the nurse bringing him to her afterwards. She couldn't understand how something so small and quiet could have caused her so much pain. The nurse tried to get her to hold him and to nurse him. Eventually she tried. It ended with both screaming. Her body was numb. She pleaded with the nurse to take him and then she turned away. It was the same the next day and the next. Eventually she had to go home.

The doctor assured Florence that her feelings were nothing to worry about after a traumatic pregnancy and once her body healed all the normal feelings for her son would arrive. She waited. Her body did heal. Much quicker than she expected. But instead of normal motherly feelings a feeling of pure dread about what could happen to her baby engulfed her. These were the memories that kept coming into her mind. Then she remembered how it all began. Desmond had put a radio into their bedroom. A man began to speak to her directly, telling her terrible things from the radio. She knew it sounded crazy, but it was true. He told her that she must clean and clean and scrub and scrub and whatever she did she could not sleep. Sleep was the enemy. Terrible things could happen if she slept and terrible things could happen if there was any mite of dust. She did everything she could to stay awake because she knew that sleep was when the worst of the darkness could come.

She remembered endless hours of trying to make everything perfect for her son. Checking that his clothes had no sharp edges. Edges could cut his skin and she had seen visions of how the blood could pour as if from a river. She allowed no one to clean the nursery, terrified that it could contain something that could contaminate her child. She scrubbed it herself until her hands would bleed. She agonised over how to feed him, how to bathe him. He was a quiet little baby and looked at her with big blue eyes like saucers. Then terrible voices arrived seeping through the walls, telling her that something was going to happen to him if she fell asleep. Terrified, she watched him day and night. She stopped sleeping or eating and began scraping wallpaper from the room in case it could poison her child. Desmond had told her that she had peeled wallpaper for thirty-six hours. She scraped the gold-embossed paper from the walls, scrape by scrape, then she banged her head against the wall until it bled. Anything to stop the thoughts, the bad thoughts. Then she saw her mother, her lovely mother, who had crawled from the dark grave to help her. It was then that her husband had sent her to that place. Taking her away from her baby. She recalled little of this except that she prayed again that she would die.

Now she hated her husband. She was silent about it

though. Was she insane? He thought so – why have her locked up in a madhouse if not? She began to scream internally when she saw him. Now she tended to sleep and sleep, with some concoction of drugs that her doctor gave her. But it was a different type of sleep, it was only in that deep sleep that the voices came and somehow she could feel them here. They were watching her. They had found her in this strange, beautiful house with the lake and the mist. Why had he brought her here? When he had collected her from the hospital, instead of going home he drove miles to this place. There was something about it. Something that frightened her even more than the madhouse had. She knew that they were all afraid to let her near her baby – they had taken him away – taken her baby from her. But maybe she could harm him? She knew that Desmond would foolishly be looking at her, hoping there was a change. It was a beautiful house and the lake was almost mystical. It seemed unnatural to be here when she felt so desolate. But there was also something else here or was it that her reality and her unreality had become intertwined like plaited hair? She could not recognise one from the other at times. But she felt something as she walked up the stairs of this house. Something almost pushing her back, telling her to run. The purple colour mixed with black. Big splotches of it across the walls and floors.

The voices. If only they would stop. Maybe they were right, and she was insane. How could she explain to anyone what she was feeling? The aroma of orchids and roses wafted up into the room and for a minute she could feel herself floating. As if her spirit was leaving and looking at her, telling her to leave. But she was as captive here as she was at the asylum. There were no padded cells but she could feel she was being watched, by the seen and the unseen.

There was a soft knock on the door, and she tried to bring herself back to her reality.

The door opened a little. It was Desmond. 'Florence, I'm just going for a walk with Ida,' he said, 'but Vonnie will be here and will check in on you. I'll be back soon.'

Thankfully, he didn't come in.

Ida insisted that they keep up a good front. Any scandal of any kind could damage the long-standing Griffith name. A name that was intertwined with Irish politics. The fact that she had spent three months in a mental asylum for electroshock therapy was not something they wanted anyone to know. Ida had informed her that Desmond was always discreet. Politely refusing invitation after invitation where he could. She wanted to scream at Ida that she didn't care. But Demond never spoke to her about what he told their friends. He spoke only about what the doctors said about her health. Who was she anymore? Not the wife of Desmond Griffith. She was the madwoman in the bedroom. The mad wife out of the madhouse. She began to cry. Cry desperately for the memories that she had that were disappearing. Julia was here. How she wanted to hug her and hold her! Tell her not to worry, that she loved her more than anything. But she was afraid to. Then the voices would know. She couldn't let them know how much she loved the child. The voices destroyed love. That was the key to their existence.

Half an hour passed and she heard a soft knock on the door. It was the same girl, not Vonnie. This girl had a soft warm voice with a lovely lilt to it.

'I have a lovely light chicken soup for you, Mrs Griffith. It smells delicious.'

Florence did not reply. But for once the aroma did not make her gag.

'Perhaps just a little. To keep your strength up,' the girl said gently.

The soup was on a tray with a glass of water and a spoon and napkin.

She waited until the girl left and then she sat up. She put the spoon in the soup, forcing herself to take a small sip. With her hand shaking she forced herself to take a spoonful and then tried another. She took another spoonful and then pushed the bowl away and climbed out of bed. Her legs were like jelly. Barely holding her up. Somehow, she managed to wash in the small pretty washroom adjacent to the bedroom. It took her a long time, but she managed it and then she pulled on a fresh nightgown. Again, she sat in the chair beside the window. Such a setting. She should feel peaceful but instead feelings of pure suffocation almost smothered her. It was as if she was in free flow. Not really part of her body anymore. Desmond had given her pills earlier. It was a struggle to take them but somehow she had managed to. The medication made her drowsy. She was glad of it. She closed her eyes. At least with the drugs her sleep was not invaded. It was a different type of sleep.

There was a knock on the door, and it opened. She didn't look.

'Florence, are you alright? Would you care to join us to sit at the lake later?' Ida's crisp voice asked. She didn't come in.

Florence did not reply. Truth was, she couldn't. When she tried to, it was as if someone was choking her.

'I gather no is the answer,' Ida said.

Later Desmond came in with a slice of cake and a glass of milk. But Florence ignored it. He sat down on the chair that was beside the bed. She could smell his cologne and it made her feel nauseous.

'I will just sit with you for a little while, Florence. Julia

101

is happy downstairs drawing some pictures for you. But I think until you are better it is best to keep her downstairs with us. If you could come down and sit by the lake it would make her so happy. I was thinking of Joseph and how, when he is a little older and you are better, we can come here – it will be a proper guesthouse then. It is beautiful here. I think you will love the rose garden and there are quite exotic trees and plants. Did you notice the beautiful oak on the lawn? Harry told me that it is one of the oldest trees in Ireland. Not sure how he knows that, but it's majestic. You have always loved our garden. The roses that you and Julia sowed last year have blossomed. We will come as a family here again. Just the four of us.'

He put his hand on hers. She wanted to pull her hand away and run as fast as she could away from him and this house.

'Joseph is such a good baby. He has grown so much. I'm so looking forward to having you home. The doctor insisted that you get some fresh air. Will you please let me help you and we can sit at the lake?'

Florence made no reply. Instead, she pulled her hand away and turned so that her back was to him. She closed her eyes, hoping that he would leave.

'I really think you need to try, Florence. I told Julia that you would be up and sitting outside. You need to get some strength. Joseph needs you too. He needs his mother.'

Now he was talking of her son. Her baby. Her Joseph with the big blue eyes. They had taken him away from her and locked her up because she was mad. Why was he talking as if it had not happened?

'He's such a jolly little boy. The nanny is great, but he needs you, Florence,' he said gently.

She could feel her body stiffen with fear. What nobody

knew was that she was terrified to be near her son. What if she harmed him? She was clearly mad. She had just come from a madhouse. What if she did something to her baby? Tears flowed down her face as terrible images of him being harmed flashed through her mind. She reckoned they should have left her in that asylum. How could she ever tell anyone that she was afraid of what she might do to her child? They would lock her up and throw away the key. The best thing for her to do was stay silent and stay away from her son.

Eventually he left and she dragged herself back to the seat at the window. She looked out again at the lake. That woman who had arrived with Ida was playing with Julia again. They were near the lake and they were following the ducks as they swam peacefully along. The woman was holding her hand. Then she heard someone whisper something to her – but she couldn't make out what the voice was saying. She felt her body go limp with fear. A new voice had found her! But this was a different voice, one that was warning her – a female voice whispering to her. *Run, run, run!* She crawled back over to the bed and lay down, putting her hands over her ears, trying to block it out. Had she gone mad? She had no idea. Suddenly she could hear a noise, like a banging sound. It became louder. Was this real or unreal? She rocked herself to and fro on the bed like a wounded animal.

Darkness had seeped into the room since she had fallen into a medicated sleep. Someone had turned on a lamp and an amber glow emanated from it. The door opened and Julia crept slowly in. She walked over to her as if she weren't sure if it was her mother. Florence wanted to scoop her up and hug her, but the voices were back whispering and laughing at her. They were telling her that she would harm her. No, not Julia. No. She wanted to scream that she would never harm her daughter. She pulled the covers over her head and prayed to any god that the child should go out of the room. She knew without even looking that Julia's bottom lip would be quivering. She always did that when she was upset and she was upset, terribly upset. Her mother was not acting like a mother. But Florence knew that she had somehow lost the ability to be anything other than a madwoman who could not speak or eat.

'Mummy, will you come downstairs and play with me? I miss you so much,' Julia whispered.

Then Florence began to see the dark shadows as if they were coming out of the walls. She was screaming but nothing was coming out.

Just at that moment Vonnie arrived in.

'There you are, little pet! Your daddy is looking for you.' Vonnie looked at Florence. 'Maybe we'd better leave your mummy to have some rest. Is there anything I can get you, Mrs Griffith?'

'Would you like some cocoa? Moira made some for me,' Julia piped up.

But Florence closed her eyes and turned away, thanking any god for taking her child away from her.

CHAPTER 12

Rosemary gathered up all the fashion magazines that Ida had thrown haphazardly around the library room. They had been trying to choose what she would wear and what kind of look they were going for to put on the cover. Rosemary had thought that the photographer or the editor would choose that but, according to Ida, she would have the final say. Rosemary suspected that they knew it would be easier to allow her to choose, as to change Ida's mind on anything was quite an undertaking.

They had spent the afternoon discussing how best the shoot might work and more importantly how Ida would look. Rosemary thought that the grounds were so beautiful that it really should be outside. But Ida was not so convinced, believing that it should be on the grand staircase where the light from the stained-glass dome was so flattering. Then they had both agreed that at least one of the photographs needed to have the house in the background. They had tried numerous outfits and they had agreed on a rather equestrian-style outfit and an evening peach-silk gown that really flattered her complexion. Rosemary had tried out numerous hairstyles and they had decided on a simple half-bouffant style, some false lashes, and strong eyes. With her blonde hair and creamy skin, Rosemary knew she would look sensational, and the backdrop of the house would add elegance. But she was exhausted from it all.

Ida was gone to take a long bath before dinner. She pitied poor Vonnie as she heard Ida's bell ringing. It echoed through the house. It still amazed Rosemary how the sound carried through the thickness of the walls but somehow it did. She surmised it was because of the acoustics of the grand hall and staircase. There was a baby grand piano in the hall, and she imagined that many dinner parties had ended with some music in the hall. She heard the bell ringing again. This time relentlessly. It seemed so rude. Ida knew that there was very few staff but she seemed to think that poor Vonnie had nothing else to do but wait on her. Rosemary tidied everything and made sure the room was just as it was, one less thing for Vonnie to do. Ida was certainly demanding, and she could see that Vonnie was run off her feet with her.

But she did enjoy discussing fashion with Ida. It somehow reminded her of her mother. Not that Ida was anything like her mother, but her mother had so loved talking about clothes. Rosemary had learned everything about style from her. She had taught her how to walk and how to wear clothes. She knew that her carriage was just as important as the clothes. She taught her how to dress her hair and she had watched her so many times putting on make-up that it sometimes played in her memory like an old film reel. She looked out of the window and admired the view. She wanted to get out for a walk on her own before dinner. It was a beautiful evening and she wanted to explore the grounds a little more before Ida would be demanding her attention. Ida liked to have at least two cocktails before dinner. Rosemary noted the smell of furniture wax. Vonnie had been busy dusting the hallway. In ways it reminded her of the house she was born in. That too had been beautiful. It had not been near as grand as anything like this, but her mother had made it beautiful. She had loved to polish and keep it spick and span. Her mother's innate sense of style had transferred to the house, making it fit for a king.

If she closed her eyes she could still see her as she whirled around the room in a new dress. Ellen and their father clapping. Her father telling her that she was beautiful and their mother smiling. They had never known that it could end, their little family. How could they have? And so cruelly.

She grabbed a light red cardigan with a big collar from the back of the chair and slipped out the front door. She knew that if Julia saw her, she would want to come. How forlorn the little girl was! There was something about her that reminded her of Ellen, those big blue eyes amidst a dusting of freckles on skin like satin. The lip that quivered when she was upset. But her hair a rich red where Ellen's was white-blonde.

She needed a little time on her own this evening, to try to figure out what was going on in her head. Harry Williams had invaded her thoughts since she had met him, and she knew that he had no place there. His almost hypnotic voice and his rugged features like granite were filling her mind. Her life was complicated enough without adding Harry Williams to it. She questioned herself – why had she really come here? She tried to convince herself it was because of the money that Ida had already given her for the trip and the fact that she felt she deserved a little break from the floor of Brown Thomas. In fact, Ida had demanded so much of her attention that she had not had any time to herself. Ida had clearly no interest in the outside world and, other than sitting at the lake with a cocktail, she spent all her waking hours indoors. Rosemary adored the outdoors. It reminded her of her younger years. Perhaps a little too much.

She walked out the front door onto the vast lawns and past the grand oak tree. Beneath the oak there was a large sprinkling of buttercups and daisies and she inhaled the evocative aroma of wild orchids. She made her way through the vast lawn then stepped down the stone steps across the small footbridge to the lake. She paused for a moment to take in the view, admiring the lily pads that were peeping up through the water. How peaceful it all looked. Perfect peace, she thought to herself.

She took the path to the left that led through the thickest wood. As she walked, on one side was the lake and on her other side the woods. The scent from the woods peppered the air with a hint of jasmine that mingled with the light rain of earlier. A family of swans were gliding effortlessly across the water like the king and queen of the lake. The evening was balmy, and she could feel a sense of calm envelop her. The constant swish of the birds on the lake and the trickle of a stream somewhere in the wooded area kept her company. There were stone statues and little stone benches dotted along the path. Some of the statues had pieces missing like a hand or even a head, their faces mottled with white and grey splotches. They gave a regal sense to the place. She could hear the ducks as if they were squabbling and, when she turned a corner, she watched them as they ducked and dived, turning themselves upside-down in the water, chasing each other and fishing for their supper.

She could hear horses in the distance whinnying. Ida had told her that there was a stable, but she still had not had time to have a look as far as there. A memory hit her as it always did when she heard horses. Her father had loved horses. He spent most of his time with them, either racing them or bartering them or talking in pubs about them. They were a beautiful animal but as a child the horses that her father kept looked wild and fearsome. She could see him now lifting her high onto his shoulders to protect her as he checked on his stock. If she closed her eyes she could almost inhale his scent, that scent of the outdoors, of horses, of leather saddles and of laughter. Did laugher have a scent? When she was a child, she used to tell her father that it did. The scent of laughter was the same scent as hard-boiled sweets and butterscotch, she used to say. She listened again as she heard the whinnying of horses, making her feel lonesome for the father that she had so adored. How she missed him! It seemed in some ways like a dream now – the memories that she had, could they really have been that happy? Or with time had she imagined that they were? She tried to bring her mind back to the present. The past always had the power to pull her back.

'Need some company?'

She jumped.

'Sorry. I didn't mean to startle you,' a distinctive voice said behind her.

She knew it was him before she turned around. His voice was embedded in her mind. This was the last thing she wanted, as to be seen with him on his own here on the estate would only raise suspicions. She could smell his cologne before she turned around.

He was smiling, his eyes crinkling and his mouth in that sideways smile. His eyes were drinking her in, making her feel uncomfortable as well as something else that she dared not name. She could feel her heart beat a little faster and knew that her face must be flushed and signalling the effect he had on her.

'I am just walking to clear my head.'

She walked on, and he fell into step beside her.

'It's a lovely evening,' he said.

'It is,' she replied.

'I hear Ida has kept you busy.'

'Oh, it's fine. I enjoy discussing fashion,' she said.

Just then two large collie dogs appeared and made her jump. They were panting as if they had been chasing a rabbit or a hare through the woods. They seemed excited to see Rosemary and pushed their bodies against her legs.

'Don't worry, they're simply curious,' he said, rubbing their heads.

'I had no idea that there were dogs here. Come to think of it, I did hear dogs barking last night but I assumed they were somewhere else.' She laughed as she bent down and nuzzled them.

'I'm afraid Ida is allergic to dogs, well, that's what she tells me anyway.' He grinned. 'I have them out in the stables. I have just a few hunters down here. I hope to have a few more horses soon – maybe breed a bit. I'm looking at land that joins the estate – it was sold years ago but I am sure with the right money it could be bought back.'

'You like the countryside?'

'Yes. You sound surprised?'

'No ... I ... it's just ...'

'You're surprised because I'm an inner-city man. But my mother is from a farm in Galway and my father was born to a fisherman in Donegal, so the country is in my blood. They moved to Dublin to earn money and my father worked for Guinness all his life. They stayed and reared ten children.'

'Oh, I hadn't realised.'

'Yeah, I am an inner-city Dub, but the country is thick in my blood. How about you?'

'What do you mean?' she asked, a slight anxiousness creeping in. She had no intention of discussing her parents with anyone or her upbringing.

'Well, where were you reared?' he asked, a strange knowing look on his face

Normally she was able to brush this question under the carpet. Ida had asked her once and she just said that her parents were from the countryside, but she had moved to the city. Ida had not asked any more. But she could feel him staring intently at her as they walked, waiting for an answer.

'I was born in Roscommon and lived there until I was almost eighteen. Both my parents died young.

'I'm sorry to hear that. What happened?'

'I … don't really talk about it … very much … if you don't mind.'

'Of course. It must have been difficult for you. Do you have any siblings?'

Rosemary could feel her body tense.

'One – lives abroad, I don't see her.'

'I see. Family falling-out?'

'Something like that. This is such a beautiful place.'

She could see him smile out of the corner of his mouth.

'I gather you don't want to talk about her either?' he said.

'No, I don't.'

They walked in silence for a few moments and Rosemary hoped that he would let it drop.

111

'I bought this place over a year ago, I fell in love with it,' he said. 'It was in the spring when I first saw it, just as the bluebells were in bloom here in the woods and the gorse was bursting into colour along the hedges. It was a sea of blue and it took my breath away. Then I came back in another month or two and the crocuses and azaleas were in bloom and the pink rhododendrons were all along the avenue. It was a sight for all the senses. I had thought we could have it and use it ourselves, but Ida has made it clear she has no interest in spending any time here. That's why I've decided to turn it into a country house for paid guests – equestrian-type holidays.'

'I can imagine how pretty the bluebells must have looked.' Rosemary was relieved that they had moved on from the earlier conversation.

'I think it's a little piece of heaven here but, if it wasn't for that fashion shoot, I doubt Ida would have come down.'

'She does love the city,' Rosemary said, feeling disloyal. Here she was, out walking with Ida's husband. She didn't feel it was right to be discussing her in any way.

'Yes, she does,' he said quietly.

They came to a place where the path divided, and he took the one that was narrower. When they turned a corner, she could see a haze of wildflowers, a cornucopia of rainbow colours with bees buzzing in a frenzy, the pops of colour like coloured candy scattered around. They kept walking and soon they arrived at a rusted gate and a rusted railing around a small enclosure. Inside the area it looked overgrown with roses that had grown wild and untamed. A labyrinth of weeds and briars. The grass was unlike the kept lawns and was high with nettles and weeds. The rosebushes were huge with flowers that were dead and black, and the body of the trees had wrapped themselves around each other in a rather strange embrace. Then she gasped as she saw a tomb inside the enclosure almost hidden behind the gnarled rosebushes and beside it a stone angel, mottled with one of the wings broken off. The face of the angel was almost erased, giving it a ghostly look. Harry opened the gate and they walked in. He broke a branch and made a path through the nettles and weeds.

'My goodness, who is buried here?' Rosemary asked.

'Sophia Elizabeth Harris. I'm afraid Jimmy Berne is a bit afraid to come in here, says he is afraid he will be cursed.' Harry laughed. 'That's why it's so wild in here. I'm surprised the Harris Family allowed it to be so neglected.' He pointed to a place on the tomb where an inscription was engraved in the stone, almost faded now but just about legible.

Rosemary read it.

Here lies Lady Sophia Elizabeth Harris who died on November 2nd, 1845. Formerly of Devon, England. Aged 19 years. Lovingly remembered by her devoted husband Lord Henry Harris.

'Why is she alone here?' she asked. 'Strange that there are no more graves. What about her husband? Is he buried here, I wonder?'

'No, she is very much alone here. He was not quite as devoted to her as the inscription implies. Her husband remarried and is buried in France, according to the solicitor who looked after the sale. Local folklore is that she drowned, and he would not allow her body to be taken away to be buried but eventually allowed her to be buried here on the grounds. The husband left and remarried and had three children – all of them died before him, including his second wife and he died in terrible pain. He believed he was cursed from his first wife, so he never returned.'

'Why cursed?'

'Not sure really. But this is Ireland, and I'm sure the townspeople had lots of superstitions at the time. But the solicitor said that he believed she had cursed him for forcing her to marry him. She had wanted to leave but he wouldn't let her. The Harris family were a very wealthy family and had numerous estates, but he brought her here which was according to what I have heard the smallest of them. When he died a cousin of his inherited Lenashee. All the rest of the family are buried either abroad – mostly in France – or in the local Protestant cemetery in Druid that the family had helped to build – well, financed. They have a private area there. Part of the arrangement is that this plot remains, of course.'

Rosemary looked at it. How sad to think of this poor girl who died at such a young age. She made the Sign of the Cross and said a silent prayer for her.

'Where did she drown?'

'Here in the lake. I'm afraid it was at her own hand, went mad they say. Local legend says that she still walks the grounds, trying to find the way out. He was known as a bit of a brute. Not sure what is truth and what is folklore. Legend has a way of growing legs and arms.'

'Oh goodness, so she never escaped. Even in death her body was kept here. That's so sad.' Instinctively she picked some wildflowers that were growing amongst the wild plants and placed them on the tomb, trying to imagine what it was like to be so unhappy here. She knew what being trapped felt like and she shivered.

They silently left the enclosure and began walking a little further along the path.

'There are lots of portraits of the family in the small room off the drawing room, if you are interested,' he said.

114

'There are loads of other things too – candles and books and even some burial clothes belonging to the people.'

'What kind of clothes?'

'Well, I'm not sure. They seem to be some sort of shrouds and clothes used for waking and burials.'

'Shrouds?'

'Yes, that were used when they died. I keep meaning to sort it all out. I'm going to send the portraits to France to the ancestors there. They expressed a mild interest in them. I have no need for them. I'll auction them if they don't want them. This place might have been owned by the English for generations, but it's owned by a proud Irishman now and I have no desire to look at their painted faces. They were lucky the house was not burned at the time of the burnings in the 20s.'

Harry obviously had more than a hint of resentment about the fact that the Anglo-Irish had owned many of the great Irish estates across the land.

'What about the hunting pictures that are hanging everywhere?'

'They are part of the house. And I love horses. I will keep them.

'Is there a portrait of the young woman who died?'

'I don't know. If you would like to have a look at them, feel free to … now that I think of it there is a portrait of a young lady. It could be her. Very beautiful.'

'Really.'

'Yes, a beauty, but the artist obviously knew she wasn't happy as she looks sad in it. Probably is her, now that I think of it.'

'I would love to see them – if that's alright?'

'Feel free. The key is hanging above the door.'

A sprinkle of rain began to fall, making the scents of

the woods even stronger. Rosemary was aware of the closeness of Harry. At that she tripped over a loose branch and just managed to save herself from falling flat on her face by putting out her hands. Harry went to help her up and the absurdity of the fall made them both laugh out loud. He pulled her up and then she was in his arms. She couldn't remember afterwards how they had become so close. Feeling his breath on her face, his closeness. She pulled away.

'I have to go,' she said breathlessly.

'I'll see you later.' His voice was quiet but definite.

She saw the look in his eyes. It mirrored how she felt. But she was not going there, she was no mistress. And she did not intend on becoming one.

'I have to go,' she said. 'Ida will be looking for me.'

Rosemary almost ran away.

The mist was closing in on the house as she walked swiftly back, and she thought how mystical it looked. She should never have gone out there alone. She would not have stumbled upon him if she had stayed in the house. As she came closer to the house, it seemed different to her. She now knew a little more about the people who had lived there and the story of the young girl, and somehow it didn't feel as peaceful as it had felt earlier. When she looked up at the house it was now darkened because the sun had shifted, and the windows looked lonesome. She imagined the young girl looking out at the lake, the lake that she would drown herself in. Somehow it all looked a little sinister now.

She saw Vonnie looking out at her through the dining-room window that overlooked the lake. She was setting the table for dinner. As she drew closer, she was taken aback at the stern look on the housekeeper's young face. She looked behind her – thankfully, he had not followed her. There was no way Vonnie could have seen that she was walking with Harry Williams. And she had not done anything wrong, even if she did see. However, it could be interpreted differently, and she could imagine what Vonnie might read into it. But even before Harry had arrived, she had noted that the housekeeper was very sullen with her. For whatever reason, she had taken a dislike to her.

The guilt that she felt almost engulfed her. What was she doing? Playing with fire? Once the shoot was over, she would leave and get the train back to Dublin and she would make sure never to put herself in the same place as Harry Williams again. She didn't really trust herself with him because, although she hated admitting it, she knew she was falling for him.

CHAPTER 13

2019

The next afternoon Julia left for her cottage in Wexford. They had bought it over twenty years before and bit by bit they had restored it. It had a view of the sea and was near the village of Blackwater. The road to it was very narrow which ensured that very few people came down. It really was a little piece of heaven and not far from Dublin. It was evening by the time she arrived. She had telephoned David the night before and he had promised to cook dinner. As she got out of the car she looked out at the Irish Sea. Wild and majestic with light foamy waves and seagulls soaring. She would have a long swim tomorrow. She grabbed her bag and went inside her home.

Julia had the knack of finding gems in antique shops and flea markets and the cottage was furnished in a whimsical way with lots of soft cushions, throws and rugs in burnt oranges, rich reds, and dusky pinks. Nothing matched, from the thick brocade curtains to the scattered ornaments and photos. It was the essence of uncomplicated pure comfort and she adored it. It was also full of mementos of her life. She hoarded even the smallest thing that reminded her of a time or a place. From a map of

Scotland that she got when she first went backpacking to a doll that she had as a child. She knew why she did it – it was to remember – because she had tried all her life to regain some memory of her mother but never really managed it.

David was cooking when she arrived. He gave her a bear hug and in a moment the months apart were wiped out. He had cooked a roasted red pepper and ricotta lasagne and, after they had eaten, they curled up on the sofa beside the fire and caught up on the last two months.

It was late when Julia told him about her father and the strange feeling she had about this woman called Rosemary.

'That's quite a coincidence,' David remarked.

'Why?'

'I was looking for a book to read and wanted something different. Remember those books that you found in your father's bedroom that you brought home on your last visit? You were getting the room ready for your father's return from hospital and you borrowed a book of poetry of his. It's by Robert Frost. You said that your father loved his work.'

'I know it, but what about it?'

'I took it to have a look at it and inside the cover was a small cut-out of an article. From a newspaper. There was a photograph. It's of a woman – but you can't really see her face. But something about a fashion show – I am nearly sure her name was Rosemary. She was a model, I think, in Dublin. Must be years ago though.'

'Where is it? This article.' A glimmer of excitement awoke in her.

'*Hmm*, I think I put it back in the book.' He got up and retrieved the well-worn poetry book from a row of bookshelves. 'Yep, here it is,' he said as he opened it and took out the article. He handed it to her.

Julia took the worn piece of newspaper and examined

it. It was a small cutting, and the image was faded. It was of a dark-haired woman in a long cloak-type coat. The picture looked many decades old. She read the article. It said that the woman in the picture was Rosemary Purcell. The article was about a fashion show being held in Dublin by Sybil Connolly. It went on to say that Rosemary was working in Brown Thomas and, when one of the models became ill, she stepped in and literally stole the show.

Julia grabbed her laptop and googled her name. Nothing came up. She kept scrolling and scrolling but nothing. She had subscribed to the archives of the *Irish Times* and scrolled through that. But nothing. Then she tried fashion shows and Sybil Connolly. She scrolled and scrolled.

'Right, I'd better lock up,' David said.

But Julia was too engrossed in her laptop.

Eventually – *bingo!* – she found something. It was about the same fashion show in 1967 but this time there was a close-up of Rosemary Purcell. She was striking with very dark hair and dark eyes with long lashes. Julia could feel herself holding her breath as she stared at the smiling face.

'You okay?' David asked as he put the damper on the stove.

'Look at this! It's her again. She just looks so familiar to me. I have seen her before, I am sure of it. It's her smile – I feel I know her. I wonder if Dad knew her. I'm afraid of upsetting him. Might be too much to show him this, if this is who he is talking about. And *why* is he talking about her?'

'Who else could you ask?'

'I'll ring Aunt Ida in the morning and tell her I am planning to visit.'

'Oh, I might let you go yourself. I might get another lecture on how well her son's law business is doing. Not sure I could hack it. But your aunt plays her cards tight to her chest. She won't say too much if your father had a wild affair with this woman.'

'I know – and she could just brush me off if I ring. That's why I will ask her face to face. Then I will know.'

CHAPTER 14

Aunt Ida, her father's sister, a widow now in her eighties, lived in Rathgar in Dublin. Julia had telephoned her to tell her that she was coming to visit. Aunt Ida was not the type of person you could just drop in to. She would find it most discourteous. So, the arrangement was made under the pretence of just a visit. Julia had read an article about her aunt recently in the *Gloss* magazine. It said that in her younger years Ida was the queen of the social diary and had held numerous honorary positions. She was also well known for her fashion sense and it was said that she never left the house unless perfectly turned out. She was known for impeccable dress. There was no casual dress in her wardrobe – every day was a day to be dressed properly. Although in her twilight years now she was often quoted as saying: 'There is no excuse for letting your sense of style lapse.'

She lived in a large Georgian townhouse. Julia was met by Margot when she rang the bell. Margot was Polish and was one of the most efficient people that Julia had ever met. She was also very pleasant. Margot came in every day and took care of Ida and the house. There was also a cleaner who arrived three times a week and a gardener that looked after the rose garden at the back. At one point Ida had a butler but sadly he had passed on. Her aunt complained that it was impossible 'to get staff that are trained today' but then she had found Margot. Margot oversaw the other staff and looked after all Ida's personal arrangements as well as preparing her meals.

Ida's husband Harry had left Ida extremely well off. There had been some scandal about how he had obtained some of his wealth but Ida had rubbished that. The evidence was too thin to carry for a tribunal or any criminal charges. But the rumours had tainted his name. She had one son Laurence and the less Julia had to see of him the better. He was a lawyer and one of the most pompous people that Julia had ever met. She had loved her Uncle Harry and often thought that Laurence was the opposite to him. Laurence was a snob of the highest order, something that her late Uncle Harry could never be accused of. But her Aunt Ida was someone who believed in class distinction and was extremely disillusioned about how the world was going. She was known to almost faint in horror when she saw how some dressed. Women's leggings she maintained should be burned as well as cycling shorts and tracksuit pants.

Once inside the elegant entrance, Julia walked into a rather grand reception room with large expansive windows revealing the rose garden. There was a pink sofa with a gilded coffee table, set with china cups and plates. A decorative marble fireplace was the centrepiece. A large flower arrangement in different shades of roses welcomed her. Around the room were small mahogany tables with silver-framed photographs of Ida and her husband over the years at various events. Ida possessed some oil paintings of note that hung around the large room, including two Jack Yeats paintings.

The aroma of Chanel Mademoiselle signalled Ida's arrival into the room. Today she was dressed in a gold bouclé jacket with a cream ruffled silk blouse underneath and cream palazzo pants. Her blue-grey hair was pinned into a perfect chignon, her make-up light with a hint of blush on her high cheekbones. Her lips were a rich pink and her green eyes lit up when she saw Julia. Even now she was a striking woman. She stood rather grandly and waited until Julia came over to her and gave her a peck on each blushed cheek.

'You look wonderful as always, Aunt Ida.'

'We must try. That is an interesting outfit, Julia – I'm not familiar with the designer?' Aunt Ida's voice was elegant and clipped. She scanned the full length of Julia, openly examining her.

Julia immediately wished she had made more of an effort.

'It's something I picked up on my travels. Not designer, I am afraid. A boutique in Berlin actually.' Julia was wearing a rather bohemian-looking long grey-linen dress that she had actually bought at a Berlin market, but she wouldn't tell her aunt that. Ida hated trends and fast fashion. Like the Parisians she believed only in buying the highest quality. The perfect capsule wardrobe with a couple of new quality pieces added each year. Although Ida had bought a lot more than a few in her heyday. There was a large, mirrored room upstairs now dedicated to her clothes. She called it her boudoir.

Ida pursed her lips at the mention of 'not designer' and pointed to the sofa for Julia to sit.

'Sit, my dear, and we will have coffee.' Then she held up a small gold bell and rang it. Within moments Margot returned. Julia surmised that Margot was waiting outside

124

for the ring – Ida insisted on proper procedure to any social calls.

'Or would you prefer tea?' Margot asked, looking at Julia.

'Coffee is perfect. Thanks, Margot.'

'Could you check on Coco, please, Margot? She was in a deep sleep on my bed and I did not want to waken her,' Ida said worriedly.

'Of course. I'll bring your coffee shortly.'

Coco was Ida's Bichon Frise and was taken for a shampoo and hairstyle every week. She had several pink outfits including a diamante-encrusted one.

'How is your father?'

'I'm afraid he deteriorated quite a bit while I was away. Joseph rarely leaves him.'

'Joseph is such a blessing. But I do worry that he will forget how to live himself. I still cannot believe it when I see your father. He was always such a wonderful conversationalist and so handsome. I miss talking to him so very much.'

Julia knew that her aunt had a close bond to her father. To her they were chalk and cheese but there was no denying that they had always been extremely close.

'It's heart-breaking.' She wanted to come straight out and ask her about this Rosemary person, but she thought it better to wait. If there was something in the recesses of her aunt's memory she wanted to know it. Did her father have an affair? She would never have dreamed of it. But she was ruling nothing out. Somehow, she felt Aunt Ida would know. Whether she would tell her was another thing.

'How is David? Still a sculptor?' Ida pursed her lips.

Being an artist was not a profession that Aunt Ida would encourage. Politics like her own father's or business like her husband's were notable careers. Or law like her son's. Medicine would be next. Julia recalled the first time she had told her about David.

'*A sculptor? My goodness! You poor girl!*'

'*You make it sound like I will be destitute.*'

'*Well, won't you?*'

Over the years David had slowly won Aunt Ida over.

'Where is he today?'

'Oh, he's meeting a friend for coffee and then visiting the art galleries. We're meeting for lunch afterwards.'

Julia handed her aunt a gift of a bottle of cognac. Quite an expensive one.

'Thank you. Julia, you look tired. I believe you've been travelling again. Alone! Just like your father. He was never happy to stay in one country. Surely you can write about other stuff now. I worry about you. You're not as young as you were. A woman of your years can't be hopping around the world like a backpacking teenager. I can't even think about how you are going off to those awful hot countries with no chaperone. Your father was the same, dragging you all off when you should be at home. Taking you out of boarding school to go gallivanting to those tropical places. I was terrified something would happen to you. Could you not stay a little more in Ireland and stop all that travel? I know that it can't be good for your illness.'

'I'm fine, Aunt Ida. I have never felt healthier. My medication is working and my last visit with my doctor was good. There is no need to worry about me.'

'You have been worryingly ill many times. I will always worry,' Ida replied a little too sharply.

Julia tried to stay calm. Unfortunately, Ida had seen her at her worst. She was first diagnosed after a visit to India when she was nineteen. Up until then she had suffered with different episodes of depression and manic behaviour. But after India she was hospitalised and eventually diagnosed as bipolar. Since then, she had some episodes but with her medication and her health regime it was under control. But there were difficult times. The heartbreak of not having children had almost pushed her over the edge. They were told that there was no hope whatsoever of her conceiving. She had tried numerous invasive treatments but all in vain. But she had made peace with it and so had David and she knew that what they had was special.

Julia knew that arguing with Aunt Ida was futile. To say that it was the most fabulous childhood she could imagine and that exploring other countries and writing about them was her dream job would only start an argument.

Luckily, Margot arrived in just then with a silver tray bearing a silver coffeepot and a coffee cake.

'I just checked Coco and she is still sleeping. I will check her again shortly.'

'Thank you, Margot dear. She gets upset when she wakes up alone. She is tired, the poor little mite. The beauty parlour takes a lot out of her. She finds it exhausting.'

Julia hid a smile at the thought of the little dog needing a nap after her day in the spa. 'Thank you, Margot. That looks wonderful,' she said.

Margot poured some coffee into china cups with delicate hand-painted flowers on them and then cut slices of the cake and handed them out.

Julia tasted the cake. It was light and moist with hazelnuts and pecans.

'My goodness, did you make this, Margot?'

Margot nodded.

'It's absolutely delicious.'

Margot beamed and thanked her then left, closing the door gently behind her.

Julia decided it was a good time to ask Aunt Ida the question that she had come to ask. It would not do to just ask her. She would come around it.

'Actually, Aunt Ida, there was something I wanted to ask you.'

'Oh!'

'It's about Dad.'

'You say he has deteriorated?'

'To be honest, he's not good at all,' Julia replied quietly. 'But I wanted to ask you something?'

'Go on. I thought this was more than just a social call?' Ida said dryly.

'Well, Dad's illness is so difficult, and he gets so anxious all the time.'

'That's hardly surprising.'

'He is constantly asking about someone and we don't know who it is. He seems to be heartbroken over her. He wants to know where she is. We thought you could shed some light on it.'

'Go on,' Ida said cagily.

'Well, he keeps mentioning someone called Rosemary. He keeps weeping over her. Did you ever know anyone of this name? Perhaps someone from my father's past?' She thought it better not to mention the article that David had found just yet.

Aunt Ida put her cup down and dabbed her mouth with a napkin. She took a long hard look at Julia.

'I have never heard of a person of importance in your father's life called Rosemary. It means nothing to me. The man is ill, for goodness' sake. Dementia as well as terminal cancer. It could be a secretary or maid. Even one of his nurses or carers. Did you come up from Wexford just to ask me this? You could have telephoned.'

Julia was taken aback by the annoyance that seemed to have come into her aunt's voice. But she decided to pursue it.

'Of course not, I wanted to see you. But we are worried about him and he is so distressed over this person. I thought that if there was someone who could shed some light on it, we could somehow ease his mind. Also, David found an old article in a book of poetry belonging to my father and it was about a model called Rosemary Purcell. Perhaps it's some sort of coincidence and means nothing. But I googled her and there was such a person. She was a model in the sixties. I thought you might have heard of her as you knew Sybil Connolly the designer. She modelled for her at a show in Brown Thomas.'

'Well, I certainly don't recall any models and I can tell you there was never anyone of that name in either your father or your mother's life. I would be certainly aware if there was an important person of that name. I have never heard of her. This dreadful disease. I advise you strongly to think no more of this and try to distract him. I'll go over to Howth to see him next week.'

'Really, you have never heard of the name?' Julia pressed.

'I have never heard the name. Is that definite enough?' Ida replied adamantly.

'I was really hoping you would because the name seemed to trigger something for me. Dad hummed a song too and I know I heard it many years ago. It was like déjà vu. It's an old Irish love song. "My Lagan Love." Somehow I thought it was all connected.'

'Your father is Irish – I'm sure he sang you Irish songs. You are reading far too much into this, Julia. Perhaps you have jet lag from your trip.'

Julia knew she was getting nowhere. Aunt Ida was definite about the fact that she had never heard of this woman. But there was something about just how definite she was. She changed the subject, and her aunt began to tell her about a charity do with a hospital that she was involved with.

'We have raised so much I am hoping that they might even honour Harry and name something after him. He did a lot for this country, creating and building jobs and all the charity work that he was involved in,' she said rather defiantly.

Julia knew enough about Uncle Harry to know that anything he had done for the country was soiled with rumours of large amounts of money being given to influential political people by him. There was little hope of anything being called after him except a tribunal investigating his shenanigans.

They finished their coffee and chatted, then Julia air-kissed her aunt goodbye. Ida was not someone who would appreciate a hug.

'I will go over to see your father next week. Remember his mind is weak now. Just distract him and give this name no more thought. It's only nonsense.'

Julia drove back into the city and got a parking space on the Green. But she was feeling disillusioned about getting no further. She called David to see if he was finished in the art galleries.

'Aunt Ida denies knowing her.'

'You say denies?'

'I felt she was hiding something. She was so adamant. Just a little too adamant.'

'Well, I changed my mind about going to the galleries – I have just been to the national library, looking at records and guess what I found?'

'What?'

'I found our Rosemary Purcell in an article from the *Sunday Press*, society page, and she is with no other than your Aunt Ida.'

'*What?*'

'A photo of Rosemary Purcell and Ida Williams. Two socialites. Your Aunt Ida was quite a looker. But I recognised her. It says that they are at a charity dinner dance in the Shelbourne in 1967 and they were judging some best-dressed competition.'

'She lied. I knew it. But why?'

'We need to do another bit of digging before you go back and tackle your aunt. There is no doubt but that she is hiding something.'

CHAPTER 15

She checked her phone. It was just after three in the morning. Her sleeping pattern always took a little while to settle after being in a different country. But she'd had a dream that had awoken her, and she knew there was no way she was going back to sleep. She crept out of bed, threw a robe on and went downstairs. The kitchen was still warm. She popped on the kettle and took out a teapot to brew some camomile tea. She felt a bit shaky after the dream. It had felt so real and so clear. In the dream she was a child sitting in a room with bookcases. But it was in a different house than her own and there was a woman singing the song that her father had hummed. The Irish lullaby. She couldn't see the woman's face, but she had a red dress on, and her voice was haunting. Then she could see a lake and the lady was sitting on a blanket and Julia was listening to her. She was talking to her and they were laughing. Then it changed, and the lady was on the stairs and her father was there. Her father said that he had never heard a voice as lovely as hers. Then she awoke. Her heart was racing. It seemed ridiculous but she knew the dream meant something.

She poured the boiling water into the teapot and grabbed a mug. She took the teapot and mug into her office adjacent to the kitchen. She sat down at her desk and flicked on her laptop. She searched again for Irish models in the 60s. She found lots of articles on Sybil Connolly and how she had really put Ireland on the map for fashion. But there was little about the models and nothing about Rosemary Purcell. She was about to shut it down when she came across a blog by a writer called Kate Wilson who was looking for information on historical cases of women who died at their own hand during the 1960s. She was looking for anyone who might know anything about a Rosemary Purcell who had once been a model in Dublin. It was assumed that she had drowned by suicide as her shoes and her coat were left on Howth Pier. But her body was never recovered. It seemed that this writer questioned why there was no investigation into Rosemary Purcell.

A shiver came over Julia. Why was her father talking about her? Why was her aunt lying? This woman was presumed drowned off Howth Pier. A few hundred yards from her father's house. But in the dream there was a house that she did not recognise. She knew that was where she would begin. She needed to find out where that house was.

She sipped the tea and eventually went back to bed, only to slip back into another dream. One that was confusing and erratic and left her exhausted. When she did get up, the first thing she did was retrieve the piece of information about the writer Kate Wilson. There was an email address for anyone with any information. But what could she say? She didn't want to say that she thought her father and her aunt knew something about this woman. Eventually she said that she had found an article about Rosemary Purcell in a library book a year earlier and thought it might be significant. She also said that she was interested in the whole topic and would love to see her thesis or perhaps talk to her about it.

She checked her email every half hour but there was no reply. Then at six o'clock there was one. The writer said that she was familiar with Julia's work as a travel writer and would love to talk to her about the article that she had found. Would she like to call her?

She dialled the number.

'Hi – this is Julia.'

'Hello, Julia.'

'This sounds an interesting project, Kate.'

'I'm so delighted that you contacted me. I adore your work.'

'Well, your thesis sounds so interesting and especially this part about this Rosemary Purcell. I can send you a copy of the article. Do you think there was foul play with this girl?'

'To be honest, I've no idea. But I did speak to a nun who knew her sister. She said that there was a letter that was discovered years afterwards, addressed to the sister who was a nun in the convent. It was dated around the week that Rosemary had disappeared. But somehow the letter went missing in the convent and the nun never actually got to see it.'

'How?'

'The letter arrived at the convent but was not given to the nun and it somehow got put in a drawer and was not found until the building was sold, and the furniture was emptied. But it is dated the week that Rosemary went missing and her shoes and coat ended up on Howth Pier in Dublin. It's a bit mysterious because she wrote to her sister saying how wonderful everything was. She said that she was in the West of Ireland at a lake house with a friend and she –'

'A lake house?' asked Julia, startled.

'Yes, you know, a house by a lake – apparently a rather grand house on an estate. Well, the nun took the letter to the police but as far as I know there was no investigation into it. There was some mystery too about Rosemary Purcell – I have tried to find some relatives, but I can't seem to trace where she came from before she worked in Brown Thomas. Anyway, I managed to have a read of this letter. The sister died in 1989 and is buried at the convent. But the strange thing was that the nuns never knew she had a sister. In the letter Rosemary said that she was away for a week in the West of Ireland. She was helping at some fashion shoot. But the letter is mostly about the food that she ate. She describes the food in detail – French-inspired dishes as well as roast lamb and lemon blancmange. She mentions that it was cooked by a young girl called Moira. This was a bit of a long shot, but I wrote to Moira Fitzpatrick to see if it was her. But I've heard nothing back from her. To be honest, I'm at a bit of a dead end. Please do send me the article. It might be a link.'

'Yes, of course, and good luck with your thesis. I would love to read it when it is finished.'

David walked in just after she hung up.

'Coffee?'

'Yes, please.'

'What's up?'

Julia told him about the phone call and the presumed suicide.

'Are you sure you want to go digging anything up? Maybe he did know this girl and had some sort of brief encounter with her, but your aunt has a point – your father is on so much medication he's not in his right mind. You hardly want to go digging into his past.'

'But it feels important. I can't explain it. I feel that I knew her too. I had a dream last night about a house with a lake and my father and I were there with a woman. I'm sure it was this Rosemary. *Feck*, I have just thought of something.'

'Go on.'

'Remember I told you that Uncle Harry had bought up some old houses over the years? It was Matthew Carty the photographer whom I used for my last book who said it to me. He said he had heard in conversation that Harry had a property somewhere in the country that had a lake. But I told him that he didn't and that all his properties were sold other than the house that Ida is in.'

'Where is this going?'

'I asked Ida about it and she was very cagey with me and told me that Uncle Harry's properties were of no concern of mine. I know that he did have a development under a lot of scrutiny over the years but that was in Galway. But she was certainly sensitive about it all.'

'Probably revenue was after him and he was trying to avoid them knowing about some of his properties. Your uncle was certainly a man of many interests. He had property in London, didn't he?'

'Yes. He had to go over there quite a bit actually.'

'There were enough rumours about him being a bit unorthodox.'

'*Hmm* … but that dream last night has really got me thinking. I am not sure – but it's like a bad case of déjà vu.'

'I'm not with you. What do you mean?' David asked, slightly worried.

'Well, this writer said that Rosemary said she was in a house in the West of Ireland, in Clare, with a lake. Well, in the dream I was at a house with a lake. I don't remember any house with a lake but there is something in my memory about one.'

'It's a bit of a farfetched hunch.'

'I know but I have to follow it up. Especially with the link to Howth Pier.'

'I don't know, Jules, maybe you should leave well alone. I'm not sure I like the sound of all this.'

'I know … but just let me see about the house. I promise I'll leave it after that.'

'Try the internet. Look up County Clare. There can hardly be that many big houses with a lake.'

She turned on the laptop and looked for lake houses in County Clare. She scrolled through a few things and then she found an old photograph of Lord and Lady Harris at their summer residence in Ireland at Lenashee near the village of Druid in Clare in 1965. But it wasn't the lord and lady that drew her eye – it was the house and the lake in the background. In an instant she knew she had visited that house. She scrolled, looking for information on it.

'*Lenashee*. I wonder what that means in Irish?' Julia said as she squinted at the computer, trying to decipher why the place seemed so familiar to her.

'I don't know but it's in the song that you said your father hummed.'

'What?'

'The word *Lenashee* is in "My Lagan Love" – the song your father hummed.'

'Oh, yeah, you're right!' Julia looked up the song and scrolled through the lines and then stopped as she read a line. '"*Like a lovesick Lenashee*".' She could feel a rumble of excitement. 'Look at it. David, it's beautiful. I was there. I know I was. Why does it seem so important to me?'

137

'Why not ask Ida about it? She might recall you visiting.'

'She'll blow me off. She is still annoyed about why I asked about the name Rosemary. Gosh, I wonder could I visit it?'

'What? You are hardly going to drive to Clare on some notion that it might be important to you?'

'Why is there no more information on it?' Julia said, oblivious of what David was saying.

'Maybe ring the County Council down there and see if it's state-owned. They will hold any records on it and even maps.'

'Really?'

'Well, it's somewhere to start. Oh, Jules, I am not sure about this. You seem … very …'

'*What?*' Julia asked, a bit too sharply.

'I don't know but you have talked of little else since your return and your father is not going to be around too much longer. Can you not just put all this on hold and look after yourself and spend some time with your father? I'm worried about you, I really am.'

'I have to go and see it,' Julia said, barely registering what David was saying. She was engrossed in the image on the screen.

'What do you think you are going to find there?' David asked.

'Possibly nothing but I have to go.'

CHAPTER 16

Lenashee 1967

Moira soon realised that having Ida Williams in the house was quite an undertaking. Vonnie had warned her that she would insist that she called her 'Madam' and she certainly lived up to the name. The small gold bells that were dotted around the house seemed to be constantly ringing – in her bedroom, the library and the drawing room. The sound of the bell echoed right through the house and then Vonnie had to figure out where the sound was coming from. Ida Williams thought nothing of calling on Vonnie for the slightest thing. If the flowers decided to think of wilting or if she needed the blinds drawn. Vonnie answered it most of the time but sometimes Moira had to leave whatever she was doing and run to attend to whatever Madam deemed an emergency. It might be that she wanted some cold cucumber to put on her eyes or it might be that some bees had found their way into her bedroom and were being a nuisance. But if either Vonnie or Moira did not immediately attend to it, she would ring the bell constantly until they did. She liked to bathe morning and night in her bath adjacent to her room, and she drained all the hot water from the boiler and poor Vonnie had to drag extra up to her. But Moira loved the scents from the bathroom that seemed to linger in the air for hours. Vonnie said that it was the bath oil that Madam used that was sent over especially from London. Moira thought the scent was like being in a field of roses and lavender.

Moira had found Rosemary quite unassuming, contrary to what Vonnie seemed to think of her. Even though she was dressed very fashionably and walked like she was brought up very fancy, there was also something about her that Moira really liked. For a start, she made a point after every main meal to come down to the kitchen to thank Moira and talk to her about whatever dish she had served. She told her that it was the best cooking she had ever tasted. Moira couldn't help but admire her style and found herself complimenting her on her outfits. At first she had felt a bit awkward when Rosemary arrived down and started chatting in the kitchen. Vonnie was clearly not happy about it and said as much but it didn't stop her coming down. Moira loved to see what outfit she had on each time. Moira wore the same old skirts and blouses every day and was delighted to see Rosemary wearing colourful trousers which she called Capri pants – she told her that the film star Audrey Hepburn wore them a lot. Moira thought they were terribly stylish and planned to buy a pair the next time she was in Dublin. She knew that Katie would love them. Katie loved clothes, but those for sale in Jefferies Drapery store in Druid or in Ennis were far from Capri pants. They really needed to go to Dublin to get some style. She couldn't wait to tell Katie all about Rosemary. She had never thought much about clothes and style but there was something so elegant about Rosemary that inspired interest. She loved how everything seemed to fit her perfectly. She found herself relaxing in her company and, as she told her about how she had cooked something, she found herself asking for a little advice on clothes. Moira thought herself very average in appearance. She was an average height and an average size and her fair hair was cut short. But Rosemary told her that she had very blonde curls, honey-coloured skin and blue eyes with hazel flecks. She advised her on some simple changes to her wardrobe that would not cost too much and a little make-up. Moira had never really looked on herself as pretty, but she took the advice and promised to herself to buy a little make-up and get her hair professionally cut when she went to Ennis next and maybe get one of those Capri pants in a pale blue and a new blouse in Dublin.

She had taken the train to Dublin with Katie a few times. She had been in awe of the lovely windows of the select grocer's, the fancy clothes in the windows with no prices on them and the lights as they lit up O'Connell Street like a fairyland. She had watched the big friars as they walked along in their long brown cloaks. She had seen buskers and watched people whizzing by on bicycles and had felt very grand as they ordered tea and scones in a tea shop on Grafton Street.

Her mother did not approve of paint and powder, but she would try to get a bit of lipstick and some powder for her nose when she was in the chemist's in Ennis. Rosemary had thick false lashes that curled, and she told Moira that she applied them every morning. Moira couldn't imagine spending very much time getting ready in the morning, but she loved listening to Rosemary, and it was nice how interested Rosemary was in her cooking. She was not used to getting personal praise for it. If there were any compliments on her cooking, she doubted that Mr Hunt passed many of them on.

But Vonnie made it known that she was not impressed with her chatting to Rosemary. It was causing a bit of a strain in the kitchen, but Moira tried to ignore it.

But it was the little girl that most concerned Moira – she seemed so forlorn and it was obvious that she was missing her mother terribly. Thankfully, Rosemary seemed to have noticed too and was spending time with her – taking her out to the lake and even walking as far as Druid to the post office. As far as Madam was concerned, she ignored the child, only speaking to her sporadically and mostly telling her to be quiet as noise brought on her migraines. Her father was spending most of the time horse-riding and, if not, he was busy working in the small study just off the library. At least they had not brought back any wild grouse for her to cook just yet. She had overheard Mr Griffith telling his daughter to go play, that he was busy writing something. He seemed nice and very gentlemanly but a bit distanced from the fact that his child was left alone a lot of the time.

But Moira was pleased at how her cooking was going down – apart from complaining that she was getting them to eat too much, the compliments were plentiful. Except of course for Mrs Griffith who to her knowledge had eaten little or maybe even nothing.

Moira was busy in the kitchen when Vonnie walked in for a much-needed tea break. Then Madam's bell began to ring.

'There she is again. What could be wrong now?' Moira said crossly. 'I know it's not my place to say but I really think that Madam needs more staff if she requires the attention that she seems to be seeking.'

She was making a soufflé earlier when Vonnie was

tending to other chores when Madam's bell had begun to ring incessantly. Because she had to run to attend to her, the soufflé had been ruined.

'Well, she certainly has more staff up in Dublin,' said Vonnie. 'I really don't know what she was thinking. I think she thought that Mrs Berne would be here to do most of the housework, but the poor woman can hardly walk with her back. I'd better go to her. I was wondering too if there is something I could take up to Mrs Griffith? Anything that I can try at all that might be different and appeal to her?'

'Maybe a little ice cream. I made some yesterday. It's in the freezer. Anything would be something,' Moira said, shaking her head.

'She looks very frail.'

'Too frail to be here, to be honest.'

'I'll get a bit of the ice cream and see will she take a few bites, but it is hardly up to us to see if she eats anything. Maybe they should have hired a nurse to look after her … she was just released from the nuthouse after all.'

'*Shush*,' Moira whispered.

'Well, she was … and I'm not convinced she is cured. She is staring into space any time that I go up. Staring like a bit of a lunatic, to be honest. I think she's still mad, and they haven't cured her at all. Maybe it's hard to cure madness. It's not like curing a sore throat.'

'*Vonnie, whisht!* They might hear us,' Moira said worriedly.

'Well, there should be a nurse just for her and, as far as Madam is concerned, I'm so fed up. She's so busy in Dublin that she's rarely in, always gone to some lunch or show, but here she seems to have far too much time on her hands and Mugsie here has to answer to her calls.'

'So much of the stuff that she calls you for could easily be done by herself.'

'Spoilt! That's what's wrong with her,' Vonnie said crossly.

'It's the poor woman upstairs that's worrying me. I don't think anyone other than us two realise how poorly she is, though. Or how demanding Madam is for that matter!'

'Hopefully Mrs Griffith might perk up today – we have enough to do without worrying about her,' Vonnie whispered. 'Whatever you're cooking smells lovely.'

'I have my roast on for the main course for this evening's meal. I had planned to cook it earlier until Mr Williams brought in trout from the fishing for lunch.'

The bell began to ring again.

'How on earth can we hear that bell throughout the house,' Moira said, not for the first time. 'The walls are three feet thick.'

'I really don't know,' Vonnie said, sighing.

'You'd better go before she blows a fuse.'

'I bet she wants the afternoon tea earlier. So much for my cup of tea. Have you everything ready?'

'Yes, I have some gooseberry tartlets fresh from the oven and some freshly whipped cream to serve with them, a chocolate-and-raspberry cake and some delicate vol-au-vents with minced chicken and cream sauce in case they need something savoury.'

'Hide a few of those vol-au-vents for me. I'll be in dire need of that mug of tea once I have them sorted.'

'I will and a gooseberry tartlet too.'

'I know you're busy, but would you have time to take up the ice cream to Mrs Griffith? Then at least I can get the tea to the library.'

'Leave it to me,' Moira said, glad that the frostiness that was there earlier seemed to have disappeared.

She laid out the afternoon tea so that Vonnie could take

it to the library. Everyone seemed to love sitting there. The drawing room was nice too but there was something so opulent and cosy about the library that it was where they went if they were not in the dining room.

She spooned some strawberry ice cream into a bowl and put it on a tray with a spoon and a napkin. When she got up to the room, Julia was sitting outside with a small teddy bear. Moira put the tray on the wide windowsill and went over, kneeling down beside her. She noticed that the child had been crying again.

'What's your teddy's name?' Moira asked.

'Chocolate Bear,' Julia replied in a whisper.

'Oh! Does he like chocolate?'

'Yes.'

'Is Chocolate Bear sad today?'

'I dunno.'

'He looks a little sad.'

'His mummy doesn't want him anymore.'

'Why ever not?'

'Because she's sick.'

'Oh, I see. But when she's better, she'll be so glad to play with Chocolate Bear again. I'm going to make some little fairy cakes now – would you like to help me, and we can ice them? I have some lovely decorations. Some little golden iced balls and some coloured flowers. I'll make some soft butter and sugar icing for the top.'

'Yes, please,' Julia replied, her eyes lighting up.

'Well, you can go and have some tea in the library and when you're finished you can come down to me in the kitchen.'

The child scampered down the stairs.

Moira knocked on the bedroom door and opened it. She could see that Mrs Griffith was awake, but she was alarmed at her pallor. She looked grey rather than pale. She set down the ice cream, knowing that she probably wouldn't even touch it. Again, it struck her that this woman needed to be in a hospital of some sort. But she reminded herself that it wasn't her place to say it. Surely her husband had noticed? Madam didn't seem to have spent any time with her at all – the shoot was the next day and she was busy picking out clothes, having Rosemary styling her hair and making sure that Vonnie was run off her feet. When she was not doing any of this she was talking on the telephone or chatting to Rosemary about fashion and drinking copious amount of gin cocktails or elderflower tea laced with gin.

'Can I get you anything else, Mrs Griffith? A cup of tea perhaps?' Moira asked gently.

But there was no response. The woman kept staring into space. There was a strange sense in the room and Moira felt almost relieved when she stepped back outside onto the landing. Then she realised that she had meant to take down the jug and replenish it with some fresh water. Reluctantly she knocked on the door again and opened it.

When she walked in Mrs Griffith was sitting up in the bed with a very frightened look on her face. Moira looked in the direction that she was staring but she could see nothing there. But she was staring into the corner as if there was someone there. Yet there was an eerie feeling as if they were not alone. But Moira knew that was daft. Just because the woman looked like she was imagining someone in the room with them did not mean that there was someone or something there.

'Mrs Griffith, are you alright?' Moira asked gently.

But she just kept staring. She then put her hands over her face as if to shield herself and lay down, turning her back to Moira.

Moira took the jug and went downstairs and refilled it with fresh water. When she arrived back up Mrs Griffith was still lying down with her eyes closed. She put the water down on the bedside table and walked back towards the door. Just as she was about to go out the door closed, making her jump. She looked to see if the window was opened. It was but it was a calm day, one of the calmest that had arrived. She tried to shake the uneasy feeling that had come over her. She looked back at the bed and Mrs Griffith. She had a terrible urge to waken her and try to take her down to the library where the scent of the orchids was so beautiful. She could lie on the couch and look out on the garden and the lake. Although the bedroom was quite beautiful in a very ornate way, there was something about it. Maybe Vonnie was right in her claim that there was a feeling of sadness about the place. It was certainly true of this bedroom. She opened the door and quietly let herself out.

She went back into the kitchen to get the ingredients ready for the fairy cakes. At least with most of the prep for the meal that evening out of the way, she had a little while to spend with Julia. She spent the next hour happily mixing and baking the little cakes. She then prepared the icing. Rosemary arrived down looking for Julia and when she saw what they were doing she asked if she could help. Moira had all sorts of colours to add to the icing and they spent a happy hour icing buns to their hearts' content. When Mr Griffith arrived down, Moira could see how relieved he was to see his daughter giggling and laughing.

After they left and she had cleaned up from the cakes, she began the evening meal.

The evening passed and again her cooking was a huge success. She nipped up with some homemade lemonade to

147

Mrs Griffith and was taken aback when she saw her out of bed in a light nightgown. Her poor bones looked skeletal, her mane of red hair falling over her frightened face. She was staring at the wall as if there was something there again. Moira set the lemonade down and ran down the stairs to tell Vonnie.

Vonnie threw her eyes to heaven when Moira relayed how Mrs Griffith was. 'Madness to bring the poor woman here. I don't like it one bit. Sitting by the lake and getting sun they thought she would be. It's a hospital she needs not a holiday in the wilds of Clare. She was only released, and they brought her here. They should have waited before bringing her off somewhere like this. I'll go tell Mr Griffith. He's having a cocktail in the library.'

As Moira was driving home, she could not get Mrs Griffith out of her head. There was something not at all right with her. When she had gone into the bedroom and seen her standing there, the woman looked like she was not aware at all. Her heart went out to her. She had a terrible look of fear about her. If she still refused to eat in the next couple of days that they were still here in Clare, a doctor would need to be called. Again, she felt slightly annoyed at having to worry about this. It really was the concern of her husband but to Moira he seemed slightly blind to just how sick his wife was. She hoped that he would realise in time.

CHAPTER 17

The next morning after breakfast Vonnie got a message to say that her mother was poorly, and arrangements were made for her to get the train back to Dublin from Ennis. Moira couldn't help feeling a little sorry for herself when she heard the news. It was busy enough as it was and now Vonnie was leaving. How was she to manage? She didn't want to seem insensitive to Vonnie though – her mother was very poorly, it seemed, and the message was to come home immediately.

Moira was preparing the vegetables for lunch when Vonnie arrived into the kitchen to say goodbye. She was ready to leave, with her coat and hat on.

'I know it leaves you in the middle of this,' she said. 'It's not right really. If Madam wanted to have the type of holiday that she seems intent on having, she should have much more staff. Mr Williams is getting two staff down from Dublin – there's a nice girl Bridget that works for us and her sister Nora. They come whenever we are having a party or anything. So, he has already got in touch with them, but Bridget is working today and they will be down on the early train tomorrow. So, if you can just get through today and some part of tomorrow … I can have a word with Mr Berne and see if his wife can come up and give you a hand.'

'No, the poor woman needs rest by the sounds of it. I will muddle through,' Moira said worriedly.

Vonnie put on a pair of gloves. 'Will you be alright?'

'I'm going to miss you. If Madam would stop ringing the bell I could manage. I thought the house was on fire earlier when she was ringing it looking for her breakfast to be brought to her. When you were getting packed, I went up to collect her tray and she took the nose off me. She was in a right strop and told me that she didn't want to be disturbed for a few hours. Why would I want to disturb her anyway? I am trying to cook for her, that's all! I was hired to cook not to wait on Mrs Williams. Also, it's not my concern but that poor woman upstairs seems intent on starving herself and I don't think anyone realises just how little she is eating. Nothing that I have made seems to be eaten by her – the bowl of porridge came down untouched this morning.'

'You just do what you are supposed to do,' Vonnie said. 'Let them worry about poor Mrs Griffith. You'll have to serve the food too, but I am sure they'll help you. All the linen has just been changed and the house is spick and span. And I spoke to Mr Griffith and he said that you are not to worry at all. I think he plans to take his wife back tomorrow. I know he was talking to the hospital and she might be going back there. If Madam starts ringing the bell you will just have to ignore it – don't worry, she will get the message.'

'Oh!' Moira didn't like the idea of having to send her any message.

'Stop worrying, Moira, it'll be fine. Just let them know when the food is ready and ask for help if you need help taking it up. But you might be better to stay tonight. You'll be busy enough and I expect if they are going back to the hospital they will set out early and need an early breakfast. I have put fresh clothes on my bed and cleaned the room. It's by far the nicest room up there. You might as well use it. It's very pretty and has its own washroom. Once you know what the noises are, it's fine. I have got so used to them I don't even hear them – old pipes always make noise and those are certainly old. I did sleep but probably because I was pure exhausted from lugging extra hot water up to Madam. But at least if you stay you will be here early in the morning and not driving home late this evening.'

'Oh. I'm not sure my mother would be happy with me staying here.'

'Really, why ever not?'

'My mother … she's very suspicious of people. She wouldn't approve of me staying away from home.'

'Even if it's for work?'

'I'm afraid not – let's just say it would be easier just to go home.'

'Well, it's up to you, but it seems a shame not to stay. You could pick up your clothes when you go into Druid today to pick up your messages. You know, I meant to say to you that I am sure the butcher's might deliver your meat to you.'

'I like to see exactly what I'm getting. I know the butcher and I would not put it past him to send me fatty bacon or a goose that is too old for roasting. He can't put anything by me if I am there myself to see it. I'm a good judge of meat and I know what's good and what's not.' The idea of staying was appealing but she had no idea how she would get around her mother. 'I get the feeling that you will be glad to get back to Dublin?'

'I told you that ever since I set foot in this house I have had an uneasy feeling. A strange sense to the place, as if when I run up and down those steps I am not alone, as if someone is watching me. I know that sounds silly, but I'm glad to leave it. I know the house is old, but it's as if the stories of the house are still here in it. Ah, listen to me! Sure, I must sound cracked ... and we already have one cracked woman in the house!' She winked. 'I can't explain it. I wonder what really happened within these walls over the years. Somehow, I feel it was not always good. I'm worried too, like you, about Mrs Griffith upstairs. They brought her here thinking a break away would do her good. Well, we can see how that worked out. If I were her husband I would take her back to Dublin straight away – not tomorrow. I went up to say goodbye and the poor woman is rocking herself to and fro. Gosh, I remember her before she got sick, so pretty with that long red hair, with beautiful clothes. You would not recognise her now. She was always playing with Julia, like two kids they were. She would come to visit Madam and Julia would always be by her side. The poor child is lost without her and it must be so hard for her to understand what is going on. Sure, I think they were afraid to bring the baby down with her here.'

'Why ... afraid?'

'Well, she's not right in the head and shouldn't really be near a baby, I suppose. But sure, she hasn't been out of that room since she arrived. Oh, before I forget, I will tell you why Madam is in a strop. A phone call came earlier to say that the big fashion shoot had to be cancelled until later in the week as there was a mix-up or something. Madam was disgusted. I wouldn't be surprised if she leaves too and cancels it altogether. But don't worry – they will still pay you if they leave. Handsome Harry is very generous. So at least you won't have the photographers to feed today. It leaves Madam at a loose end so try to not let her get to you. I'm sure once she has a sleep she will be ringing that bell. Just ignore it. She will soon stop. The two girls from Dublin will be down by lunchtime tomorrow and then at least one of them can attend to Madam. That is, if she hasn't run back to Dublin.'

'I'm going to miss you,' Moira said.

Mr Berne arrived at the kitchen door.

'There's a storm on the way. Best to make sure you have everything that you need in the house,' he warned Moira.

'I will. Thanks, Mr Berne.'

'I'll take your bag, Vonnie.' He grabbed it and left.

'I hope you get back safe and sound,' Moira said to Vonnie.

'I hope so too. My mother is low. I hope she will pull through this time, but her heart is bad a long time.'

'I'll say a prayer that she does.'

'Thanks, Moira. Will you remember to tell Mr Griffith that his wife ate nothing again this morning? As you say, she is intent on starving herself. I would say it to him myself, but he is gone fishing.'

'Do you think he will mind me saying it? Is it not above my station as such to be saying things like that to him?'

'I think you have to, Moira.'

'Alright. She must be as weak as a kitten.'

'Just mention it to him if you get the chance. I'm not sure about the storm that Mr Berne is talking about. It looks quite calm out there now.'

'I'm a bit surprised that Mr Griffith went fishing, leaving his wife here,' Moira whispered.

'He said to me that Madam was looking after her and Julia. *Ha!* As if! But sure, I couldn't say that to him. He would think me disrespectful, but what rubbish. She hasn't looked in on the woman all morning or the child for that matter.'

'Well, thank God they are taking her back to the hospital,' Moira added. 'I wish there was someone here today though to look after her.'

'Mr Griffith, nice and all that he is, does not seem as worried as he should be. Madam is not much of a sister-in-law. I was told that they would all be looking after her. But all she cares about is her big fashion shoot. She pays me well. I won't complain and she looks after me but there is not much love lost between her and her sister-in-law. I have it on good authority that her and her brother were inseparable and then he met his wife – well, I am told that Madam tried to come between him and his new wife. But it didn't work. Before she got sick, they seemed so happy as a couple. I often saw them when they were heading out to parties and they would call for Madam and Mr Williams. Mrs Griffith's hair was always piled high on her head and she had gorgeous dresses. She was always nice to me and made a point of asking me how my mother was. The poor little child needs her so much. I will give that one her due – Rosemary – at least she is spending some time with her. It's not right, though, the poor little child being left to her own devices. It can't be easy having her poor mother gone cracked in the head.'

'No, it must be hard on her.' Moira agreed but didn't feel she should gossip anymore about her employers in case they were overheard.

'You'll be fine, Moira. Just do the cooking and after today you will only have Madam, Rosemary and Handsome Harry to look after. I have a feeling Mr Griffith will take Julia home with him. Madam has a cook back at their house called Mrs Flaherty. She will be under pressure after they sampled all your lovely food. I would not be surprised if they offered you a job. Mrs Flaherty should be retired years ago. She worked for Madam's mother before that. Madam entertains a lot and Mrs Flaherty's food is not always fancy enough for what she wants and Madam orders food in. The guests never know this. Mrs Flaherty goes mad, though, at the insult that she is not good enough. There are often fireworks in the kitchen. But, if you were there, she would not need to order food in.'

'I really want to work in a French restaurant someday, so I won't be taking up any jobs in houses so Mrs Flaherty can rest her mind.' Moira grinned.

'Maybe we will meet again, Moira.'

'I hope we do, Vonnie.'

'Come to Dublin and we will go to one of the showbands. You can stay in my mother's house. I will show you where to buy those trousers that you so admire on that one. You could look for a job in that fancy French restaurant that Madam loves on Nassau Street.'

'I'm not sure I would have a hope of a job there.'

'You're forgetting that you are cooking for Mrs Ida Williams and her husband. Believe me, if they put a word in for you, you could be working there. Handsome Harry seems to know everyone, and his word carries a great deal. Sure, they are constantly having Ministers and important people for dinner. Charlie Haughey was over recently. Now he is very charming. Likes his fine wines and his cigars. The Archbishop has even dined with them on different occasions. I always make myself scarce when he is around – he gives me the jitters in his big red cloak. Not sure Mrs Williams really likes him, but I overheard her saying that he has a lot of clout. If he doesn't like something, you'd better watch out. It's not that they are religious in any way. But Handsome Harry likes to keep in with the big powerful people in Dublin and there is hardly anyone more powerful that the archbishop. I would say that Mrs Williams would love to see Mrs Jackie Kennedy before she goes back to America. I hear she is staying in Waterford. But I heard nothing about an invite. If Madam gets an invite to visit her we will know all about it. The fussing over what she will wear will be unbelievable.'

'I'd love to visit you and come to Dublin,' Moira said, excited at the thought.

This could be the opportunity that she was looking for. Secretly she was seriously thinking of leaving home. She had put up with enough of her mother's taunts. If only she was not leaving her father there. But there was nothing she could do. For her own sanity she was beginning to think that she would have to – sooner rather than later. But she needed enough money to get a place to live and feed herself until she got some work. A job in Jammet's would be a dream come true and some day she would make her way to France. It would be one step closer.

'You do that. Write to me and I can meet you at the station when you come up. Take care now, Moira. I'd better be off. Mr Berne is waiting to drop me to the station. Write to me and tell me how the rest of the week goes. I left my address over there on the dresser. I will be dying to know.'

'I will.'

The late morning was hectic. The men had gone fishing and Madam had completely ignored the fact that Vonnie was gone and was constantly calling Moira for the least little thing. Moira was trying to remain calm, but it was becoming hard to. She had brought Madam her midmorning coffee with some seed cake that she was partial to and had requested.

Julia arrived into the kitchen, looking rather subdued. Moira had noticed an old china tea set with blue violets painted on them in one of the presses in the kitchen that was not in use and she washed it and set it up with some cookies and homemade lemonade for her to play with in the library. Julia was soon content, having tea with Chocolate Bear. Just as Moira was heading back into the kitchen Rosemary walked in dressed in a lime-green pencil skirt and bright-yellow silk blouse. Moira thought it was a very striking look and admired it.

'Thanks, Moira. What a lovely tea party you have set up for Julia. May I join in?' she asked a beaming Julia.

'You can sit between me and Chocolate Bear,' Julia said, clearly delighted with the company.

'I have to make a quick run to the town, is there anything that I can get you?' Moira asked before she left.

'No, thank you, and don't worry about Mrs Williams. I will go to her if she rings the bell. I heard about poor Vonnie – I hope her mother is alright.'

'Thanks, Miss Purcell, that would really help as I am worried how I am to manage on my own until tomorrow.'

'Don't worry. I'll help you and I can help in the kitchen too if you need it.'

'Thanks. It's just Madam's bell really.'

'Don't give it another thought, I will handle Mrs Williams,' Rosemary said as she sat down, and Julia poured lemonade into a china cup for her.

'Thank you,' Moira said, relieved. 'Right, I'd better be off. There is some more fresh lemonade in the fridge. I will be back soon to prepare lunch.

'My clothes are getting tight with all this amazing food,

Moira. I will have to go for a long walk today,' Rosemary said, grinning.

'I took up some fresh water for Mrs Griffith, but she's asleep – so I left it beside her,' Moira said.

'I'll keep an eye on her, Moira. You have enough to be thinking about.'

'Great, right, I'd better be off.'

Julia was so engrossed in organising her tea party that she barely noticed Moira leaving. Moira was glad that Rosemary was there because, if not, the child would be alone and there was no one to keep an eye on Mrs Griffith. She tried to stop feeling annoyed at the fact that her husband thought it was alright to leave his daughter and his sick wife in the care of Madam. Madam who had not set foot outside of her bedroom since her strop earlier.

She got into her mini and drove the couple of miles into Druid. The market was on today in the village and the place was overrun with geese, hens, calves, cows, and goats. It was quite a small town to hold a fair, but it was an immensely popular one with people coming from the neighbouring villages and towns. The pubs were busy, and she could see lots of the menfolk were sinking pints of porter and the women, all dressed similarly in skirts, coats, and headscarves, were talking in small groups, with children climbing in and out of prams.

She watched Naggie Nelligan wheel a big, rusted pram with a fine fat goose sitting in it. Naggie was known for speaking her mind and this morning was no different.

'Hello, Moira, I hear you're up in Lenashee cooking for the grandeur.'

'I am indeed, Naggie. I'm rushing now to get some stuff from McDaid's.' Moira really didn't have time for a big chat with Naggie today.

'Did you see any strange things up there?'

'In what way strange?' Moira asked curiously.

Naggie stopped and coughed, then she pulled an old handkerchief out of her pocket that needed a wash and blew her nose with gusto.

'Me mother used to work up there. She was in the scullery, but she said that there were strange things in that house.' She put the handkerchief back in her pocket and secured her green wool headscarf under her chin. Her eyes were slightly sunken into her puffed-up red face.

'I don't know what you mean by strange?'

'On a black night in the dead of winter she said she saw a young woman with a long dress walking past the kitchen window – then she vanished just like that!'

'Vanished?' Moira asked.

'Vanished! Then she saw the carriage – the black carriage with the horses coming for a soul. Then that too disappeared into the night. Another time there were footsteps on the top landing and, when the woman in the house looked, she saw a woman walking there who vanished and she swore to the Lord Himself that her face was the same as the one in the picture.'

'What picture?' Moira asked.

'Over the mantelpiece in the library there is a big picture of a young woman – the finest woman in Ireland. She was meant to be so good-looking that a man could faint just looking at her.' Naggie came closer and whispered in Moira's ear. 'She drowned at the bottom of the lake but something in that house drove her to it.'

Moira thought of the story that the Master had told her. Vonnie had told her that she was convinced that there was something odd about the house. But Moira couldn't recall any portraits hanging in any room.

'There are no portraits of any young women in the house. You must be mistaken, Naggie. There are only big hunting pictures.'

'Well, the house was once full of them. I know that for sure.'

'I have heard about the young woman who died in the lake.' Moira could smell whiskey off Naggie but, even if Naggie was partial to her little whiskeys and the odd drop of poteen, Moira had never known her to lie about anything. 'I'd better go, Naggie.'

'Watch yourself up there,' Naggie warned as she wheeled her pram off.

Moira felt slightly unnerved after Naggie's revelations. As she passed the chapel, she blessed herself and tried to forget the conversation. Her day was far too busy to ponder on it, even if it had shaken her a little.

She went into McDaid's and got what she needed and then she drove home for her nightgown and a few things. She had decided that she would stay the night. Her mother was not impressed when she said she would not be home.

'There's no way that a daughter of mine is staying away in a house with people that don't even attend Mass. Heathens the lot of them. Do they have no religion?' her mother shouted at her.

'I don't know!'

'*That's it!* There's no way you are sleeping there tonight. Spreading their evils ways! No daughter of mine is staying the night in a house with no bit of religion in it. I asked Mrs Berne if there was a Sacred Heart lamp burning in their parlour or a holy picture on the wall and she said she didn't recall! Didn't recall! Surely you would notice if Our Lord was on the wall in the house or Our Holy Mother's picture was there! "No," says she, "I don't recall!" She would tell you nothing. A sleeveen is all she is. I'm telling you now, Moira, I am not having you there! It's bad enough you are there at all, let alone at night. I'm not having my daughter up there with jezebels and men in flash cars and a Mission on in the town. You better not miss Confession tomorrow!'

Moira had had enough. 'Their religion is of no importance to me and it is my job to stay there tonight and maybe for the rest of the week!'

'I warn you, Moira, not to go against me!'

'I'm not! I'm doing my job.'

'You were always trouble. The boys never gave me an ounce of trouble. But you were always looking for it.'

'How can you say that?' Moira cried, knowing she had never given any trouble.

'I've tried to warn you, but you won't listen to me. Staying away tonight so you can get up to no good. I'm no fool, Moira, so don't take me for one!'

'Well, I'm sorry you feel like that. But I don't know what you think I will be doing that is so bad. I have to work and then go to bed and then get up and go to work.'

'Don't lie to me.'

'Ah, I'm sick of this. Every time you have a chance you are at it. What the hell do you think I'm going to do? What kind of mind have you?'

'*How dare you answer back to me!*'

'*I'm sick of it!* Sick to the teeth of you getting on to me. Making me feel like dirt on the street. Get out of my way!'

With that Moira walked out of the door and into her car.

'*Don't think you can darken this door again! Troublemaker is all that you ever were!*' her mother roared at her.

'*Don't worry, I won't!*' Moira cried.

She was shaking and tears were flowing down her face as she drove away, knowing that her mother's anger would spill onto her quiet father and he would bear the worst of it. Guilt rose in her for her father. Frank Fitzpatrick looked years older than he should have. He worked far harder than a man of his age should, and Moira was worried that it would send him into an early grave. But he did whatever it took to try to keep his wife from giving out.

As she drove back up the avenue to Lenashee she stopped at a break in the trees that gave a glimpse of the lake to try to calm herself. A grey heron was in the distance and she thought how graceful it looked. It was like a sign. There and then she reminded herself that she had no choice. She would have to stay with Katie for a few days after her stint here. She couldn't stand it anymore. Then she would plan to leave. How, she had no idea. But she would find a way. She stopped and took a few long breaths to try to calm herself. She felt better now that she had made the decision. Then she spotted some moorhens amongst the longer grass. There was something quite magical about the lake but a dark sky in the distance signalled the storm that Mr Berne had warned her of.

She hurried on and got back to the kitchen with her supplies and the promised goose for the following night. She had some fresh vegetables too. She was serving lemon blancmange and baked blackberry pudding for dessert. She had a chicken roasting for lunch with some summer salad. She made some chicken soup and hoped that Mrs Williams might just have some.

She was just about to prepare the rest of the lunch when the men returned from their fishing trip with a large salmon and asked if it could be cooked for lunch. Vonnie had warned her that if they went fishing she would be expected to cook their big catch straight away. She put aside her other plans for lunch and began preparing the fresh salmon. She took the head off and gutted it and then poached it. She assembled it on a silver platter with some fresh vegetables around it. She made a butter and parsley sauce to go with it. She had a light green pea soup to start and a raspberry-and-custard tart with the rest of the deserts. There was some elderflower wine, and the men had some whiskey and ice as an aperitif. When she brought the platter in, they made a great deal of taking a photo of her with the silver platter in her hands holding the fish.

'You're spoiling us, Moira, with your wonderful recipes. This meal is fit for a king and, yes, I will have a slice of that raspberry tart,' Harry said cheerily when the meal was over.

Moira freshened up their drinks and brought Julia a comic book that she had bought in the town.

'You're very kind, Moira,' Mr Griffith said.

'No problem. Sure, I was in the shop and saw it and thought of Julia.'

'I popped up to see Florence before lunch – she might have a bite when she wakes up?'

'Hopefully,' Moira replied.

She wanted to talk to him about his wife, but she wanted to speak to him alone. She made a cup of tea and brought it up to Mrs Griffith just to see if she was indeed still asleep. She was. She was sleeping so much that it was even more concerning, and Moira was again slightly annoyed that she seemed to be the most concerned.

Rosemary had helped with the serving and brought the plates down to the kitchen with her.

'I can help wash and dry,' Rosemary said.

'Oh, there's no need.'

'I would like to help – you can't be expected to do everything, and I can see that you are busy.'

'Well, thank you – I might take some fresh water up to Mrs Griffith.'

Moira was not sure how comfortable she felt having Rosemary alongside her in the kitchen, but she was right – it was all too much, and she was not going to say no to a helping hand. She fetched a fresh jug of water that she had cooling in the fridge and went up the long stairs.

Then she saw Mr Griffith walking into the library, and seized her chance to talk to him.

'Excuse me, Mr Griffith, but might I have a word?'

'Of course.'

'Vonnie asked me to let you know that Mrs Griffith has eaten little. I'm afraid she ate none of the chicken soup that I brought her – or anything else. She has actually eaten hardly anything in the last few days.' Moira didn't feel it was her place to be talking to him about his wife but the woman had really eaten nothing since she arrived.

Mr Griffith was still dressed in his outdoor clothes and looked very relaxed with a brandy now in his hand.

'I had so hoped that this little visit here would help but instead it seems to have made her even more withdrawn. Her not eating can't really continue. Thank you for telling me, Moira. I am taking her back up for a check-up with her doctor in the hospital tomorrow and I am expecting him to admit her. So, we will leave early in the morning. My wife seems to have really withdrawn from me. I can't get through to her at all and the fact that she refuses to speak is devastating.' He said this almost to himself.

Moira couldn't help feeling sorry for him yet a little annoyed too, as well as embarrassed that he was talking to her so personally. He seemed an intelligent man and very sophisticated which made her wonder even more about his decision to bring his sick wife to the wilds of Clare.

'I think it's best that she gets to see her doctor. I'll try bring something else up today,' she said kindly.

'Thank you, Moira.'

Moira brought up a small bowl of bone broth and some toast to see if she could tempt Mrs Griffith. When she opened the door, she was sitting on the bed, rocking herself to and fro with her hands on her ears. She was making small whimpering sounds like a wounded animal.

Moira put the tray down and went over to her. The poor woman looked so distressed.

'Mrs Griffith, what's the matter?'

But Florence just stared at her with eyes that looked as wild as a wild animal's. Moira went downstairs to look for her husband. This could not continue. Someone needed to be with this woman today.

She knocked on the library door and Mr Williams coughed and then told her to come in. When she walked in, she stood respectfully a few steps away. He was sitting sipping a large whiskey and a cigarette was smouldering in a crystal ashtray.

'Moira, I was just thinking what a wonderful cook you are. Have you had any training other than the hotel?'

'No, but I do hope to one day. I want to go to France to train.'

'Well, it's great to have ambition, Moira. It really is and you should go.'

'Thank you.'

'Now what can I do for you?'

'Mrs Griffith looks very unwell. I thought it best to let Mr Griffith know.'

'Well, he just left with my wife and Julia for a walk along the lake.'

Then Moira noticed that Rosemary was also in the room. She hadn't noticed her at first as she was almost behind the door. She had finished in the kitchen and said she was going to freshen up. But she must have been having some sort of private conversation with Mr Williams instead.

'I can go after them,' Rosemary suggested.

Moira thought that she was somehow glad of a reason to leave the room. Perhaps Vonnie was right all along? She did seem a bit cosy with Mr Williams.

'Oh, would you mind? I have some pots boiling on the hob and I don't want to leave them unattended.'

'No problem. They can't be far. I'll be back soon,' Rosemary said.

Moira wasn't sure but she sensed that she had walked in on something in the library. And she also noticed a kind of private look that passed between Mr Williams and Rosemary.

She went back into the kitchen to heat some hot milk for Mrs Griffith. She was taken aback at how dishevelled she had looked. She should be in a hospital today and not tomorrow. She had a large pot boiling with dishcloths in it and they were creating a lot of steam. She grabbed a cloth and moved the pot off the hob. They had a big lunch, but she knew by the time dinner came around they would all be hungry again, and she needed to organise afternoon tea.

She heard the kitchen door opening but she couldn't see who it was with the steam. When the steam cleared, she gasped as she saw Mrs Griffith in a nightgown, and she seemed to be walking as if in a trance. It was as if she was not aware of anything around her. Then Moira noticed blood on her face and her hands.

'Mrs Griffith, what's happened to you?'

It was then Moira noticed that she was pulling at her hair, taking it out in clumps, the rich red hair falling around her shoulders and on the floor. Her face was scratched and torn. But it was the expression of pure black fear on her face that frightened Moira the most.

CHAPTER 18

Blood was coming from her scalp onto her face. Moira held her breath in shock. If she left her, anything could happen. She watched in shock as Florence's empty gaze rested on a large array of knives that Moira had left out earlier on the butcher's block. Moira wanted to scream for Mr Williams, but she was afraid that she would startle her, and God knows what she would do then.

'Mrs Griffith, you're not well, let me help you,' Moira said as gently as she could.

She walked over to her, seeing the full extent of her ravaged scalp that was now bald in places and gently pulled the woman's hands away from her hair. But she still seemed unaware of her presence.

'Let me take you back to your room. You'll feel better when you lie down, and I'll bring you a nice cup of tea.'

She gently caught her hand and began to steer her towards the door and then to the stairs that led up to the grand hall. From there they mounted the main staircase. All the time Florence kept staring up to the top landing as if she were looking at something or someone. She looked so afraid and she began to whimper and cry.

'There, there, Mrs Griffith, everything will be fine,' Moira said as reassuringly as she could. She looked up the stairs but other than a stream of light from the stained glass there was nothing to see. The poor woman was imagining things. Vonnie had said that they had to lock her up for that before, so unfortunately it looked like she would be locked up again. Moira talked soothingly to her along the way, but she knew that this woman was gone beyond hearing anything. With a huge sigh of relief, she reached the bedroom and took her over to the bed. She felt more annoyed than ever. There was more hair and blood on the bed and on the floor. This woman needed to have someone watching her permanently. She sat her in the chair by the window, put a blanket around her and quickly stripped the bed.

Then she heard someone come up the stairs and rushed to the bedroom door. It was Mr Williams.

'Mr Williams, Mr Williams, come quickly!' Moira called out softly.

'What's the matter, Moira?' Harry said.

He took two steps at a time until he got to the door.

'It's Mrs Griffith. She's really sick. She came down to the kitchen in a kind of trance. She came down the backstairs but I managed to bring her back up. I was afraid to shout for help as I thought it would frighten her. I felt her brow and she seems very warm. She's pulled out some of her hair and she's bleeding.'

Moira said all this as quietly as she could, although Mrs Griffith had closed her eyes again and seemed to be falling asleep in the chair.

'Is she bleeding badly?'

'Her head is covered in blood. I had to strip the bed. I'll get a basin downstairs and a cloth to bathe her head. Will you stay with her? But don't go in – that might frighten her further. I hope her husband will be back soon.'

'Christ! I'm sure he'll be back soon. Yes, of course, I'll stay at the door and keep a watch until you come back.'

When she was hurrying back down the stairs through the open front door she saw Julia running ahead of Mr Griffith, Rosemary and Madam who were walking a good bit behind her. Moira rushed to the front door to try to stop her, knowing that she might run up to her mother's room. The poor child would be in shock if she saw her poor mother like that.

Julia came rushing up to Moira, her curls tumbling around her face after coming loose from her ribbon. Her eyes were worried, and her bottom lip was trembling.

'I want to see my mummy. Rosemary said she is feeling bad.' Two big fat tears began to fall.

Moira felt a stab of annoyance. Why did Miss Purcell say this in front of the child?

'Julia, your mother is not very well. Let your father look after her and then you can see her,' Moira said softly.

Julia began to cry, big wet tears falling down her face.

'Why? I want to see her.'

'I know.' Moira gave her a hug as Desmond came in.

She didn't want to say anything in front of Julia.

'I think it's best you see Mrs Griffith first,' she said to Desmond, trying over Julia's head to covey to him by her expression that there was a serious crisis afoot.

He nodded in acknowledgment and knelt beside Julia. 'Mummy will be fine – she just needs lots more rest. You can see her later,' he said gently.

Moira left them and hurried to the kitchen where she quickly gathered together a cloth, antiseptic and some hot water to bathe Florence's head.

Upstairs she found Harry walking up and down the

landing and Desmond sitting in the bedroom beside his wife's chair, talking soothingly to her.

Florence had her eyes open again and was calmer now.

Desmond approached Moira. 'I rang the doctor at the hospital,' he whispered, 'and he advised me to give her an extra sedative and hopefully she will sleep. We will leave as early as possible in the morning. I'd leave tonight but that storm is brewing.'

'If you need help packing let me know, or if you need me to sit with her,' Moira said.

'Thank you.'

Moira went and began to gently bathe Mrs Griffith's head.

Ida had arrived and overheard the conversation. 'Goodness. What has she done to herself? Desmond, I have some stronger sleeping tablets – I'm sure they will help her sleep. I'll get some for you. I got them in New York on our last trip.'

'*Hmm* ... not sure I should.'

'Nonsense, they are perfectly safe, just not available here.'

'I'm not sure, with the medication that she is on.'

'These will knock her right out until morning, and you can take her back as soon as she wakes up. You should never have brought her here,' Ida said sharply.

'Well, hindsight is a great thing, Ida,' Desmond said but he followed her to get some of her so-called sleeping pills.

The rest of the evening was a quiet affair. Only Ida, Harry, Rosemary and Julia sat down for dinner. Desmond didn't want to leave his wife and Moira kept his food warm in the stove. He came down eventually and Moira prepared his meal.

'Is Mrs Griffith alright on her own? I can go up and stay with her?' she asked worriedly.

'She's in a deep sleep. I gave her two of Ida's sleeping pills and they have really knocked her out. Thank goodness. I really should have left this morning.'

At that the wind blew some old branches against the window, making Moira jump.

'The weather seems to be gearing up for a rough night. I hope that the roads are clear in the morning,' Desmond said. 'I think I have most of her clothes packed – Ida has gone for a bath. I wonder would you mind packing Julia's clothes and things?'

'Of course, whatever you need. And I can help you to look after Mrs Griffith this evening.'

'Thank you. But I think it's fine – she should sleep through the night now and I have another sedative if not. I can't quite believe she is so ill again. I really thought that she would get better here. I assume you know that my wife has been unwell since the birth of our last child?'

Moira could feel her face redden. 'Yes. Vonnie did say that she was unwell and that the little break here was meant to help her.'

'Unfortunately, it seems to have done the opposite. Thank you, Moira, for the meal. That was particularly good. I'll miss your cooking. If you ever want to move to Dublin do get in touch.'

'Thank you, Mr Griffith. I hope to one day go to France, but there is a French Restaurant in Dublin, I believe. Do you know it?'

'Jammet's. Yes, of course. Fabulous oysters! I can put a word in with the owner for you if you like. Harry is good friends with them too. He and Ida are constants there. I will say it to Harry.'

'That's so kind of you.'

'Not at all. You are hugely talented, Moira, and talent deserves to be treated accordingly. I'd better go back upstairs now.'

She could feel her whole face burning. She hated the fact that when she got nervous her face was such a tell-tale sign and became as red as a tomato. But she wanted to scream in delight. Leaving for Dublin might happen sooner than she thought.

She cleared up the kitchen and began to braise some beef that she planned to cook. It was one of her French-inspired dishes with good red wine, onions, bay leaves and a good drop of brandy. It was better after a day or two so she thought she would get started on it now. She was half afraid that her mother would have sent her poor father to make her come home but there was no sign.

At ten o'clock Moira made some tea and was about to have something to eat when a clap of thunder made the electricity go out. Mr Berne arrived and warned them that they should not venture outside. They lit candles and oil lamps around the place.

Ida was not impressed, and Moira heard her telling her husband that she regretted coming here and she was going to bed. With that she banged the door of the bedroom so hard some of the paintings on the wall shuddered. The telephone lines were also down.

With the wind howling the storm began to rage. Moira finished all her prep for the next day and tidied up. She had offered again to sit with Mrs Griffith if her husband needed the relief.

'I think I'm fine, Moira. I'm afraid Julia is quite upset about her mother though. Rosemary is reading her a story. But my wife is sleeping peacefully.'

173

'I'll bring Julia some hot cocoa. I'll heat some milk on the stove. It might settle her.'

'Thank you.'

She made some cocoa and took it up to Julia. The child looked pale and small in the bed with her red curls around her face.

'Is Mummy better?'

'Yes, she's sleeping, and she will be much better soon.'

'Promise!' Julia pleaded.

Moira was not sure what to say. How could such a little child understand that her mother was far from being well.

'I promise she's trying to get better.'

Rosemary tucked her in and they both walked out, leaving a small oil lamp on her bedside table as she was afraid of the dark.

'The poor child is upset,' Rosemary said.

'The poor little mite. Is there anything I can get you?'

'No, thank you. I have never eaten so well. I really do hope that you get to France someday, Moira.'

'I hope so – the more I learn about it the more I want to go. But I might go to Dublin first.'

'Well, if you do make sure and contact me and I will help you find those styles that you admire. Don't worry, I know shops that have great sales.'

'Oh lovely!'

'I forgot the book that I am reading so I am at a loose end. Do you need any help?'

'No, I'm finished really for the night. I'll probably turn in early. I just want to look for some more candles for Madam. I am sure Mr Berne left them in, but I can't seem to find them.'

'Mr Williams mentioned that there were more candles in the room beside the drawing room. If the storm continues it might be good to have extra candles.'

'Mr Berne was up earlier checking everything – he says that we are in for a rough night – it's bad already out there. And Madam seems to need quite a few candles!'

'She certainly does.' Rosemary grinned. 'He said that the key for the room is in the hall. I might just have a look with the oil lamp. Would you mind coming with me?'

'Not at all,' Moira said.

They walked down the stairs and looked around the hall but could see no keys. Just as they were about to give up Moira noticed a key hanging up over one of the doors. They had to get a chair to reach it. There was a small tag attached saying *The Blue Room*.

'Will we try it?' Rosemary asked.

'Alright.'

They walked into the large dining room and put the key in the door adjoining it. It creaked but with a firm wrench it opened. They went in and looked around the room. It was a square room full of paintings of people from long ago. Some were hanging on the walls and some were left down against the wall.

'They look a bit ghostly all locked up in here,' Rosemary said. 'I wonder who that was?'

Moira was holding a torch up at a portrait hanging on the wall of a young woman in a full ball gown with her dark hair piled high on her head. A heart-shaped face, almond-shaped eyes and ruby lips.

'Naggie Nelligan who lives in Druid was talking about her today. I think this portrait used to hang above the mantelpiece in the library.'

'She's incredibly beautiful.'

'She … drowned here on the lake,' Moira said.

'My goodness, yes, that must be her, Mr Williams was

telling me about her. She drowned herself and she's buried in a tomb on the grounds all by herself.'

'Really, I didn't know that.' Moira wished she didn't know now. 'The poor girl. Vonnie said that there was a sadness to this house, and I am starting to believe that she was right.' Her hand began to shake and the torch in her hand looked like it was going to fall.

'Moira, you're trembling.'

'I'm alright, but I think we might lock this door again. Leave the spirits of the past where they are.'

'Why did you say spirits?' Rosemary asked.

'I don't know. It kind of just came out. I really don't know. I think I need to get to bed actually. It's been a long day.'

'Oh, look, there's a box of candles! Yes, you just get yourself to bed and I will drop the candles up to Ida. Oh, look at that!' Rosemary was pointing at a very delicate-looking piece of cloth. She picked it up. It was like a long nightgown.

'Is it a nightdress?' Moira asked.

'A shroud according to Mr Williams.'

'A shroud – as in for the dead?'

'Yes. Look there are other bits too. I'm locking this room back up. You get yourself up to bed. If anyone needs anything I'll be here.'

'Thanks, Rosemary. Goodnight.'

Moira was walking back to the kitchen when Madam's bell began to ring from her bedroom.

Rosemary called out, '*Ignore it! I'll look after her!*'

'*Thanks!*' Moira replied. She couldn't really deal with Madam right now, so she was grateful for Rosemary's offer.

Back in the kitchen she sat down and made a cup of tea and put some sugar into it. She felt a little in shock and she had no idea why. It was as if a strange feeling had come over her when she had opened that door. She knew she was possibly imagining it, what with Naggie Nelligan and her stories and Vonnie saying that the house was full of sadness, but it was as if once she had opened that door a feeling that she couldn't understand weighed her down. Perhaps she was only tired. She washed the cup and left.

She made her way up the narrow servants' stairs that led to an opening onto the top tier of the landing of the grand staircase. She was so busy earlier she had not had time to even drop her bag and nightdress up. As she reached the top of the stairs, she opened a door that brought her to the top floor. To get to the top floor the people in the house could also use the grand staircase. Moira walked along the landing to have a peek down the grand staircase. It was difficult to see with just her torch but she imagined that it looked quite beautiful from there when the light from the dome was shining down. She put her hand onto the bannister and was about to lean over when she felt it move under her hand. She gasped. The bannister was broken. If she had leaned on it she could have fallen. She remembered Vonnie saying something about it that first day when she arrived. Mr Berne should really get it fixed. Not that any of the family used the top floor but it was still dangerous. She would mention it to him in the morning.

The light through the stained-glass window was completely gone. She could hear rain pounding down on to it. She felt weak suddenly. She thought she might be coming down with some sort of summer cold. She walked back and opened the door that Vonnie had described to her. The room was small and cosy and papered in a light pale-pink flowered wallpaper. There were clean sheets, a blanket and a patchwork quilt on the bed, a small washroom adjacent. She washed her face and brushed her teeth, took off her shoes and clothes and put on her

177

nightgown and got into the bed. She turned off her torch and closed her eyes. She could feel her body completely drained. She heard a rattle and knew that it was the pipes. Madam must be having another bath, she surmised, as she rested her eyes.

The wind was getting stronger outside and there was a flash of lightning that lit the room. Then another crack of thunder hit and rain like she had never heard before began to pour down. But, despite everything, her eyes were tired. It was strange to sleep in a different bed to her own, but she decided that it was a good kind of strange and soon she drifted off to sleep. All memories of Naggie Nelligan had vanished and she was dreaming of cooking Crêpe Suzette and fresh cream.

But it didn't seem long before there was a knock on the door. The room was in darkness and the wind was still howling. She searched around for her torch but couldn't find it. Luckily, she had put a candle and a box of matches beside the bed. She struck a match and lit the candle, then put on her robe.

'Who is it?'

'It's me – Rosemary.'

'What time is it? Is something the matter?'

'Please open the door and I'll explain.'

Moira turned the key and held the candle up, it quivered with the draught in the hall. Rosemary was standing there, dressed in a dark-brown coat and a hat and she was dripping wet. A puddle was forming that was falling from her clothes.

'You're soaked. Why? Were you out in that?' Moira asked, amazed.

At that a clap of thunder sounded that seemed strong enough to knock the house down.

'Mr Griffith went for a quick lie-down and when he went back his wife was missing.'

'What do you mean *missing*? She can barely walk.'

'Well, she's gone.'

'Gone? She must be in the kitchen or somewhere else.'

'The latch is off the front door. We have searched the house from top to bottom. I assure you – she's gone.'

CHAPTER 19

2019

Julia was beginning to get consumed by her interest in this lake house that she had dreamed about. Much to David's dismay she booked into a guesthouse in the small town of Druid in County Clare and headed off. David then offered to come with her, but he was busy and it seemed such a foolish wild goose chase that she had talked him out of it.

It took over three hours and by the time she got there she was wondering if she should have done a bit more research first. The lake house was just outside the town, according to the information that she had managed to obtain. Looking around, she decided it was a town with a feeling of the old and the new. Ice-cream shops, coffee docks and pubs advertised their wares. She had spotted a sign for a pretty coffee shop with a large blue wooden sign saying *The Nook, Everything Freshly Made*. She made a mental note to come back there for a coffee and a bite to eat.

The guesthouse was a modest house with ivy covering it and a big white cat sleeping in the window. She was met by a young girl who showed her a simple bedroom and a bathroom that was fresh and clean. She showed her where to get her breakfast in the morning.

'Full fry-up?'

'No, just some poached eggs if that's okay?'

'Fine. If you need anything let me know.'

She freshened up and decided to see if she could find out a little bit about Lenashee. She went out and walked back to *The Nook* and ordered a salad and a coffee. It was busy with waitresses bringing down lattes, sandwiches, and sumptuous deserts.

An older lady took her order. She had a pen behind her ear and another in her hand. She smiled at Julia as she put some cutlery down for her.

'Excuse me, I was wondering if you could help me? Have you ever heard of Lenashee? It's an old house on a lake a few miles from here?'

'Lenashee! I haven't heard anyone talk about that in years. Belonging to some big lord but sold decades ago. Could be after falling down at this stage. The land around it is owned by the estate. I'd say there must be about ten acres with it, but it must be gone wild now. I don't know who owns it now. I would say no one has been down there in years to be honest.' She then had to go as a large group of American tourists arrived in.

Another waitress brought down a mango and avocado salad and a coffee for Julia.

Julia had rung the Clare County Council before she left to see who now owned the house. They had directed her to the Land Registry and the Registry of Deeds, but they told her that she would have to wait for a week or so to find out. But she had found an old map of Druid and the surrounding areas so she could see exactly where it was.

She finished up and paid and then left to find Lenashee.

181

CHAPTER 20

The road was small and winding with only the odd car. Trees almost embraced each other, meeting in the middle, forming a green cathedral to drive through. She knew she must be near to it now. Sure enough, as she turned the next corner there was a rather grand old entrance with a lodge that looked abandoned. The windows of the lodge were boarded up and it looked like nobody had lived there in a long time. The entrance had grey mottled stone pillars with a pair of austere wrought-iron gates locked with a rusted chain and padlock which looked like it had been untouched for decades. She was surprised to see that there was no name in evidence on the gates or the pillars – nor on the high stone walls which curved out from the gates and then led away on each side. The walls had wrought-iron spikes on top of them. Julia hadn't noticed the wall as she had driven along. The trees had become one with it, hiding it. Creepers had found it and clung too, gnarling its way over it, disguising it further.

Looking at the padlock, her heart sank. There was no way in. She had driven all the way down to look at some high gates.

She could think of nothing else since she had the dream. She had rung Joseph and asked him if he ever remembered her father talking about visiting a house in Clare that Uncle Harry might have owned. But he said he had no recollection of it. She parked the car and decided to at least have a walk to stretch her legs. She needed the break. It had begun to sprinkle a light rain, but the sun was continuing to shine, making the road glisten. She walked on, admiring the wild primroses, hawthorn and fuchsia that grew thickly on either side. A white butterfly flew out from the hedge.

She had only gone a couple of hundred yards and was about to turn back when she noticed that part of the wall had come away. If she tried, she would be able to get over it. A ripple of excitement stirred in her stomach as she looked up and down the road to make sure no one was about. But there was only the sound of insects humming in the thickets. She carefully climbed the wall, holding on to scrub that had gripped it. At fifty-two she was as fit as she could be, and the climb was easy. She climbed to the top and looked at the other side. There was little she could see because of the thickness of the trees. She hoped that she would not be caught for trespassing. She held on to the top of the broken wall and eased herself down straight into some nettles and briars and let out a yelp of pain as the sting began to take hold on her hands and arms. A large briar wrapped itself around her leg like barbed wire. It had dug into her jeans leaving a tear and a small gash below her knee. Her eyes began to weep with the sting from the nettles. She carefully pulled the briar away from her leg.

She picked her way forward and stepped into a thick wood of beech, ash and oak which had grown wild and unruly. It was a labyrinth of trees and wild bushes and plants that had all become one.

The grass was wild and thick, mixed with nettles and a yellow flower that she knew was a poisonous weed to animals. Nature had grown wild and neglected, taking over any order that ever might have been there. She made her way through it but not before getting stung even more by another throng of nettles. She began to wonder how wise her decision was to jump from that wall as she winced in pain.

The trees became a little less thick and she heard something rustle through the high damp grass. She held her breath in fright. Someone was behind her. Slowly she turned around only to see a red deer stare at her as if staring into the headlights of a car. The deer looked much more frightened than she did. It was one of those glorious moments that she knew she would store in her memory to recall like a precious jewel. Then the deer ran through the thick grass and around the trees and disappeared. She could see a path that was almost grown over. She broke off a branch from a tree and used it to beat down the nettles as she made her way. It was perfectly still except for the humming of insects and the call of wood pigeons. She began to see a clearing through the trees and the air became thick with the smell of stagnant water. There was a small pool of water that had got clogged with hanging branches and a horde of insects were hovering over it. She walked on, glad of the sunshine that had now begun to peep its way through the trees. The wood was becoming clearer and the thick nettles were replaced by long grass that was damp from the sprinkle of rain. A bigger clearing became visible and she could hear the district chatter of lots of birds. Then underneath a flowing willow tree she caught a glimpse of a lake, the water murky with flies hovering over it. She could see it was a large lake that was a cornucopia of ducks, waterhens and moorhens ducking and diving and passing their day in their oasis of calm. It was lined by what seemed to have once been a terraced walkway with stone statues dotted along the way.

As she continued there was a break in the trees, and she got a clearer view of the lake. She looked up, somehow knowing what she would see. She could hear herself gasp as there in front of her was a view of what might once have been an expanse of green but was wild now like a field – but above, with its windows twinkling in the light, was a grand old house with the backdrop of a heather-covered mountain. A mist seemed to be circling it. A strange feeling of being here before crept over her. It was not the first time that she had laid eyes on this house. She continued as best as she could on the path. It was still very overgrown and wild, now with big ugly rhubarb-looking plants that seemed to have wrapped their bodies around other plants, keeping them captive. Plants that looked like rose trees and rhododendrons that had gone large, black, and ugly and had grown across the path like giant green and black monsters. Somehow, she made her way through. She looked out on the lake.

In some places it was covered in a green moss that looked so thick it probably reached the bottom. Parts of it were clear and this was where the birds were gathered. She could see a small footbridge that would bring her across a narrow part of the lake to the expanse of green that she thought was definitely once a lawn.

Gently she put her foot on the bridge. It seemed sturdy. Carefully she began to walk across. Halfway across she wondered was it a wise decision, not knowing how deep the lake was, but it seemed okay and despite the place looking untouched the bridge was not broken. She stopped to look at one of the stone statues that were dotted around, some with arms missing. They had a lonesome eeriness about them, but she imagined that the lake would have once been beautiful. There were some wide stone steps that led up to the house. In the quiet, with the sun shining directly on to it, it seemed to glitter. Walking closer, she realised the glitter effect was golden sandstone on the front. It was a very grand house but like a lady who had once been beautiful and now only clung desperately to her high cheekbones and blue eyes, showing a hint of a rare beauty of before.

On her travels she had loved studying the buildings that she encountered. She was no expert but from the highly pitched roof this looked Victorian with its gothic features. The steeply pitched roof had a multitude of ravens and blackbirds that had made their nests there. A flock of magpies flew up beside the house. Weeping willows were dotted here and there, some dead and some so heavy that they were falling. It was so perfectly quiet that she felt very much the intruder as she approached the house.

She walked up the steps to the porch which had four stone pillars of cut sandstone. She looked up into its roof and a large raven flew out, startling her, and she shrieked. The front door and windows were all still intact. There seemed to be a basement and then four storeys. She looked though one of the porch windows and could see a large hall with black and white tiles and, amazingly, a piano. She could see a rather grand staircase at the back.

The walls were covered in wood panelling and wallpaper. She admired the floral-embossed wallpaper which looked still intact. If she strained her eyes she could see into some of the rooms. On one side she could see into what looked like a library and that feeling of being there before became overpowering. Despite years of dust and cobweb, it looked beautiful. She could see what were probably floor-to-ceiling glass bookcases. Some of the cases were broken and the books had come tumbling out. There was a marble fireplace and a round coffee table with armchairs scattered around.

She looked again into the entrance hall, but the sun had begun to shine directly on the window and she had to put her hands together to try to shade her eyes as she stared in again. Suddenly she could hear a strange repetitive sound and it seemed to be coming from inside the house. She looked around to see if she was mistaken and perhaps it was something else outside. But then the noise became louder. She knew it was possibly a loose tile that was hitting off something, but that didn't make it any less eerie. Besides, there was only a slight breeze – not enough to blow a tile. Was there somebody in the house? She wanted to stay and look around more, but the noise was unnerving. She decided to leave.

She walked back through the grass over the footbridge and made her way along the path beside the lake then back through the woods. It was easy to see her way back as her footprints had made a path in the wildness. Then she saw another path and couldn't help but follow it. It was again overgrown but with her stick she beat down the brambles and nettles.

She came to a small enclosure with a gate. She peered in but with the thickness of the shrubs it was difficult to see what it was. Then she saw what looked like a tomb. Just one. She could feel her body shudder.

Suddenly she just wanted to get out of there. She went back and followed the first path and, moving hastily, tripped and fell into the same nettles as before. This time the nettles had got her face and tears ran down her cheeks from the pain.

Her phone rang and made her jump even more. It was David.

'Hi, I was just worried about you? Did you find the house?'

'Yes,' she answered breathlessly.

'Where are you?'

'I jumped over the wall of the estate and now I'm trying to get back out. But, David, I was here before. I just know it. I have seen this house before.'

'Why on earth did you jump over a wall? You are fifty not fifteen!'

'I'm fine. I need to hang up. I'll call you from the car.'

Julia had travelled the world on her own and had often met danger but looking back she knew that, as beautiful and familiar as this place was to her, it had also spooked her a little. She could not really put her finger on it. Perhaps it was the noise that had spooked her – and, well, there was the eerie tomb.

She managed to pull herself up and over the wall. Then she ran, half-stumbling, back to the car.

A farmer on a small blue tractor with no hood on it stopped and asked her if she was okay. She knew she must look a mess with the stings on her face and the tears. He had what looked like a cowboy hat on. His skin was brown as a berry and two bright eyes looked directly at her. He turned off the engine. Julia reckoned he looked at least eighty years old. A sheepdog with one paw missing was sitting beside him. Julia was worried in case a car would come as he was not exactly pulled in but rather stopped on the road – but the road was quiet, and she noted that at least she would hear one coming in the distance.

'Hi, I'm fine but thanks for asking.'

'Are you lost? You don't look to be from around. Are you hurt?' He was looking at her torn trousers.

'No, just a few scratches.'

'You one of them hikers?'

'Kind of.'

'Town is full of them. Lots of Yanks around too.'

'Yes, I suppose there are.'

''Tis a good spot, I suppose, for city people. You a city person?'

He pulled out a pipe and lit it and, as if this were a signal, the dog sprawled across his lap and settled down for a snooze. Julia thought she had better wrap this conversation up as it looked like it could go on for quite a while. But then it struck her that this local man might be a mine of information.

'No, I'm not from the city,' she said and pointed at the gates. 'Do you know anything about the estate here or the house?'

'It's called Lenashee.'

'Yes. Do you know much about it?'

'How do you mean?'

'Well, does anyone go there?'

'Sure that's falling down! No one has been there since it was sold in the late sixties. I remember when it was sold. To Harry Williams.'

'Really. You remember that?' she said, delighted. 'Do you remember anything about him being here?'

'I surely do. He used to come down on his own sometimes at first. He had a few hunters. Oh, he was a city boy, but he liked to play the country squire too. A great character. I met him once in Burke's pub and, would you believe, he stood us all drinks for the night. But sure, he was seemingly a bit of a cod, giving politicians money they say to get special favours. But I liked him. Never did me any harm except to get me drunk.' He sat back and pulled hard on his pipe.

'Is there anything else that you might know about it? Where you ever there?'

'I wouldn't go there if you paid me.'

'Why do you say that?'

'Ah sure they say it has bad luck, kind of cursed,' he said, pulling on his pipe.

'Why do they say that?' Julia asked, alarmed.

'To tell you the truth, I don't know. Aw, sure, that's what they say, the people of Druid. But saying that, there might be some truth in it.'

'Really?' Julia asked cagily.

'Well, when he bought it, he was full of plans and then they say something happened there during a storm in '67. Oh, a fierce storm. I remember it well. The roof nearly blew off me own farmhouse.'

'What happened there? What was it?' Julia asked eagerly.

'Ah, there were stories. That's all. But shortly afterwards Harry Williams ordered the house to be locked up and put that big padlock on the gates. There was a big sign saying that trespassers would be prosecuted and to keep out. The signs are gone. Young ones took them, I would say, over the years. But he need not have bothered with the signs – when people think a place is cursed it's a good way to keep people away.' He laughed.

'But he ordered it to be locked up? For how long?'

'For good, missus! To my knowledge not a soul has passed through that gateway since. Poor old Berne who used to mind the place got sick and he and the wife moved to Ennis to the daughters. Aw, he's dead now, God rest him, and her too.'

'But why would he do that? Lock it up. He was a property developer, wasn't he? Surely this was a prime property. Are you sure he never sold it?'

'No. Never did. I suppose that's why they say something happened there – there was no other reason he would lock it up and order it to stay that way.'

'But Harry Williams is dead, years ago.'

'Well, it was never sold.'

'Are you sure?'

'I'm living only a couple of miles away. I would have heard. Sure, his wife must not be short of a penny if she's alive – she must own it.' He took another deep pull of his pipe. 'She was a fine woman to look at. I remember seeing her in the papers. Not sure if she was ever here though.'

'I was down there just now. I heard some strange noise coming from the house. Like a broken tile or something?'

He nearly dropped the pipe in surprise at this, his eyes like bright brown buttons in his tanned, lined face. 'You were down there? By yourself? How did you get in?' he asked, his mouth open, holding the pipe in mid-air.

'There's a break in the wall, just down there.'

'Well, my God! There has been no one there in over half a century.' He whistled, shaking his head. 'You shouldn't have gone somewhere like that on your own. Jesus, Mary and Joseph!'

Julia felt foolish now. This man thought she was cuckoo. 'Anyway, I'd better go and thanks for stopping.'

'No bother. But go home now and mind yerself and don't be traipsing off on your own to the likes of Lenashee! Come on, Benji, the wife will have the spuds ready for me.'

The dog sat up and his master started up the tractor. For a moment Julia thought it wasn't going to start, but then with a sudden burst of smoke the engine came to life.

'*Good day to you, missus! Lenashee is better left alone.*' He tipped his hat and drove slowly off.

Julia jumped into her car. David was ringing again.

'I'm okay. I'm in the car.'

'What happened?'

'I can't explain. I was at the house and it was quiet and peaceful. The house looks like it was once beautiful. Then as I was peeping in the window a strange banging noise started up. Kind of freaked me to be honest.'

'Why did you go there alone like that? I knew I should have gone. Maybe there is someone living there. Squatting.'

'I don't think so. There is no path to the house. I would have noticed – it's full of nettles. Probably it was just a bird. It's a haven for them. And get this, I think Aunt Ida still owns the house. I met a farmer and he told me as much. Harry did buy it and never sold it.'

'She's a dark horse. I never heard her mention it. Probably trying to keep it from that vulture of a son of hers. Strange it's not sold though. What would she do with a property like that?'

'I think Uncle Harry's wishes were that it was to remain locked up.'

'Why?'

'I don't really know. There are some rumours that it brought bad luck, according to the farmer.'

'At least you're back in the car. Are you sure you won't come home tonight?'

'I know it all sounds ridiculous, but I want to see if I can find out anything about this woman.'

'Okay. But be careful – don't go anywhere like that on your own again.'

'I won't. Thanks for ringing but I'm fine.'

She hung up and then dialled Ida.

'Aunt Ida, I need to ask you something.' She thought she would see what her response would be before asking exactly what she wanted to know.

'Go on.'

'There's a house in Clare that I think Uncle Harry used to own. Do you know it? A house on a lake?'

There was silence from Ida.

'No, I don't recall it. Your uncle owned many properties. I didn't keep a log of them.' Again, that sharp tone.

'Oh, I was hoping you might remember it or if we ever visited it?'

'No, I don't ever recall a house there or visiting it. Why do you ask?'

Julia knew she was lying but she also knew that if Ida didn't want to tell her something nothing would persuade her to.

'I just wondered.'

'No, never to my knowledge did we go to Clare as a family. Is that clear enough for you?'

'Did Dad ever or my mother?' she pushed.

'What's this about?'

'I don't know, Aunt Ida. I asked you about that woman called Rosemary Purcell and you said that you never heard of her. But I know for a fact that you did know her and somehow I think that the house in Clare is somehow connected.'

'Are you calling me a liar, Julia?'

'I saw a photograph of you with Rosemary Purcell on the social diary in the *Irish Times* in 1967.'

'What is this about? I was photographed at many events over the years. I certainly don't remember with whom and I know no one of that name.'

'But it says you are with your friend Rosemary Purcell.'

'I am telling you I don't recall anyone of that name. If I did have my photograph taken with her it was just by chance.'

'Okay, I'm sorry. I'm just stressed over Dad and the fact that he is still talking about this woman. I somehow thought the house was connected.'

'Well, it isn't. I can imagine how worried you are. But remember how ill your father is. Now no more about this. I plan to visit him on Thursday.'

'Okay, I'll be there too so I'll see you then. Bye, Aunt Ida.'

Julia hung up. But the more her aunt denied it, the more she knew that she was hiding something. Something that her aunt was determined not to tell.

CHAPTER 21

Luckily, no one saw her as she parked and went into the guesthouse and up the carpeted stairs to the quietness of her bedroom. She ran a shower to wash the blood from her leg then wrapped herself in a clean white towel afterwards and was glad that she had a tube of antiseptic to attend to her stings and cuts. She decided to get dressed and visit the restaurant bar, O'Brien's, which was across from the guesthouse. She got dressed, grabbed a book, and headed over.

She ordered the chowder, a green salad and some mineral water and sat in a small alcove. She rarely drank alcohol, but this was one of those times that she would have loved a large glass of wine, but she resisted.

But, instead of opening her book, her mind began to wander. What was it about the house that was drawing her to it? After today she knew she had been there before and somehow she knew that Rosemary Purcell had too. The fact that Ida possibly still owned it added an extra layer of mystery to it all. She wished she could remember if she were ever inside. That glimpse of the library seemed familiar. She felt that if she saw the rest of the interior, she would remember.

She lingered after her meal and had some tea. She often dined alone while she travelled. It suddenly hit her that she had written so much about other countries but nothing about Ireland. Her love of travel was for the unknown places. The places that people only thought they knew. The West of Ireland was surely well documented over the decades and had seen numerous tourists. What was left for her to write about? But there was something quite mystical and unlike anywhere else in the world about the West of Ireland. The ruggedness, the history and the sheer beauty.

She returned to the guesthouse. She had lots of work to do but her concentration was not good so in the end she decided to try to get an early night.

She wanted to go back to the house the next day but this time with her camera.

She awoke early and was the first down for breakfast. The guesthouse was run by a woman called Bridie who told Julia that the house was originally her parents'. Julia admired the small dining area with spotless tables covered in oilcloth with a pattern of red roses.

She reckoned that Bridie must be at least sixty-five so she might know something about the house and now was a good time to ask her as the other guests hadn't arrived down yet.

When she came to put orange juice and a basket of bread on the table, Julia struck up a conversation.

'I'm trying to find out a bit of history about a house not far from here. An estate really. Well, it once was.'

'Oh, where?'

'Lenashee.'

'I have not heard that name in a long time. Not since my mother's time.'

196

'Really? Do you know anything at all about it?' Julia probed.

'It was meant to be very fancy in its day. I'd say it must be after falling in. It's been locked up as far back as I can remember. My mother used to bless herself when she passed the entrance.' Bridie grinned, remembering.

'Why would she bless herself?'

'She used to bless herself and say a prayer to Saint Agnes. She was devoted to Saint Agnes. She used to tell us not to look up at the gates for fear of bad luck. Ah, sure, it just had that reputation. There was a bit of a scandal up there too.' Bridie winked.

'How do you mean? Scandal?'

Bridie squinted her eyes and, with one hand on her hip and another to her chin, she paused for a moment as if trying to think back.

'Well, I remember my mother and my Aunt Gracie talking about it. Sure, it must be back in the sixties it happened. There were rumours that a young woman was seen running through the woods naked, screaming, during a terrible thunderstorm. The locals said that there were some strange goings-on up there. It's rumoured to be haunted too – but, sure, people are full of old stories like that. My mother believed she heard the banshee the night before she died. She said it to me. "Bridie," she says, "I'm going to my Maker. Will you go and wash out the kitchen floor and get the place ready?"'

'Ready?'

'Ready for a wake! But sure, it was an old vixen that she heard. They would scare the living daylights out of you when they are in season, crying like that.'

'Did anyone know who the woman was, who was running in the woods?' Julia asked, half-dreading the answer.

'I don't even know if it happened. Again, just old stories that were told around fires when we were young ones.' She laughed. But then her face took on a more serious look. 'To be honest, I'm not sure what I believe but I wouldn't like to go there all the same.'

Julia tried to ignore the side of her brain that was telling her to leave well alone – her gut was telling her otherwise.

She hurriedly ate the poached eggs on toast that Bridie brought her and went upstairs to pack.

There was a hardware shop outside of the town and she bought some wellington boots and some thick work gloves. Then she took the road back to the entrance of Lenashee. She parked in the curved space in front of the gates. Then she got out and pulled on her wellingtons and gloves. She would be ready for the nettles this time. She hoped she wouldn't meet her farmer friend today as he would be sure to give her grief about going back into the estate. She locked the car and grabbed her phone. Her boots sounded squeaky as she walked down the road.

She found the break in the wall and climbed over and took her time getting down the other side so as not to land in the nettles. It was better today though as she had already trampled lots of the nettles down the day before. She began to follow her own track, stopping at times to look at the trees and the wild bushes and grass. There were small paths where the nettles were trampled by small animals. At least the gloves now were able to protect her hands from any bee sting or nettle rash.

As she trudged along, she spotted things she had not noticed the day before. The cornucopia of wildflowers that had grown amongst the briars and the gorse. Patches of blue whimsical flowers in the shade in the woods. Then she heard the buzzing of insects and knew she was near the opening to where the lake was. The lake was again a hive of activity of ducks and waterhens going about their day. The sun was shining directly onto the house and the glass of the windows glittered back. Julia stopped to look at the sandstone as it shone like gold dust from the brick. She took out her camera and began to take some shots.

When she got to the house, she walked around it slowly, taking lots of shots at all sorts of angles. It was then she noticed a window that was broken on the basement floor. She reckoned that she could fit inside but there was still glass embedded in the frame. She used her gloves to pull the remaining bits of glass away.

With trepidation and a bit of excitement, she carefully climbed in through the window. She found herself in a concrete-floored rather dark passage. Thankfully, there was no noise today. It had probably been a loose tile or something similar. She felt foolish now for being so spooked.

There was a nest of bees in the passage and she moved slowly so as not to disturb them. Her father had kept bees and he had thought her how to react with them.

She went through an arch and looked around. She was in a kitchen. There were copper pans hanging with years of cobwebs and dust, an old range, a dresser with ornate plates covered in cobweb. Lots more presses. A large table and a butcher's block. She thought how extraordinary it was that all these objects were just abandoned in this house. As if some catastrophe had made the inhabitants flee for their lives, never to return.

There was a door that led to a passage with a narrow staircase. With her heart beating, she climbed the stairs. The dust and dirt and stench made her want to vomit, but she felt compelled to go on. She climbed, pushing through thick cobwebs. She could hear scratching and scuttling, and she let out a small whimper, hoping the scampering and scuttling was from mice rather than rats. She put her hand to her nose as the stench was becoming overpowering. Then she came to a small landing with two doors to the side of the staircase which continued upward. She expected them to be locked. She turned one of the large black doorknobs and smiled when she heard it click. She pushed the door open and gasped as she walked into a beautiful dining room with heavy dark furniture, probably mahogany.

She caught her reflection in a large grimy expanse of mirrored glass along one wall. Then she turned around and marvelled at the hunting pictures that adorned the other walls. She walked the length of the room and looked out of the large bay window – it had a stunning view of the lake. How wonderful it must have been, to sit and eat with such a view! There was a large heavy door and she opened it and walked out into the grand entrance hall which had a large glass case full of stuffed pheasants and ducks that looked like they were decaying behind the glass. She never really understood why people stuffed animals and she quickly walked on past. She looked up and took in the carved grand staircase that seemed to have three landings, looking up she stared at a dome-shaped ceiling with stained glass that allowed the most magical light through. Again, that feeling of being here before was overpowering.

She went into the library room that she had seen through the window the day before. Books in cases with thick glass lined the walls. Another wall had open bookcases, some of whose books had fallen out or been knocked out onto the floor over the years – perhaps by rodents – the thought made her shiver. The years of dust made her catch her breath and brought on a fit of sneezing.

She noticed a motheaten red cardigan covered in cobwebs on the back of a chair. A large spider walked across her foot and made her scream. A bird flew around her and made her jump even more and she left the room and arrived back in the hallway.

She went into a room across the hall – a magnificent drawing room with a huge fireplace, luxurious drapes now heavy with dust and faded sofas.

Then she went back out into the hall and walked on to the stairs.

It looked solid and as if in a dream she began to climb. She walked on slowly and gently. She went into the first room. She put her hand on the rose-coloured wallpaper. It felt textured, almost like velvet. A wooden four-poster bed sat in the centre. Sheets that had become eaten and covered in dust seemed to be pulled over other pieces of furniture. There were two small rooms off the bedroom, one seemed to be some sort of washroom and the other a dressing room. How very grand, she thought. Then as if something were pulling her, she walked down the corridor to the last room and walked in. She closed the door behind her and paused, looking at the door handle. It seemed a strange thing to do. She was unclear as to why she had closed the door and was about to open it again when she thought she heard something. She swung around as her heart beat faster.

She stood with her back to the door. A strange scent filled the room. It was becoming more powerful. She had a strange sensation that she was not alone. There was a gold-edged mirror with years of dust on it in front of her over the fireplace. She looked at the grate and saw a decayed bird. It was possibly where the smell was coming from. Then something on the floor shone back at her. She walked over, leaned down and picked it up. It was a small gold hatpin of a peacock. She put it in her pocket. It was then that the scent of decay became even stronger.

There was a sash window and she pushed it up, soaking in the fresh air. But, as soon as she stepped away, the window came crashing down, and she watched in dismay as it fell to the ground outside. Then she heard the faint sound of something banging. The same sound as before. Probably something loose but today the air was still, the wind was not blowing a loose tile or anything. She could feel her heart beat in her chest. She went to open the door, but it was locked. Alarm bells went off in her mind. She was about to try it again when it swung open. She shrieked in fright. She rushed out and legged it down the stairs. She rushed through the dining room, catching her image again in the mirrored walls and half afraid she would see something else. She took the stairs down into the kitchen and back to the broken window. With difficulty, she began to pull her body through. The banging was getting louder. She caught her hand on a piece of remaining broken glass and it ripped her glove, cutting her hand. She fell through and scrambled to her feet.

She ran as fast as she could across the lawn. While she was running, she looked back. She looked up to where the window had fallen and for a split second she thought she saw a shadow there. Then it was gone.

She ran across the footbridge and through the woods, tearing her face on a briar.

Relieved, she got back to the gap in the wall and climbed over it.

Back at the gates, she jumped into her car and locked it. She pulled off her gloves and saw that her hand was still weeping blood. She grabbed a cloth and wrapped it around it. Glancing in the rear-view mirror, she was shocked at her appearance. Her face was ghastly pale and blood streaked across her cheek.

She pulled off the wellington boots and put her shoes on, then started the car and drove away.

She drove for an hour and eventually stopped at a petrol station that had a coffee kiosk and a bathroom. She went in and washed her hands and face. She realised her hands were shaking as she paid for the takeaway tea. She tried to steady herself, but it was useless. Her whole body began to tremble.

The shop assistant, a thin woman with deep furrows on her brow, came around the counter and put the takeaway cup of tea at a small table with a chair.

'Would you like to sit for a moment? You look a bit shaken.'

'Thank you – I think I will,' Julia replied, glad that the table was discreetly away from most of the customers. Slowly the overpowering feelings began to settle. Watching the humdrum business of people coming in and paying for petrol or grabbing something to eat settled her. Normality. The woman arrived back over, a look of concern across her face.

'Can I get you anything?'

'No but thank you. You are kind. I'm fine now.'

She picked up her bag and left.

When she got home it was late. She sat in the car for a while. Had she only been gone for one night? It seemed so much longer.

David was still working in the studio. He arrived in just as she was taking off her jacket.

'Did everything go okay? Jesus! You look shook! What happened?'

'I ... I'm not sure.' Suddenly she started to cry.

He came over and put his arms around her.

'It's okay. You need some rest, Julia. Between your father and all that travelling, you are out of sorts. Your face! And your hand! What happened?'

'Nothing. It looks worse than it is. It's just some scratches. I need to go to bed.'

'I'll bring you up a hot drink. Do you want something to eat? I have some soup made.'

'No. But a hot drink would be good.' She crept up the stairs and lay on the bed.

David brought up some tea.

As she sipped it, David asked her again what had happened.

'I was in the house.'

He sighed. 'How did you get in?'

'There was a broken window and I climbed through.'

'Jesus, Jules. That's breaking and entering.'

'The place has been deserted for decades, David! Believe me, there is no one there monitoring it in any way.'

'Okay. Just tell me why you're so upset.'

'It's hard to explain ... it was all very emotional. It was as if I was there before. In fact, I'm sure of it. But it's strange – the feeling that I have for it. I cannot get it out of my head – or this woman. I feel compelled to find her. I know it sounds a bit ridiculous, but I can't stop thinking of her and the house.'

'I'm worried about you.'

'I know.' She suddenly didn't feel like telling him the rest of the experience ... the noises ... her panic. Oh, don't listen to me, I'm just a bit stressed. I think I'll have a bath. It might calm me a little.'

'Okay. There's lots of hot water. But I am worried about you.'

'I'm fine, honestly. Nothing that a good night's rest won't cure.'

'Alright. I'll leave you to it. I'm going back out to the studio.'

She was glad to be on her own. She needed time to process her thoughts. She poured some lavender bath oil into the water and inhaled the aroma. She began to undress and, just as she was about to put her jeans in the laundry basket, the hatpin that she had found at the house fell out. She picked it up and walked back into the bedroom. Opening a drawer in her dressing table, she put it in there. For a moment she wondered what had possessed her to take it in the first place.

Back in the bathroom, she stepped into the scented bath and tried to push any thoughts of the house out of her head. The bath did calm her mind as well as soothe her cuts and scratches.

Back in bed she soon fell into a dream but in the dream she was back at Lenashee.

She heard David come to bed. But then she fell back into the dream. Soon she could feel someone shouting at her, calling her name. She felt frightened and she could feel herself clawing at something. Then she awoke, and David was standing over her – his face scratched.

'Jesus, calm down!'

'What's happening?' Julia was hysterical

'Calm down. It's just a nightmare.'

'David! What happened?'

'You were having a nightmare, I tried to wake you but you clawed at me.'

'I'm so sorry.' Julia started to cry. 'I was so afraid in the dream. I was somewhere and I couldn't get out.'

'Were you dreaming of the house?'

'Yes. I was so afraid.' She began to weep uncontrollably.

'Hush, Jules, it's okay. It was just a nightmare.'

'But why do I get nightmares? I have had so many over the years. Why?'

'I don't know – maybe it's to do with your illness. Do you feel you are slipping into that again? I'm worried sick, to be honest.'

She could see the concern on his face.

'No. I really don't think it's that. But I know what you mean. I'm obsessive about this house.'

'You know better than anyone when you are unwell. Don't ignore the signs. *Please.* You are not yourself since you came home from Africa. With your father so sick and all this about this woman, I think it's all too much. Are you taking your meds?'

'Yes, of course I am.'

'Well, something's not right. You promised me that at the first sign you would go to Doctor Phillips.'

Doctor Phillips had been her doctor for the last five years. He specialised in bipolar disorder and since she had begun attending him she had never felt better. Lithium and psychotherapy were working for her and, with her health regime, thankfully it had not raised its head. She knew that David was silently terrified that it would raise its head. They rarely talked about it. But he had seen her at her worst. She had made a promise to him that she would never ignore the signs. She could see how he would think that this was her disorder, making her slightly manic. That was the beginning of the signs that her meds were not working. She would become quite obsessed about something. Her voice would begin to sound slightly different. Her sleep would be interrupted, and the nightmares would begin. But this was different – despite

206

the fact that she *was* feeling slightly obsessed and perhaps even a bit manic. But how could she explain that finding out about the house was something that she felt compelled to do? Ever since that first email from Joseph about her father, something had been uprooted in her memory that was almost haunting her. She knew if she was to find peace of mind, she had to find out why it seemed to mean so much to her.

'David, I'm okay. I swear. You can see my voice is fine.'

'But ... it could be the start of it.'

'I know it looks like that. It's not. Please trust me.'

'Why don't you make an appointment with Doctor Phillips anyway? When are you due to see him again?'

'Not until August.'

'Please try and bring it forward. I don't think I can go away and leave you alone like this.' David was meant to go to London for an exhibition of his work.

'Alright. I promise I will bring it forward, but you must go on your trip.'

'Why don't you come with me?'

'No, I think I had better rest and anyway I'm going to Howth to look after Dad for a couple of days and give Joseph a break.'

'I'm not sure you should be looking after anyone but yourself right now.'

'I'll see the doctor and get some rest and try go up on Wednesday. Aunt Ida and Laurence are coming to see him, and I think they might send poor Joseph over the edge. It's time I took some of the burden away from him.'

'Alright but ring the doctor. Promise.'

'I promise.'

CHAPTER 22

Lenashee 1967

'She's out there? In this weather? You can't be serious!' Moira cried.

'Well, she's gone. Not a sign of her,' Rosemary replied, out of breath.

'But she has to be in the house. She's so weak. She can hardly stand with the lack of food. How could she be missing? Did you check her washroom or her dressing room? Maybe she wandered out into the hall?'

'We've searched the house. Her husband is beside himself with worry. They are all outside now searching. She's not anywhere to be seen. Vanished! Harry, I mean Mr Williams, is sure that he locked the door before he went to bed but the latch was off and the door was slightly ajar when Mr Griffith realised she was missing. We had all gone to bed.'

At that it was as if the skies opened and the rain lashed down, beating on the window. The force of the water pelted blindly, like it was coming from a rushing river.

'But the lake! What if she falls in the lake? Where's Julia?' Moira cried.

'Julia's fine. She's sound asleep. Mr Williams is trying

to see if there is any sign of Mrs Griffith near the lake. The others are in the woods and the gardens.'

'But she has not been out of that room since she arrived. She must be as weak as a kitten. How on earth could she take a jaunt down to the woods and lake? It makes no sense.' Moira was bewildered.

'There are trees down everywhere too which doesn't help,' Rosemary said.

'I'll get dressed and meet you out there. Oh, but we can't leave Julia alone.'

'I'll stay with her for a while and then we can swap around. I'm wet through and I need to change. Hurry!' She ran across the landing.

'*Be careful – part of that banister is broken!*' Moira called out to her.

'*Thanks for the warning,*' Rosemary called as she ran down the main stairs, leaving water puddles behind her.

Moira wondered for a second if she had imagined it. But no, she was fully awake. Using the candlelight, she found her clothes. She pulled on a coat and hat, knowing she would be drenched through in no time. She really didn't have the proper clothes to fight a storm. But she would change as soon as she came back. Luckily, she found her small torch that had fallen behind her locker.

She went across the corridor to the servants' stairs which brought her back to the kitchen. She made a thorough search of it just in case they had somehow missed her, calling out her name softly so as not to startle her. She could hardly believe that Florence was outside in the storm so she thought she would check the living area herself, just to be sure. She went up the servants' stairs into the main hall and then into the library where the embers of the fire were still golden. Then into the dining room and back to the drawing room. It was then she noticed that the door to the room with the portraits was wide open. Rosemary must have forgotten to lock it. She went in and, using her torch, she looked around, but nothing seemed out of place. Just as she was about to go out, she heard something crash to the ground. She jumped and with her heart in her mouth she looked around. It was the portrait of the woman. It had crashed and was lying on the floor. It was so heavy that she could hardly lift it, but it seemed important to see if it were damaged. Slowly she managed to lift it up and lean it against the wall. She gasped. The glass had broken and the face was destroyed. She shone the light on the hook on the wall. Why had it fallen? She shivered as she shone the light on the distorted face of the woman in the portrait. She decided to lock the room, but the key was not in the door or where they had found it. She just closed the door and went back downstairs and out the back door.

When she opened the door the wind almost took it off its hinges. She put her hand up to save her hat. She struggled to close the door and to steady herself against the power of the wind. She let out a small scream when she saw a thin blue light crack through the sky and heard another clap of thunder. She put her hand up to try shield her eyes from the rain that lashed at her face.

She could see flashlights moving in the distance near the lake and Mr Williams calling out his wife's name. The reality of the situation then hit, and she blessed herself and whispered a prayer, 'Mary Immaculate, look down on us this night and help us to find this poor woman!'

Moira felt her body being pushed by the wind like an almighty force. She ran through the lawn and down the stone steps towards the footbridge and then to the walkway across the lake. She looked up as another great angry bang of thunder arrived and then another flash of blue lighting. She let out a scream. The storm was far too dangerous to be out in. She remembered hearing about a neighbour Matty Hartigan who went out in a storm to try to save a trapped ewe. But he was found dead in the field a couple of hours later with the ewe, both having been struck by lightning. She was terrified of being out in this and terrified for Mrs Griffith. What kind of state was her mind in if she really came out in this? Was she totally mad? Insane? And if she did come out, why on earth did she? The thought that she had come out to throw herself into the lake like the poor woman in the portrait clouded Moira's mind.

'Dear Lord, in your mercy let us find her!' she prayed again.

The storm seemed to be circling Lenashee like a great angry monster lashing out, roaring, and flashing great streaks of blue electric light. The horses in the stable were whinnying and the sound of dogs barking could be heard in between the thunder. She almost fell over – the wind was continuing to build force. Then Mr Griffith was shouting that he had found something. He was near the stone steps that led to the lake. Moira could see him shining his torch to show others where he was. Her stomach retched. They all rushed with torches to where he was. He was near the lake. He was shining a light on something. Moira was almost afraid to look.

'*Is it her?*' Ida yelled.

Moira looked, expecting the worst, but it was Mrs Griffith's underclothes and nightgown strewn on the ground. She felt her stomach lurch in fear for her. Wherever this woman was, she was naked. Had she drowned in the lake? Had someone taken her? Was she drowned? They searched and searched all through the woods and along the lake. But the rain was making visibility with the torches almost impossible. They were all shouting her name and calling and calling. The fear that she had already drowned was chilling Moira to the bone. Thirty minutes that seemed forever passed but nothing. The thunder was still clapping and becoming even stronger. Great unmerciful bangs as if the sky were going to fall in on them.

They had all congregated in the summerhouse that was on the lawn. There was no sign of the storm easing. The large oak tree that stood in the centre of the lawn for centuries at Lenashee seemed to move from the earth. Ida screamed with the sound of the roots coming from the ground – the roots that must have reached so far under the earth. Moira remembered her father telling her that Mr Berne said it must be one of the oldest trees in the land and it was rumoured that if it fell it signalled bad luck or even death. After another crack of thunder, the tree gave out a great moan like a wounded animal and crashed to the ground. Luckily, the lawn was vast so it didn't reach them at the summerhouse. Ida screamed from where she was taking shelter behind Harry as it fell, shaking the earth beneath. Moira gasped and leaned against the wall of the summerhouse to steady herself. She wanted to get into the safety of the house – anything could happen to them out in this. They needed help.

'We need to call the gardaí!' she said.

'The phone lines are down!' Ida replied.

'The avenue is blocked – there are trees down,' Harry said. 'I can't get a car through to go for help.'

'What are you going to tell them anyway? That she is gone mad and is running naked around the woods?' Ida shouted at Moira.

212

'What if she falls in the lake? Or has already fallen in the lake?' Moira cried.

'They're not going to do too much until this storm eases,' said Ida. 'Hopefully, we will have found her by then. And I think, Desmond, you had better sign her in as soon as possible. *She is clearly mad!*'

'Ida! Quiet! That is not exactly helpful!' Harry said angrily.

'Well, she is, and we will all have pneumonia out here looking for her. We could be electrocuted with that lightning and thunder. I'm going in. I've had quite enough drama for one night. If she wants to stay out here, she can. You should have left her in that madhouse, Desmond!'

But Desmond was not listening to his sister's ravings.

'I should never have left her tonight. What if she has drowned?' he cried. He put his head in his hands.

Moira felt sorry for him but angry too. He was right. He should never have left her.

'I'm going back down the avenue on foot,' Harry said. 'Moira is right – we do need help to search and medical aid should we find her.'

'Well, I'm going in – and I think everyone else should too until it eases,' Ida said.

Moira was inclined to agree with her. It was far too dangerous, and she wanted to run into the house herself.

'Ida, will you look near the rose garden? She might have gone that way?' Desmond said.

'*Fine!*' Ida shouted. '*But then I am done!*'

They dispersed again.

The thunder was not letting up. It roared and roared, and the rain was flowing down the lawn like a stream. Moira shone her light on the big oak that had fallen. She had so admired it as it stood so majestically on the lawn. It was no more now. The lightning flashed and made her scream and run. That was it. She had enough. Mrs Williams was right. This was sheer madness. They would have to wait until it eased and hope to God that Mrs Griffith was found safe. Although the likelihood of that was decreasing every minute. She began to make her way in.

Just as she turned towards the house, she thought she heard a scream. It seemed to be coming from the house.

She saw Harry making his way down the avenue with a torch and ran after him.

'*Harry! Harry! Did you hear that?*' Moira shouted.

He turned and ran back to her. '*What?*'

'It came from the house. Someone screamed!'

'Probably Julia after waking up and hearing the storm.'

'I don't think it was. Rosemary is in there with her.'

They ran to the house. Harry opened the door, holding it against the wind.

Inside, they could hear crying coming from upstairs.

In the grand hall, they looked up. There seemed to be lights coming from the very top floor.

'*Who's there?*' Moira shouted.

'*She has Julia!*' Rosemary screamed.

'*We're coming!*' Harry shouted.

Taking three steps at a time Harry ran up to the top floor, followed by Moira. But, before they got there he stopped abruptly, putting his hand up to stop her.

The image that met Moira took her breath away and she knew she would never forget it. A candle flickered that she had lit earlier and left on a side table, a torch flashed in Rosemary's hand and an oil lamp in Julia's threw shadows that seemed to quiver.

Rosemary was on her knees about four feet away from where Julia was, with her mother's arm holding her neck in the crook of her arm. In her hand Florence held a knife that Moira recognised from the kitchen. She seemed to Moira to be holding the knife to her own throat. But what frightened her even more was that where they were leaning was right beside where the banister was broken. Julia was holding a small oil lamp and it was swinging to and fro as Julia tried to get away from her mother. One wrong move and they would both fall to the ground floor. In the lamplight Moira could see that Florence's hair was wet and strewn across her face, blood oozing from cuts that looked like briar cuts. She seemed to have some sort of thin gown on and a silver cross and chain. Moira recognised the gown. She had seen it earlier that evening in the blue room. The shroud. How on earth had she come to put that on? Had she been in the room all along? But she was soaked so she had been outside. And her clothes had been found at the lake. They had not seen her come in.

Florence seemed to be in a trance and unaware of what was happening, staring at something above her. Moira thought she looked almost ghostlike. She was leaning against the banister as if to hold herself up.

Julia was screaming with tears flowing down her face.

'*The banister will give way!*' Moira screamed. '*It's broken!*'

'*Mama, stop! Please!*' Julia cried, her hands shaking and the lamp moving around.

Moira gasped, terrified of what could happen. A slight wrong movement could bring tragedy.

'*Christ!*' Harry shouted.

'*Let Julia go, Florence!*' Rosemary cried.

But it was as if Florence couldn't hear her, she was so transfixed. She was still staring at something above her with the strangest expression on her face.

Moira wanted to run to the child but was afraid that she would startle Florence.

Harry spoke softly. 'Let the child go, Florence. Take your arm away from the child. Drop the knife, Florence. This is Harry. You're not well.'

Rosemary was on her knees, begging her to release the child.

Then the noise of the banister giving way made Julia scream even louder as Moira helplessly looked on, with her hand over her mouth in pure dread.

Florence dropped the knife. The sound of it landing on the tiled floor rang around the hall. The sound seemed to bring her slightly out of the trancelike state that she was in and suddenly she seemed to realise that Julia was there and instantly she released her grip on the child.

Rosemary lunged forward to grab Julia as the child, dropping the lamp, ran into her arms.

But the lamp had fallen on the end of the shroud that Florence was wearing. Within seconds the thin cloth caught fire and golden flames billowed around her.

Julia wrapped her arms around Rosemary, screaming.

The flames were out of control. For one second the light shone on Florence's face and Moira saw her terrible fear and knew it would haunt her forever. Then a clap of thunder shook the house and a scream that seemed to come from the house itself tore through the air.

Moira watched in utter terror as Florence fell through the broken bannister, her body plummeting like a ball of flames and crashing onto the cold tiles three floors down.

Moira knew she would hear Julia's screams forever in her memory.

CHAPTER 23

Desmond arrived in just as Harry reached Florence. Desperately they tried to smother the flames with Desmond's wet coat. Moira ran down the staircase, knowing that whatever happened now the woman could hardly have survived.

The flames at last disappeared. Harry knelt beside Florence and shone a torch to her face. Moira gasped as she saw her poor burned face with a halo of blood around her head where she had hit the cold floor. Her eyes staring right up. She watched helplessly as Harry felt for a pulse and shook his head. Desmond seemed frozen to the spot. Julia was screaming and Rosemary was trying to soothe her and hold on to her.

The grandfather clock in the hall chimed three o'clock. Moira knew that three in the morning would forever bring her here to this time and this place. No matter where she ever went.

Time seemed to stand still then. Just the chimes of the clock and the cries of Julia.

Moira knelt beside Harry and into the ear of Florence she said the Act of Contrition. She knew from Vonnie that

217

they were Catholics. She whispered the words softly into her ear.

'*Oh my God, I am heartily sorry for having offended thee …*' The scent of burned cloth, hair and skin filled her nostrils, making her gag. Her eyes had become accustomed to the dark and she watched as Desmond remained in the same spot. She knew he was possibly in shock, and he reminded her of the cold statues outside.

'*Mama!*' screamed Julia.

'*Don't bring her down!*' Harry shouted back.

Suddenly the door opened, and Ida walked in and took in the scene. She stood with her hand on her mouth, staring and shaking her head. Harry rushed to her and put his arms around her.

Moira realised she still had her small torch in her hand. She made her way down to the kitchen. There was a large press with all the linen neatly piled and she shone her light in and got a clean sheet. With her hands trembling she brought it back up the stairs and as gently as she could she left it over Florence's body. Moira wanted to cry and scream but somehow she knew she needed to hold it together. How had they all ended up in this nightmare?

Harry brought Ida, who was shaking like a leaf, into the library. Moira followed them in and fixed the fire and handed him a blanket to put over Ida. Ida took off her trench coat and, just as she was about to take her hat off, it was as if her legs lost their strength. Harry and Moira caught her in the nick of time and put her on the sofa. The storm continued to rage.

'I'll make some hot sweet tea for the shock,' Moira said softly to Harry.

Then she lit the candles on the mantel and the oil lamp and threw some dry sticks on the embers in the fireplace.

'Thank you, Moira.'

Back in the kitchen her hands shook as she filled the big kettle and put it on the hob. She dropped the sugar bowl and it fell to the floor, cracking in tiny bits. She reminded herself to try to hold it together. But the scene in the grand hall kept playing again and again in her mind. When Harry had shone the light on Florence's face Moira had tried to hide her reaction. The woman's beautiful face was damaged beyond recognition. The portrait of the young woman that had fallen earlier came into her mind, with its destroyed face, and a strange sense of fear filled her heart. The portrait falling now felt like some sort of terrible premonition. What on earth had happened to make Mrs Griffith get up and go out on such a terrible night? What was that terrible screech that happened just before she fell to her death? Then with her heart beating so fast that she thought it would explode, she walked over to the butcher's block and looked at the knives. One was missing! The one that Mrs Griffith had in her hand. She should have locked the kitchen. In some terrible way she felt she had played a part by not putting the knives away or locking the kitchen. She had known the woman was mad. A pain deep in her soul began to take hold and she fell to the floor, weeping.

Eventually she pulled herself up and managed to make a pot of hot sweet tea. Her hands were not shaking as much and she managed to gather some cups on a tray. She brought it up the stairs and into the library.

Harry arrived down from upstairs.

'We've taken Florence back up to the bedroom,' Harry said.

'How's Desmond?' Ida asked.

'Still in shock. I've forced a brandy into him. We had better just leave him alone for a few minutes. Julia is in her

219

room with Rosemary, shaking like a leaf and crying, but Rosemary is trying to calm her down.'

'Good that you have moved her. That gardener could arrive in at any stage,' Ida replied sharply. 'What about the floor? Is it cleaned up?'

Moira noticed that Mrs William's seemed to have returned to her former self. A thought struck her. Was it proper to move the body before a doctor and the gardaí were called? Surely not? But it wasn't her place to voice such a question.

'The floor is the least of our worries, Ida,' Harry retorted.

Then he took a bottle of brandy from the drinks cabinet and put some into his tea and Ida's.

He poured a cup for Moira and poured a drop of brandy in. 'Moira, drink this up – we've all had a terrible shock,' he said gently.

'Thanks. I might, to be honest. But first I think I'd better check on Miss Purcell and bring her a cup of tea. I'll see if I can do anything to help calm Julia.'

Ida was standing in front of the large mirror and fixing her hair. She made no reply to Moira.

'Thanks, Moira,' Harry said.

Moira brought Rosemary a cup into Julia's room. Harry had poured some brandy into it for her. The child was in the bed, whimpering like a small animal.

Moira took a deep breath. She wanted to cry herself. The same thought kept whirling around in her mind. What had driven the poor woman to do what she had done and where on earth had she found the strength to do it? She must have crept out of the room and gone outside while everyone was asleep. She had taken all her clothes off. Then she had sneaked back in when everyone was looking for her. But how and why? Then Vonnie's words came to her.

Vonnie had said that there was something not quite right about this house. A strange sense in it. Then Naggie Nelligan had told her about the young woman in the portrait and the vision of the black carriage. Moira had not had much time for stuff like that. But now on this night she thought that anything was possible.

The rain had eased now, and the storm was passing. But it was a storm that had left its mark on Lenashee. Moira noticed that Rosemary was shivering, so she took Julia in her arms, rocking her to and fro, giving Rosemary a chance to drink the tea. Then like a light Julia fell asleep. Rosemary got up and fixed the blanket around the child's sleeping body.

She looked at Moira.

'I broke up a sleeping tablet and gave her a little piece,' she said. 'Perhaps I should have asked her father's permission but I couldn't disturb him. I thought it was for the best.'

'You did the right thing,' Moira said. 'It was necessary to blot out that nightmare for a while.'

'She won't wake now. We can go downstairs.'

Together they walked back down the stairs and into the library.

'Rosemary,' said Harry. 'Sit down and have some hot tea with brandy. And, you, Moira, sit yourself down and have a cup too. I insist.'

They sat and he poured two cups of tea and laced them with brandy.

'Thanks,' Moira said as she took the cup. She had never drunk brandy, but she could feel the golden liquid ease down her throat and almost into her veins. Soon she did feel a little calmer. Everyone was silent. Desmond hadn't come down from the bedroom where Florence's body was now lying on the bed.

Then Moira thought of something.

'Miss Purcell, will we walk down to the gate lodge and ask Mr Berne to get the priest?' she asked awkwardly.

Harry got up and paced the floor.

'No, I'll go when the storm has fully passed,' he said. 'They would have to wait until full light anyway to come here, as I imagine the roads are flooded from the storm.'

'I can't believe this has happened,' Rosemary said as if to herself.

'I know. It seems even more unreal because we are so cut off. But soon people can come and help us,' Moira said.

'People?' Rosemary asked.

'The gardaí and the priest and I suppose the doctor and the ... undertakers,' Moira suggested softly.

'The doctor?' Ida scoffed. 'What do you think he can do?'

'It seems only right to call him – isn't he supposed to issue a death certificate? And he might like to see Julia and Mr Griffith, to help them with the shock.'

'The gardaí!' Rosemary said, a little alarmed. 'Do we need to call the gardaí? Why? What can we tell them? That we heard an inhuman sound and then she fell to her death? There was nothing we could have done.'

'I believe that sound was just the storm,' Harry said. 'Possibly another tree falling. I know it sounded like it was in the house, but it was an almighty storm and goodness knows what damage was done outside. The sound just echoed inside, possibly frightened Florence and made her lose her balance.'

'Exactly! And I don't want to hear any other hocus-pocus stories about what happened!' Ida added.

Moira found it hard to imagine that it was a tree but anything else seemed unbelievable too. But for that moment when it happened it seemed like something not of this life screamed in the grand hall. But she was wise enough not to say this now. If this is what they wanted to say to the gardaí, she would not argue with it.

'The sergeant in Druid is a decent man. He will come straight away, I'd say. I suppose they'll just need to know what happened,' Moira said reassuringly to Rosemary.

'You know how things can get twisted though,' Rosemary said as if to herself.

'Twisted?' Moira asked.

'Yes, twisted. Things can get twisted once the gardaí get involved.'

Moira could see that Rosemary was still shaking.

'I'll make a fresh pot of tea,' she said.

She gathered the tea things onto the tray and went back down to the kitchen. She could hear the storm still roaring but it had lost its strength. She felt a lump in her stomach, knowing that news of what had happened would soon filter into the village once the gardaí arrived. Or the priest. The young curate would possibly be the one to come, she thought. He seemed nice and gentle. She wished Vonnie was here. It would be good to have her to talk to. She knew the family well and she would know what to do. Her mother would get wind of it. God only knows what she would say. Moira's resolve to leave was never stronger.

She wondered should she ask anyone if they were hungry. On second thoughts she decided to just make some more tea and a tray of light sandwiches. She sat down for a few minutes in the kitchen. Maybe it was the brandy, but her body felt heavy. She knelt and said some prayers aloud for Mrs Griffith, her words echoing in the silent kitchen. Eventually she got back up and busied herself making a tray of sandwiches and tea and brought them up to the dining room and through to the library. Rosemary had left. Only Ida and Harry were in the library and they seemed to be having a very intense conversation.

'Sorry to disturb you. I just want to leave these with you. I might ask Mr Griffith if he would like some tea.'

'Maybe leave him for now, Moira. I think we will try to bring him down soon and give him another good strong brandy,' Harry said.

'Very well. If there is anything at all that I can get you, just let me know.' Moira felt very shaky and she wasn't quite sure how she was holding it all together. She wanted to run away from Lenashee and all that had happened there.

'Moira, we need a word,' Ida said.

'Of course.'

Harry got up and shut the door.

'Have a seat, Moira.'

'Thanks.' She sat down.

'We have all had a harrowing night and we need to make some decisions before more people arrive to the house,' Ida said.

'Decisions?' Moira asked. 'How do you mean?'

'Well, what exactly to say to Mr Berne for example. He'll be sure to make his way to us as soon as the storm passes,' Harry said.

'What to say to him? I don't understand.'

'What we say is extremely important,' Harry said.

Moira had a strange sense of foreboding.

Harry got up and paced the floor. He lit a cigarette and took a deep drag of it.

'We've decided that it's best not to say exactly what happened here tonight. I've discussed it with Ida and we've decided, with Desmond's blessing, that the actual circumstances of Florence's death should well ... stay within these walls,' Harry said, never taking his eyes off Moira.

There was silence then – possibly only for a few seconds but to Moira it seemed forever. She looked at Ida who was lighting up a cigarette. She watched as she took a long drag and puffed small circles of smoke into the air.

'I don't understand,' Moira eventually said.

Ida sat up and looked directly at Moira.

'My sister-in-law is dead and there is nothing going to bring her back. But if the details of how she died gets out into the public it will have huge consequences.'

'I don't follow,' Moira said.

'Surely you have read the papers at some stage, Moira! The newspapers love nothing more than a juicy scandal. This story will double their sales. Do we really want the private details of this dreadful fiasco splashed across the front pages? I can see it now. *Florence Griffith released from a lunatic asylum runs naked through the woods of Lenashee and then tries to kill her child and falls to her death after the child set her on fire and a terrifying scream from the Devil himself.*'

'But ...'

'But what?' Ida snarled.

'But the oil lamp was a terrible accident. The poor woman didn't seem to even know that Julia was there. I really don't think she would ever have intentionally harmed her. It was as if she was in some sort of trance. Mr Griffith, you saw her. It was as if her mind had left her. She was not aware of what was happening. I'm no expert, but her mind was gone. That is the truth and, as Mr Williams said, the scream was possibly a tree falling.'

'Well, that might be well and good – but life is not always as simple as that,' Ida retorted.

'How do you mean?'

'Oh, for goodness' sake, do you really think that is how it will be reported? *You silly girl!*' Ida shrieked.

'Ida! Calm down,' Harry said evenly. He sat next to Moira on the couch, making her feel even more uncomfortable. 'Moira, I know this is hard to take in, but my wife is right. Julia's life is going to be difficult enough now with what has happened – attach a scandal to it and – well, I think she will have no chance.'

'I always knew that there was something not quite right with that woman,' said Ida. 'But he wouldn't listen. He had to marry a pure lunatic and leave us in this mess.'

'Ida!' Harry said sternly.

'Well, it's true. He should have never married her. And he should have put her into the asylum and thrown away the key.'

'There's no point talking like that now,' Harry replied sharply.

'But the gardaí will surely understand when we tell them what happened,' Moira said.

'*Ha!* Once the gardaí get in on this, it will be a circus. I doubt this one-horse town Garda Station will be left to cope with it. Pearse Street will possibly get involved.' Ida stood up and looked at Harry. 'You have to stop this madness. Now! The newspapers will never leave us alone if they get hold of it! I will not have this for our family. She might be dead, but she will not turn our family into a calamity.'

'Are you really saying that we should keep quiet about what happened here tonight?' Moira asked incredulously.

'Moira, we need to deal with all of this without it turning into a field day for scandal,' said Harry.

'But – she's dead,' Moira said.

'But we can say that she died naturally,' he said. 'Or something else. It could be several things. We don't have to say what really happened. Or where it happened.'

'But – it's what happened. There's nothing we can do about it!' Moira cried.

'There's too much at stake here,' Harry said.

'I'm sorry, Mr Williams. I don't follow you. The poor woman is upstairs, and I think at the very least she needs a priest.' Moira spoke quietly although she felt like screaming.

'Destroying everyone's life will not bring her back. If the gardaí get here and begin examining her they could order an inquest and then they could say that we drugged her and burned her. My sleeping tablets are ... not prescriptive, shall we say!' Ida cried hysterically. 'You were there, you heard me tell Desmond to give them to her.'

'But surely they didn't cause this?' Moira gasped.

'They could think that Desmond and I conspired to drug her. Set her mad! Not that she needed any help!'

'But ...' Moira could hardly believe what she was hearing.

'Ladies, calm down, please,' Harry said. 'What Ida is saying is true, Moira. We could all be implicated here. Desmond could be in trouble for giving her those pills. Think of what could happen to Julia. And no matter what we say to her about the lamp being an accident, it still killed her. There is no denying that. It will destroy the child. There's another way.'

'How?' Moira felt weak.

'I know people. People who could help me and all this could remain very discreet. But you must promise to keep quiet about what happened here tonight.'

'The Archbishop, you need to talk to him, Harry,' Ida piped in.

'Leave all of that to me.'

'So – I am not to say that she's dead?' Moira whispered.

'Not a word,' Ida said.

Moira felt sick. 'No, I need to tell the gardaí and get the priest. She deserves some respect.'

'We are not asking you to lie outright – we will slightly fabricate the truth,' Harry said as he lit another cigarette. He pulled deeply on it and poured a glass of brandy.

'But we can't lie,' Moira said.

'Oh, Moira dear. We cannot tell the whole truth,' Ida said irritably.

'But …'

'If we tell the truth, it affects lots of things,' Ida said.

'But a woman is dead,' Moira pleaded. 'We must let the clergy and the guards know. I don't know what the proper procedure is in Dublin, but if someone dies here a priest is called and the body is waked.'

'Waked! Do you honestly think it would be a good idea to have a wake here? Oh, let's call the villagers in and maybe a few singers. How ridiculous!' Ida scoffed.

'It's not ridiculous. It's respect for the dead,' Moira said, fighting back the tears.

'She's being absurd!' Ida cried.

'Moira, there is a little more to it,' said Harry. 'We only have our word that it was an accident. Our word! Do you really believe that they are going to believe us? We could all be under suspicion.'

'*But it was an accident!*' Moira cried. 'Why on earth would we be under suspicion?'

'So how do we explain what happened? Did she kill herself? Did the storm frighten her? I wasn't there,' Ida said.

'She lost her balance,' Moira said.

'Brilliant! I am not sure the superintendent will believe that!' Ida scoffed.

'Well, she was acting crazy of course,' Moira said.

'We can't tell the gardaí that the woman had gone mad,' Harry said, pacing the floor. 'They would go to town on it.'

'But what about Mr Griffith? Will he agree to ... not telling the truth?'

'Leave Desmond to me,' Ida replied.

'But then we are lying to the gardaí – that's a crime,' said Moira.

'The gardaí don't have to get involved. If they are, we will be smeared for life,' Ida said, raising her voice. 'Whatever happened there will be a massive interest in this. It will ruin Julia's life. So, for now no running to the priest or the guards. Do you hear me?'

'I'm sorry! I have to go the guards! It is the right thing to do.' Moira began to cry.

'Lower your voice, Ida! Think about it, Moira. Think about the scrutiny that Julia will be under for the rest of her life,' Harry said.

'Even if I were to agree to this, what about the child? She was there. She saw it.'

'Not if she believes it was a nightmare,' Ida said. 'A terrible nightmare.'

'What? You think she would believe that!' Moira said incredulously.

'She will if we all agree to it,' Harry said. 'Moira, I know it's asking a lot but think of the child. She will live her life believing that she had a hand in her mother's death and that her mother was a madwoman who could have killed her. She adored her mother and her mother adored her. Let her keep those memories. Don't have her only

229

remember her mother with her hand around her throat with a knife in her hand. The woman was clearly mad and should never have been here, but she was not always mad. She was a wonderful mother and that child meant everything to her. If you don't want to agree to this for us – do it for them. Do it for what they had. Don't destroy what they had. The child has lost her mother. Is that not enough?'

Moira felt sick. It was wrong and she knew it was, but he had a point. The face of Mrs Griffith just before she fell to her death was engraved in her mind. She certainly was no killer. She had looked utterly bewildered and frightened. Could it work? Would the child believe them?

As if reading her thoughts, Harry said, 'She will only believe us if we are all on the same page.'

'I don't know.'

'Moira, think of the child!' Harry said.

Moira began to cry. It was all too much. Now this.

Harry put his arm around her. 'We'll talk again, Moira, but for now say nothing to anyone!'

No matter what way they put it she knew it was wrong. She had never done anything wrong in her life. Every Saturday that she could she went to Confession and told the small sins that she had. How could she ever tell this sin? But perhaps they did have a point. She was so muddled she hardly knew what to think. Part of her thought it was dreadful and sinful. But another part of her was not sure. Something in her had shifted. She knew now that she would have to leave Druid. She could not live with this lie. She wondered should she just go to Dublin straight away and not bother going back to Druid. Maybe she could stay with Vonnie for a few days. She had a small bit of money saved ... so maybe she could even pay for a place to stay until she got some work. Her mind was racing so hard.

'Alright, I won't say anything now. But I need to think about it. I'm going to check on Julia.' She wiped her eyes with her handkerchief.

'Very well but don't say anything to her,' Ida warned. 'Check if she's still asleep. I will be up to see her shortly after I decide exactly what to say to her,'

'Oh – Rosemary gave her a tiny bit of a sleeping pill – she says she won't wake up.'

'Good, that's good,' Ida said.

'Are you serious about telling her that it was a nightmare? What do we tell her about where her mother is?' Moira asked.

'We tell her nothing other than she had a nightmare,' Ida said sharply. 'I will take her back to Dublin as soon as the storm clears. I am getting her out of this godforsaken place and I never want to hear of it or see it again.'

'Very well,' Moira replied.

She got up, left the room and slowly climbed the stairs, trying to stop even more tears from flowing. Julia's door was slightly ajar and when she peeked in the child was still sleeping. She looked so peaceful no one would realise the trauma that she had gone through.

The wind outside had stopped howling and the light was now making its way across the lake. Had it all been a dream? If only. Moira knew then that the nightmare had happened and somehow now she was part of it.

CHAPTER 24

2019

Aunt Ida and her son were arriving to Howth to see Desmond and Julia had arrived two evenings before. They would only stay a couple of hours. Julia had never liked Laurence and she was not looking forward to the visit. Joseph liked him even less and she had persuaded him that it was a perfect time to get away for a couple of days while she stayed with their father. Joseph had been very hesitant but, in the end, had agreed.

She had rung her doctor before she left and made an appointment to see him. She was taking extra care of her health and making sure that she got plenty of sleep. The last thing she wanted was to end up sick. The nightmares had not gone away but the manic feeling was subsiding and with meditation and light running she felt she was keeping it at bay. However, the memory of her visit to Lenashee was still very much all she could think of.

She had said goodbye to Joseph earlier that morning. He was flying over to London for a couple of nights to see some friends. She was glad to see him drive off and felt very guilty, realising that he had not taken a break in so long. She also knew that her time with her father was getting short. He was even weaker since she had last seen him. She knew how devasted Joseph and she would be when their father did pass but another part of her hated to see her father suffer so much. It was as if the medication was just prolonging everything. He was not suffering physically but in every other way he was suffering terribly.

It was strange how childlike her father had become but at least he was a little less restless now. It was as if Joseph and she had become the parents and he the child. She had tried to get the carer, Alice, to help her to bring him into the garden, but he didn't want to leave the room. He got terribly upset if he was on his own. So, he was only really on his own in the room when he was watching his programme – he was now watching only *Winnie the Pooh*. The magnitude of his illness really hit home to Julia and not for the first time she felt guilty about how devoted Joseph was. She had mentioned to him again about a hospice, but Joseph wouldn't hear of it. The doctor had told them that he was comfortable but fading. He needed round-the-clock care now. Joseph was liaising with an agency and hiring a private nurse at night. A nurse called twice a day and the doctor called three times a week. With the two carers, her father was cared for all the time.

Joseph had warned her that he was still talking about this woman Rosemary – in fact, other than that he was not really talking at all. He had become quite silent, other than fading into some trance-like state and then talking about Rosemary. Even asking Alice the carer about her. Alice had reassured Julia that it was just all the medication that he was on. He had not recognised Julia when she had arrived up to see him first. But at least now it was not a shock.

Joseph had written out his routine as to stray from it might upset him.

Maggie the housekeeper was gone home with a bad dose of migraine. But Julia was well used to cooking for herself.

The carer gave him a bed bath every morning. Luckily, with all the care he had, he did not have any bed sores. For breakfast he ate a spoonful of yoghurt mixed with a drink that had minerals and vitamins in it. His medication was carefully monitored and administered by Joseph, so she looked after that now and made sure it was all logged. Then, at around eleven she would put on the television on the wall and put on the same episode of *Winnie the Pooh*. Julia watched it with him. There seemed to be a flicker of happiness when he looked at it. She imagined he was young in his mind again for that moment. It was as if he was mesmerised by the woods that looked so pretty and knew that in a strange way it was as if he was transported to that hundred-acre wood and she was glad that it seemed to bring such peace to his face, even if it did break her heart.

The carer was having lunch and her father was after falling asleep. She thought she might have a nose around the room to see if she could see anything that might somehow connect the dots as to why he was asking about this woman and why she felt a familiarity about her. She had asked Joseph to look but he had said he found nothing. She started with her father's bedroom and looked on his bookshelf and even in the books. She tip-toed into his office which was close to the bedroom so she could still hear him. Alice would not be back for at least half an hour. Her father was very organised all his life and the office had nothing out of place. But after a thorough search she found nothing. All the files were neatly in folders in a large filing cabinet, but she had found the key in the drawer of his desk. She was closing the cabinet when she dropped the little key. She bent down to pick it up and then she saw something shoved under the filing cabinet. It looked like a file. She tried to get it out, but it was too far pushed in. She would have to move the filing cabinet. But it was far too heavy when she tried. She went back to the bedroom to check on her father and he was still in a deep peaceful sleep. She grabbed a wire clothes hanger from the cupboard and went back to her father's office. She wedged it in under the filing cabinet and tried to push whatever was under there out. Eventually there was enough of it out for her to prise it all out.

Putting it on her father's desk, she opened it. There was a faded clipping from a newspaper, a small yellowed envelope, and an old paper wallet for photographs. But there were no photographs in it except for an old negative of film that had at least three photographs on it. She held the negative up to the light but, other than making out that it was of people sitting at a table, that was all she could see.

She looked at the clipping. The heading was: **Missing Woman Took Her Own Life.** It said that a woman was missing and presumed dead after a passerby found her shoes and coat on Howth Pier. The missing woman was not yet named.

With her hands shaking, she opened the envelope and a small silver cross fell out. She could hear her own breath. What had she just opened? She picked up the negatives and knew that some of the answers might just lie in these. She looked at the time. Her father would be waking up. She went back and he was still asleep. The nearest chemist was in the village of Howth. Her heart was racing. She put the paper wallet with the negatives and the envelope with the silver cross into her bag, pushed the file back under the filing cabinet, replaced the clothes hanger and waited. When Alice arrived, she told her that she had to run an errand but would be back soon. Then she grabbed her bag and left.

But rather than going to their local chemist's she drove into Sandymount and parked and went into a chemist's there. She wasn't sure if the negatives would be alright after all this time but the assistant looked and said that they should be fine. However, the photos would not be ready until the next day. Julia thanked her and left.

Back at the house her father had awoken. She wished she could talk to him. There was so much about this disease that was heart-breaking. He looked at her and she realised that he was unsure of who she was.

'Rosemary, have you found Rosemary? Please tell me that you have?' he whispered.

'What happened to Rosemary?' Julia asked gently. She thought of showing him the silver cross. But something stopped her. She had promised Joseph that she would take care of him. She began to sing the song from *Winnie the Pooh* and instantly she could see her father's face relax.

Alice arrived in with some soup for him.

'Well, how are we? I have some lovely jelly and ice cream for afters but first I have some lovely soup.'

Julia left the room as Alice tried to get him to take a couple of spoonfuls. That would be all he would take, if he did take anything at all.

That night Julia found it hard to sleep. She got up early and went for a run on the treadmill that Joseph had installed. Then, after a long shower, she went into Howth village and grabbed two home-made quiches and some salads for Aunt Ida's visit as well as some cakes. She popped them in the car and hoped that the boot of the car would be cool enough for them. She drove to Sandymount.

Thankfully, the prints were ready. She waited until she was in the privacy of her car before she opened them. There were only three photographs. The assistant said that the rest of them were blank. Taking a deep breath, she opened them. The first was of Aunt Ida sitting beside a lake with a blanket across her and her father sitting opposite her. They looked young. They were smiling at the camera. But it was the lake that hit her like a thunderbolt. It was Lenashee. She recognised it. Next was a photograph of her Aunt Ida and a woman that looked like Rosemary Purcell. She could hardly believe it. Rosemary was holding a hat in each hand and it looked like Ida was looking at them. She couldn't be sure as it was only the side of her face, but it looked genuinely like her. Then she noticed the detail again. It was blurred but it looked like the library at Lenashee. So, Rosemary was at the house, she surmised.

The last photograph was at a table and it was laden with food. The people sitting around the table were looking at the camera. She recognised her Aunt Ida, her father, and Rosemary Purcell sitting with a little girl. Rosemary had her arm around the little girl who she knew instantly was herself. A young woman with an apron and a cap on was holding a platter with some salmon. She stared at the photograph, trying to catch her breath. Then she picked up her phone and googled the chef Moira Fitzpatrick. As she looked at the different images it was clear that the young girl in the photograph was the famous chef Moira Fitzpatrick and, although decades later, she knew from her visit to Clare that the photo was taken in the dining room of Lenashee. Her Aunt Ida was lying about the Lake House, lying about Rosemary Purcell and she was certainly lying about the fact that Julia knew her too. She was lying about everything. The question was, why was she lying? And why was her father talking about Rosemary and why had he these photographs hidden?

CHAPTER 25

Julia prepared lunch. She had set a table in the conservatory for the visit. She knew that Laurence would be fussing about his mother. Aunt Ida still held the strings to the family fortune and her son played his cards well. He was substantially wealthy himself, but his father's fortune still belonged to Ida.

His black shiny Mercedes arrived at ten minutes to one. Julia had thought it best to try to tackle Aunt Ida on her own. So, she had put a small plan in place to get rid of Laurence for a while. Aunt Ida arrived dressed in an elegant linen trouser-suit in ombre from Dolce Gabbana and a Chanel cream cashmere wrap. Laurence looked like he was about to step onto a golf course with a tartan pullover over a white short-sleeved shirt and tanned chinos. He looked younger than his fifty years and sported a very un-Irish tan. Joseph was convinced he either had a sun bed in the house or constantly wore fake tan.

She had put the two quiches in to heat and placed the salads in some fancy Nicholas Mosse pottery bowls. She had some crusty bread and a delicious-looking strawberry roulade and Bailey's cheesecake for afters. All were bought in. She had set the table with china cups and saucers. Maggie, the lady who looked after the house, would be appalled at Julia serving anything that was not cooked in the house. But the food looked delicious.

She heard them at the door and went to open it.

'Julia, how lovely the garden looks,' Ida remarked rather grandly.

Laurence looked as pompous as Julia remembered. His tan was verging on the orange side.

'Lovey to see you. I have lunch almost ready.'

'Well, I think we had better see Desmond first as we have come all this way,' Laurence said.

'Daddy is being looked after by his carer now. If we give him a little while, I can take you up then.'

'Goodness, poor Desmond. I hope you have manged to get good staff,' Aunt Ida said.

'They are wonderful, to be honest. Come on, I've lunch set up in the conservatory.'

Lunch passed without any hiccups and then she took them both up to see Desmond. Unfortunately, he didn't recognise either of them.

Ida was clearly shaken at how frail he had become. She sat down beside him and tried to talk to him. He looked bewildered and slightly frightened at Laurence. Julia politely asked Laurence to leave as his presence was not helping.

'I'm sorry, but he gets stressed so easily,' Julia tried to explain as she walked out after her cousin.

Then she went back into the bedroom. Her father was looking looked intently at Ida.

'Where's Rosemary?' he whispered.

Julia looked at Ida and could see her pale. There was silence in the bedroom.

'Goodness, Desmond, I don't know who that is. You poor thing. Perhaps she was in a book that you read,' Ida said breathlessly.

Julia had to bite her tongue. After half an hour she knew her father had had enough and she told Ida that she would make some fresh coffee.

Alice returned and looked after Desmond as they retreated to the conservatory.

Then Alice arrived down.

'I'm sorry to interrupt but we seem to have run out of one of his medications. It's not a prescriptive one but I do need it. Could you look after him while I nip out. Oh goodness, I forgot that I need to be here for the nurse when she arrives.'

Julia waited and sure enough Laurence spoke up.

'Why not tell me what he needs, and I can get it.'

'Laurence, you're always thinking of others,' Ida said smugly.

Julia tried to hide a grin. She winked at Alice. Her plan had worked.

With him out of the way, she tackled Ida. She would only have a few minutes as the local chemist was not far.

'More coffee?'

'No, dear. My goodness, your poor father. Dear lovely Desmond!'

'Aunt Ida, I want to show you something.'

'Oh?' Ida said cautiously.

Julia took the photographs from the pouch and laid them out on the coffee table. She watched Ida closely for her reaction. If she had paled when her father had mentioned Rosemary, she looked like she could faint now.

'Why are you showing me these?' she asked.

'I asked you about Rosemary and you said that you

didn't know her. I also asked you about the house in Clare and you said that my father was never there. This clearly shows that you did know her and that you even brought her to that house and not only was my father there, but I was there too!'

'How do you know that it is that house? It could be anywhere!'

'I know it because I was in it. It's been locked up for decades – desolate – but it's still there, and I recognise the lake and the library in the photograph.'

'You were at Lenashee?' Ida's voice was barely audible.

'Yes, I was there a few days ago.'

'I can't believe it,' Ida said, catching her breath.

'Are you okay?' Julia asked worriedly. Maybe this was not such a good idea after all. She hurriedly gave her aunt a glass of water and waited for a few minutes for her to recover.

She looked shaken. Then she looked at Julia with a fierceness that she had not witnessed from her before.

'How dare you? How dare you corner me here under the roof of my sick brother?'

'What are you talking about? I'm just asking you why you lied to me.'

'No. You are not! You are not just asking me! How dare you treat me with so little respect!'

'You're being unreasonable. You can see Daddy is obsessed with this woman. I want to know who she is.' Julia had expected her to avoid answering but not to act like this. 'What happened to her and where is she?' Suddenly she threw caution to the wind and took out the silver cross and the cutting from the file about her going missing. She threw them out on the coffee table for Ida to see.

242

'I found this silver cross and this cutting with that roll of film. Why would my father have that? Who owned that cross? Was it belonging to Rosemary Purcell?'

Ida picked it up and looked at it. She had looked overwhelmed earlier but now she stood with her eyes bulging and her face puce with anger.

'Have you nothing better to do but dig up this rubbish? My goodness, Julia, do you know how ridiculous all this is? Your brother is here every day looking after your father while you go gallivanting and then you have the gall to come back and stir up rubbish like this. Does your brother know what you are up to?'

'Leave Joseph out of this. Why did you lie?' Julia's voice sounded stronger than she felt.

'*I will not honour that with a reply! How dare you?*' Ida shrieked with venom in her voice. 'Is this your illness? If it is, I can forgive you. I have always said that you should stop all that travelling. It can't be good for your illness.'

'No, it has nothing to do with my illness,' Julia replied tersely.

At that the door opened and Laurence arrived in.

'I could hear shouting. What's this about?' he asked.

Ida stood up and grabbed her bag.

'Nothing! We're leaving.'

'But … 'Laurence said.

'Laurence, we're leaving. *Now!*' Ida replied, leaving Laurence in no doubt that they were indeed leaving.

'Please – don't go like this,' Julia tried to reason with her.

Ida eyeballed her.

'Please leave us, Laurence, and wait in the car,' Ida instructed.

Laurence looked at Julia and shook his head. 'Fine!'

'Aunt Ida, I'm sorry if all this has upset you, but I just want to get to the bottom of it.'

'Stop it! You are way out of your depth here. I warn you! *Leave it alone!*' Ida turned around and walked out.

Julia followed her.

Laurence had the car door open for her. He shut the door once she was in.

'Bye, Julia. Certainly a visit to remember,' he said sarcastically.

Ida was looking straight ahead and would not even reply to Julia as she tried to say goodbye. Julia felt like crying. What a disaster! She was not sure what she'd expected but this!

And she was no wiser except for her aunt's words to leave it alone. She went back in and flopped down on the sofa. She felt very weary suddenly. David had also told her to leave it alone. But how could she explain to them that she couldn't? She picked up the photographs that Ida had thrown down with such anger. Her eyes were drawn to Rosemary Purcell. Then she looked at the photograph with the group and the famous chef.

Then it hit her. The only other person that might be able to throw any light on it was Moira Fitzpatrick. If she was the cook in the photograph, then she must know something.

CHAPTER 26

Paris

Moira was back at Lenashee. The candles were lighting, the grand dining table golden in the candlelight. She was checking to see if Vonnie had put everything out for the meal she had cooked. They would come in shortly and take their places. She looked out through the window and she could see a flight of birds soar over the lake then in the distance she thought she could see a girl, maybe not a girl but a young woman with a rope on her neck and carrying a piece of wood that was attached to the rope, she had long flowing hair and a long cloak-like dress. Moira began running down the stairs, out through the entrance hall, through the lawns that smelt of roses and orchids and then down the stone steps shouting at the girl to come back.

'Stop please! Come back, come back!'

The girl was disappearing into the lake …

Then Moira awoke in her bed in Paris. She was dreaming of Lenashee again. She checked the clock. It was three o'clock in the morning. Strange how that hour still had power over her. She sat back and tried to calm her mind. She was dreaming of Lenashee and the story that Master O'Sullivan had relayed to her so long ago of the young woman who had drowned herself in the lake. Sitting in her Parisian bedroom she could still smell the roses in her dream and see the girl as she went deeper into the lake. Moira's heart was beating fast and she knew there was no point in staying in bed she wouldn't sleep now. Slowly she pulled on her dressing gown and made her way to the kitchen. How many times had she done this in her lifetime, she wondered? So many times, she had dreamed of Lenashee. So many times, she had sat in her living room watching the dawn as she tried to still the memories of Lenashee. How foolish to think that even if she never saw it again the memories would disappear!

It was that letter that had made the memories even stronger. They had all kept their promise. Their secret was safe. Some student was not going to unearth the secrets that they had kept for over five decades.

She sat there for over an hour watching the night sky, waiting for a glimmer of dawn to wash the dream away. Eventually she got up and made some Earl Grey tea. She needed to take her mind off it. She jotted down some ideas for her new book. Even if it was early, it was better than sitting with her memories.

Then at about eight she got up and washed and dressed and had some breakfast. She liked to be up and about before Francoise arrived at ten. It took her longer now to get ready. But she was at her desk by ten minutes to ten and began answering her emails. She had promised to write an article for *Le Parisien* about the importance of using foods that are in season. It was what she was most famous for. She had written for decades about using food that either you grew yourself or that could be sourced from a local grower. It was a simple philosophy but one that seemed to be getting lost through the generations. Even on her veranda she had herbs, garlic, tomatoes and berries. She wondered how to begin the article. She could say that she learned the importance of this from growing up in rural Ireland in the fifties when everything that you ate was sourced from your own hand or locally. She could still almost taste the big juicy blackberries that would grow on the hedgerows along the road. She would pick them and boil them with sugar for jam or make a blackberry tart and use the top of the milk for cream.

But then she thought better of it. She would stay clear of mentioning Ireland at all. If she had not mentioned it in *For the Love of French Food* that student might never have contacted her. She took out a pen and a clean piece of paper and began to write. She preferred to handwrite it first and then to type it. She still hated computers, but she had managed to learn to use one, just about.

The morning passed and all thoughts of the night before were gone with it. Rupert was calling for lunch. She had not seen him since their lunch at the Ritz, but he was back in Paris for another client and was dropping in at twelve. She finished up and went back to her bedroom.

Francoise had lunch prepared. She checked that all was set and at one minute to twelve Rupert arrived.

They sat in the living room and sipped on a dry sherry before lunch. Rupert was full of good news on book sales and the excitement of the latest project that Moira had agreed with the publisher. She was going to write a book about cooking with only fresh local produce. It was a big undertaking and she wondered if it would be her last book. But she was passionate about it so it would not be a burden.

'By the way, I had a most unusual phone call from Grace,' Rupert said.

Grace looked after all the social media to do with

Moira. Moira hated the words *social media* and had warned them not to put up anything remotely personal.

'I hope she's not suggesting that I do one of these Facebook live things that I have read about! I have told you I have no interest in anything like that.'

'No, nothing at all like that.'

'Well, what is it then?'

'She had a phone call from a woman who wants to get in touch with you but it's personal, she says. It's about some house in County Clare.'

Moira could feel her breath almost stop. Then she found her voice.

'I had a letter from her. Remember, you brought it to me. It was marked personal. I have no intention of talking to her and I have no idea who she is – some student mixing me up with someone else.' Moira could feel her chest tighten. She had thought that was the end of it when she hadn't replied to her.

'I don't think so,' Rupert said.

'What do you mean you don't think so? I am telling you I want nothing to do with her. I'll ring Grace myself and tell her to block any more calls from this person.'

'What I mean is, it's not a student.'

'She is, she said it in the letter!'

'This is someone different. It's Julia Griffith. The travel writer. Have you heard of her? She's very well known. She has written a few fascinating books. I have a couple of her books. One is about Africa and one on the Northern Lights. She must be in her fifties, I would imagine. Very striking lady. Anyways she seems to think she met you many years ago at a house in Ireland on a lake. She said that it was really important that she talk to you – but that it's very personal.'

Moira stood up and slowly walked to the window. She had known this day would come. Even if she never really admitted it to herself she knew that one day this woman would look for her. The image of that child on that night was still vivid to her – the fear, the disbelief, and the terrible loss. But their lie had worked, their deceit had worked. Hadn't it? Suddenly, her breath deepened, and she could feel herself falling. She could feel Rupert put his arms around her as she fell into blackness.

CHAPTER 27

Dressed in jeans and a light shirt Julia walked around the cottage, checking to see that all the windows were locked. Then she got a glass of water and took her medication. She knew that her need to know the truth about Lenashee was becoming obsessional. But she was no closer to finding the answer. After the fiasco at Howth, Ida had avoided her calls. She had phoned the publishers of Moira Fitzpatrick and left a message asking Miss Fitzpatrick to contact her. But she too had ignored her. Sleep was now evading her, and David had to remind her to eat.

The night before, she had not gone to bed at all. While David was sleeping she had gathered every bit of information, photograph, and newspaper article that she could find on Moira Fitzpatrick, Rosemary Purcell, her Aunt Ida and Lenashee. She had not even noticed David arrive down in the early morning. The entire floor of the living room was covered in articles and photographs. She had spent the night printing them and putting them together like a jigsaw on the floor. Trying to find some timeline, any link at all that could shed light on it. David was not impressed and was going to cancel his flight and stay at home and get her to her doctor. But eventually she convinced him to go. He grabbed a later flight and said he would call her as soon as he arrived at the exhibit and possibly catch a late flight back if she was not any better. She knew that he was terrified that her disorder was rearing its head. She was afraid herself. She was manic after all. All the signs that she was heading in the wrong direction were waving red flags. Her thoughts were at times mangled and obsessive. She had promised him that she would go to bed and try to sleep.

He had helped her to tidy up all the articles and then, when she was resting in bed, he had left. But she had only rested for a short time. After a few hours she had got back up and made her plans. The landline rang. She knew it was him checking in on her. She took a deep breath and answered it.

'Hi, how's the exhibit?' She tried to keep her voice normal and disguise the feeling of pure anxiety that was engulfing her.

'It's good, just arrived! How are you? Did you sleep?'

She could hear the worry in his voice. She tried to keep her voice even.

'I'm just about to have another lie-down. Sorry, I need to sleep some more. I might take the phone off the hook because it'll just waken me.'

'I'll ring you when the exhibit closes and see how you are. I can always get a flight back tonight, I just needed to show my face today.'

'Grand ... good luck with it.'

'Bye.'

She hung up and then took the receiver off the hook, grabbed her keys and left. She had already thrown some stuff into the car.

She was not heading for a lie-down. She was headed for Druid. But her body felt strange, as if she were slightly dizzy. She knew that she probably shouldn't be behind a wheel, but she got in and fastened her seat belt and started up the engine. Slowly she reversed the car and drove off.

At first she couldn't recall the route – only that she needed to drive towards Carlow. She put on the Satnav. It said that it would be over three hours to Druid. She drove off, her mind consumed with getting there, nothing else mattered now.

After an hour she pulled into a garage for diesel. As she was filling it up her hands shook, spilling the diesel on her hand and the sleeve of her shirt. She finished up and went in to pay, joining the lunchtime queue and grabbing a bottle of water and a bar of chocolate. A sullen grey-haired man scanned the chocolate and bottle of water without looking up at her. She took out her credit card.

'Petrol or diesel?'

She looked blankly at him.

'Did you get petrol or diesel?'

'Oh sorry, yes,' she replied.

He looked at the screen and tapped in the diesel. 'Fifty-two euro and twenty cents.'

She held her card to the machine.

'You have to put the pin in,' he said gruffly.

She could feel him looking at her intently and she knew he had noticed her hands shaking.

'It's over fifty quid – so you need to put the pin in,' he said again, irritated this time. Her mind was blank, she had no idea what the number was. She stared at the pin machine.

'The pin?' he said tersely.

'I – I can't remember it.'

'There are people waiting – step over there, please.' He waved to her to stand away from the till.

She didn't move.

'I think I've got cash.'

'Fine,' he mumbled.

She could feel his impatience building as she began rummaging through her bag. She pulled out an empty purse and a make-up bag – silently praying that she had a wallet somewhere. No sign of it. She kept rummaging.

'You will have to step aside, people are waiting,' he said gruffly.

'I have it!' She took out a black wallet, hoping that there was some cash in it. As she opened it, it fell to the floor and the money fell out. A girl standing behind her helped her to gather up the coins from the floor. She breathed a sigh of relief. There was a fiver, some coins and a fifty-euro note. She put it on the counter and looked at the man again.

'Receipt?'

'Sorry?'

'A receipt! Do you want one?'

'No.' She tried unsuccessfully to gather up the loose change that had fallen on the counter, her hands visibly shaking.

'You sure you should be driving?' he said accusingly.

She shoved the change in and left, not offering him any answer and praying that he wouldn't follow her out. She jumped in the car, started up the engine and drove off. She could see him looking out at her.

She followed the Satnav. At one point she could feel the car swaying and she almost drove into a very irate driver who blew the horn at her. She kept going. It seemed an eternity.

Eventually she saw a sign for Druid and a sense of calm seemed to envelop her. She was getting nearer. She drove straight into the town. There were people walking about, a bunch of teenagers walking in a group. The coffee shop that she had gone into before was still open and she parked on the street near to it and went in. A small bell rang as she entered and a young dark-haired girl sweeping the floor greeted her.

'I'm afraid we're just about to close.'

'Can I use your bathroom, please?'

'Of course. Do you want to order anything to take with you?'

'I'll take a black coffee please. No milk or sugar.'

'No problem. Anything to eat?'

'No, just the coffee please.'

Once in the bathroom she splashed some cold water on her face. She stared at her reflection and in some ways she barely recognised herself. It was as if she was far removed from who she was or even who she thought she was.

When she came out the girl was at the counter putting a lid on the takeout coffee. She paid for it with her remaining change and left.

It was a dull summer's evening. Cooler than it had been. She felt a chill over her body. She turned on the car and switched on the heat. The coffee made her feel a little better. She broke off a piece of chocolate and had it with it. She couldn't remember if she had eaten anything at all that day. She remembered David bringing her tea in bed, but it seemed so far away now. She finished up and drove off and soon she was back on the road to Lenashee. Her phone rang but she didn't answer it.

She had a strange feeling that every moment of her life was leading to this point. She knew herself that she felt unwell, but somehow it didn't matter. Nothing really mattered now except getting there because somehow she knew that the answers that she was unknowingly searching for were there in that house.

She parked at the gated entrance. She had a small backpack, and she threw her phone into it. She pulled on the wellingtons that she had in the boot and with the backpack slung on her back she walked towards the gap in the wall.

At first she couldn't find the gap and then, as if she were in a trance, she found it and climbed over. A strange sort of peace came over her. She had not known there was so much of her here in this place. No one would tell her why. But she knew. She walked on and a soft hazy mist surrounded her. A hint of woodsmoke carried in the breeze, the buzz of nature surrounded her and the scent of wild lilac – somehow familiar to her – made her stop to inhale it more deeply. The sky seemed closer somehow and the clouds heavy, throwing shadows across the lake. A family of magpies gathered around a dead tree and dived into flight as she neared them. Then the house was revealed with the mist hanging like a blanket over it.

She went around the back of the house and climbed in through the broken window. The nest of bees lay undisturbed. Why did this house seem to have such a strong hold on her? She couldn't understand – but it almost was tangible – her connection to the place. Perhaps houses did hold memories, she thought, because she felt the house remembered her too. She knew that she was here long before she had discovered it this summer. The photograph proved that she had been here. Once in the kitchen, she felt almost faint and sat down on a dusty chair. She felt so tired. Her phone rang again but she didn't answer it. It disturbed the peace in the room. A white butterfly flew in front of her face, startling her. She heard a scratching noise and knew it was a rodent of some sort, but she didn't care.

She took the narrow, stench-filled stairs that led to the dining room and then walked over to the drawing room where she removed a motheaten dust sheet and revealed a gramophone. She took up the records. Dean Martin, Tony Bennet, Elvis Presley and Ella Fitzgerald. She felt lightheaded. She sat on the floor and tried to remain there, trying to make sense of the last few days.

Her illness reared its head at certain times in her life, sometimes with no warning or reason, leaving her with no option but at times to be hospitalised. But this felt different.

The wind was picking up and she could hear the whistle down the chimney. She felt slightly suspended from reality. Here she was in this desolate house that she believed somehow held the key to something that was especially important to her. What, she had no idea, but she was as sure of it as she was of anything. Then like a jolt a memory came back to her. She walked back into the dining room and down the small narrow stairs that led to the kitchen. Then as if part of some other entity she walked around opening presses and looking at old tins, saucepans, and baking tins. She was searching for something, but she had no idea what. Then she came to a press that held some cups and saucers, all covered in dust. There were numerous large plates at the back. A dresser with cups and plates was placed beside an old stove and when she coughed the layer of dust was disturbed. There was a press at the bottom of the dresser with faded blue wooden knobs on the doors. She slowly opened the press doors.

She took out some old china cups and saucers of fine china. Delicate violets were hand-painted on them. She picked up one of the chipped cups and as she held it a flash of a memory hit her. The evening light shone through the window and then it was as if the evening sun shimmered through the window and a thickening of the light by the window threw shadows and an image floated in the air. There was a blue blanket set out with the china and a Teddy Bear with pink buttons for eyes and a black button for his nose. Then like a flash the image was drifting, leaving her feeling desolate and so very alone. Her body was heavy now, weary of not knowing.

She struggled to get back up and left the kitchen by the narrow staircase. She supposed that decades or even centuries before, servants were meant to be as discreet as possible and that was why the staircase was there. She walked trance-like up the stairs to the first landing and opened the second door which led her out into the grand hall. She tried the handle of a door that was near to the drawing room. But it seemed to be locked. She tried again. She pushed at the door and eventually it gave way. As the door flew open her eyes fixed on a portrait of a woman with its glass broken and her face destroyed. She walked over to it and put her hand to the face, gently caressing it. A heaviness seemed to enter her body and the sense of being suspended from reality became stronger. She reached to her neck where earlier that morning she had put on the silver cross and chain. She had no idea why she had put it on, but she felt almost compelled to. She then continued up the stairs to the very top of the house. She gasped as just in time she noticed that part of the banister was broken.

She collapsed down on the landing and took off her rucksack, rummaging inside until she found her phone. She had downloaded the song that seemed to be haunting her. She played it and soon it was echoing around. 'My Lagan

Love.' The light had now dimmed and its watery hues were shining through the stained-glass dome down onto the landing, the acoustics like a concert hall. She kept the song playing repeatedly. The light changed again, twilight in all its glory with different shades of light from the stained glass. Its pattern changing across the walls giving an ethereal feeling. She watched as patterns formed and dissolved in the changing light and then she barely breathed as the colours formed a silhouette of someone. Was it real, she wondered, or had reality become intertwined with her imagination? She knew that something was being unearthed in her memory – an image penetrated her mind, a disturbing image of a woman screaming. Then the light from the dome changed and she could see nothing only the blinding light from the stained glass, all reds and oranges. She felt afraid. She wanted to run down the stairs. She grabbed her rucksack and phone. She put her hand on her head, trying to stop the images, but they were getting stronger. Her head felt like it would explode. This time she could see a woman in silhouette – there were candles lighting. She screamed in fright. Then the image became more real and she could see the woman, but she couldn't see her face as it was covered in blood. She began to scream, and her voice echoed around the house. She ran down the stairs to the ground floor but just at the last step she tripped and fell. Her head hit the cold tiled floor and then there was only darkness.

It was dark when she awoke. At first, she had no idea where she was. The sliver of a moon was shining through the dome and the rustle of wind rattled against the windows. She watched the moon and then a cloud must have arrived and slightly covered it. Her back hurt and her head hurt. She tried to move her body but her back hurt so much that she cried out in pain. Slowly she pulled herself up, but the pain was dreadful. Then she realised where she was. Her phone … she tried to think where it was. She put her hands about her but nothing, she couldn't find it. She moved around on the floor and then her phone rang and lit up as it did. She breathed a sigh of relief but as she picked it up it went dead.

'*Damn!*' she cried and then winced in pain.

Then she looked up into the darkness. She was not alone – she could hear a voice whispering to her. She knew that either she was not alone, or she was simply going insane. She had to get out of here. It would be crazy to try to get through the woods at night. But she felt she had little choice. She began to crawl, but she could hardly see anything. She crawled across the floor and an image of a woman came like a flash again. Image after image then she heard a scream. She put her hands to her head and over her ears. Who was screaming? It was terrifying to listen to. Then she heard the scream again. Again, and again. Her head hurt, image after image hitting her like a shovel and the screams that never ended. Then the shocking realisation that she recognised the voice. It was her voice. Her screams. She wept. It had happened. She knew she had lost her mind.

CHAPTER 28

Lenashee 1967

Rosemary looked out from her bedroom window. There was a sliver of light in the distance. The dawn was coming. The rain was still teeming down but nothing like earlier. The light would fully come, and others would come to the house. Others would know the terrible thing that happened only a few hours previously. For now, what had happened remained within the walls of Lenashee. Her thoughts went to Julia. She had tried so hard to get the child away from her mother. Thank God she was still alive. It had seemed to Rosemary that Florence didn't even realise that she was holding the child.

When the others were out searching for Florence, Rosemary had stayed in the room with the sleeping child. But the storm had awoken Julia, and Rosemary had gone to the kitchen to heat some milk on the stove for her. Rosemary thought that it must have been when she was in the kitchen heating the milk that Florence had gone into the child's room. Or maybe the child followed her to the kitchen and that's how Florence found her.

Ida had told her that before her illness Florence Griffith was vastly different to the woman she had seen on the stairs earlier, but Rosemary surmised that Ida and her sister-in-law had not been close. Ida had said that Florence preferred to be in the garden with Julia rather than on the whirl of social engagements that Ida relished.

Ida was lying down after everything that had happened. The telephone lines were down and so many trees had fallen that no one could drive out or in. They were all trapped in this house with a dead woman. She knew she would never forget the terrible screams of Julia. She was sleeping, thankfully. How could the child ever cope with this horror? She was still in a deep sleep after the piece of sleeping pill but soon she would awake and how then would she cope? Ida had warned her that they were to call her as soon as the child awoke. She was going to tell her some story about it all being a dream. Rosemary had told her that she thought it was ludicrous to think that the child was going to believe that. Ida told her that if everyone told her that it was a dream, she would. But surely it was not as simple as that. The child was traumatised.

It was hard to sit still. She shivered as she pulled her cardigan tighter on her. She decided to go to the library where Moira had kindly lit the fire. Rosemary had to admire her calm though – making tea and organising the fire. Moira was a few years younger than her, but she seemed wiser than her years.

She walked in and just as she was about to sit by the fire Harry arrived in, closing the door after him.

'Rosemary, I need to talk to you.'

How good his voice sounded! How calming to know he was here! The tick-tock of the clock seemed very loud. Tick-tock, tick-tock it went, the crackle of the fire and the sound of the rain pounding gave her a sense of grounding. The events of the night seemed so unreal she needed something familiar. The simple sounds of life that she could cling on to. She could smell his cologne. If she could close her eyes and imagine this was a different time and she was here with Harry sitting by the fire, happy to be in each other's company ...

She knew she loved him. It seemed foolish really as she didn't know him very well and he was married but perhaps you couldn't help who you fell in love with, you could only control what you did about it. He looked older than he had. She watched him go to the dark cabinet which held the drinks, and he took a decanter down and poured two brandies. He handed her one and ushered her to sit beside him. He took her hand. It felt good, like a buoy in the sea. She was not a brandy drinker, but she had drunk it earlier in the tea and it had helped. She sipped the drink. She watched Harry, his eyes that seemed as deep as the ocean. He seemed so sure of who he was and so confident without being pompous. He was the type of man that you felt you needed in your corner. Someone to hold you up when you could not hold yourself up. But she reminded herself that he was not hers. She pulled her hand away, one small movement that meant so much. She wished she could leave it there.

Desmond was in the bedroom with his dead wife. She was not sure where Moira was, but she was most probably lying down or in the kitchen. She was alone with Harry. Guilt engulfed her yet she was glad of this precious time with him. A few minutes to forget the nightmare that they had witnessed. She was worried about what was to come next. She knew she must keep her distance now from Ida and Harry. He took her hand again, and this time she didn't take it away.

'How are you holding up?' he asked kindly, his eyes crinkling at the corners.

'I keep going back over it. I can't believe what has happened.'

'It's shocking alright.'

'It was as if there was someone else there screaming.'

'It was just the storm. That's all. But the fact of the matter is the woman is dead and we need to protect Julia. I'm not sure the gardaí will believe us when we tell them.'

'How do you mean?'

'Well … I don't know but it does seem all a bit farfetched. She was so ill she could hardly walk, yet she went out in that storm and then grabbed the child and a knife. It just doesn't add up – even to me. But we know it happened. I just think they will want to look into it a little more than that.'

'How?'

'Not sure. But there will certainly be questions from the gardaí. But the poor woman was clearly mad. Plain and simple.' Harry was looking at Rosemary intently.

The mention of the gardaí made Rosemary shudder.

'Will the gradaí come here?'

'Not if I have anything to do with it. I'm sure an investigation will come to nothing but still we don't want anyone surmising that something other than what did happen happened. I will make some calls as soon as I can get a line. If I can get the car out, I will take care of things.'

'How will you – take care of things?'

'Never mind, but we don't want the gardaí sniffing around here, thinking that something else happened and putting anyone under suspicion. Do we?'

Rosemary was taken aback at this remark. What if they began asking questions about who they were and their backgrounds? She could feel her body tense. She couldn't risk that. She needed to think. She should never have come here.

'I'm afraid there is something else too,' Harry said, looking kindly at her.

'What?' Rosemary said.

'I know who you are, Rosemary,' he said gently.

She could feel her heart beat so fast it felt like it would explode.

'What do you mean?'

'I know that you are Rosemary Brown not Rosemary Purcell. You are Rosemary Brown, the daughter of the late Doctor Brown and his wife Dorothy. They were both killed in an accident when you were fourteen and your sister twelve. Leaving you and your sister Ellen in the care of an uncle who was meant to look after you and your home.'

Rosemary could feel her body sway. This was too much.

'How do you know this?' she asked, shocked.

'I have my ways. I believe your uncle liked to drink and soon the drink forced him to sell your house and he moved you both into a cottage far up a hill. There were rumours that you had … a difficult time with him.'

'What rumours?'

'Just rumours. Let's say that there were two sides to his personality.'

'How do you know this? *Have you been spying on me?*'

'*Shush*, I don't want to waken anyone.'

'*Does Ida know?*'

'No, calm down. When I first met you and my wife decided to invite you to stay with us, I had someone, well, I suppose look into who you were. She was bringing you here to stay and inviting you into our home. I have many interests and connections in the business and political world. I was not about to allow someone into our lives that I knew nothing about. My wife is … more trusting that I am. I needed to know who this person was that my wife was befriending.'

264

'Well, what did you find out?' Rosemary said, trying to fight the tears that threatened.

'Your uncle disappeared a few years ago. It was thought that he went to England as he owed debts everywhere.'

'Yes.'

'Why then did you disappear too and take Ellen with you?'

'There was nothing left there for us.'

'I had a phone call from the man who researched this for me as he had some news. I was going to tell you when we were walking the other day.'

'What news?' Rosemary asked, her voice barely audible.

'They found your uncle's watch and his shoes and hat buried in a bag on the land.' He watched Rosemary without taking his eyes off her.

'Oh!' She tried to remain calm, but the use had left her body.

'The gardaí plan on searching the land in case … anything else turns up. They have not located him in England.'

Rosemary felt physically sick – she could feel the bile rising in her stomach to her throat. She put one hand to her mouth and desperately looked for a handkerchief with the other, but she must have lost it. She began to retch. Harry hurried her to the window and opened it. She barely made it as she leaned out and threw up.

She often lost sleep, terrified that this day would come. The day of reckoning and then a thought that almost suffocated her. She retched and retched, and green bile mixed with the brandy came out of her mouth.

'Ellen?' she cried.

'Don't worry, her location is safe. No one knows where she is, she covered her tracks well.'

Rosemary knew that he knew. Somehow, he knew.

'Will they come looking for me?'

'They might. Your photograph was in the paper with Ida. Someone might recognise you. I am sure some of the people from your parish know where you work. I expect the gardaí know exactly where you are, but they are biding their time to see what else might turn up before talking to you?'

She started to tremble all over, her body almost convulsing. Harry put his arms around her.

'*Shush*, it's going to be alright.'

'How? Tell me how?'

'Leave that to me to worry about. But you must tell me the truth. Will they find something on the land?'

'I don't know.'

'Are you sure?'

'Oh God!'

'You need to tell me.'

'*Yes … they will!*' she cried.

Harry held her in his arms. '*Shush*,' he whispered.

But Rosemary was almost in a trance.

'Was it an accident and you tried to cover it up?' he asked.

But Rosemary was tired of lying, so tired of it.

'No.' All she ever wanted to do was protect Ellen. She looked at Harry and wondered what had led her to this man. Who was this man? Would he protect her or throw her to the wolves? If he didn't turn her in, he would be obstructing the course of justice.

'They will come looking for me soon!' she cried.

'They will. But they don't have to find you. You need to listen to me, Rosemary. I will help you. Ellen's whereabouts are safe so far. I have someone keeping an eye on it. If it leads them to her, I will personally look after it. You have my word.'

'How will you protect me?'

'You will need to trust me, Rosemary, that's all you have to do.'

She looked at this man who was almost a stranger to her. She knew instinctively that he meant it. Could she trust him? Had fate intervened and led her to him?

'Why ... why will you help me?'

'You know why,' he said gently.

And she did. Whatever she felt for him, she knew that he felt the same for her.

'I trust you,' she whispered.

CHAPTER 29

It was another half hour before they both left the library. Moira knew this because, just before Rosemary had gone into the library, Moira had gone into the small office that was adjoining the library to look for Chocolate Bear to give to Julia when she awoke. When she had heard someone come into the library, she had remained quiet – slightly embarrassed that perhaps they might not approve of her being in the office on her own. Then once they had begun talking, she felt she had no option but to remain quiet. She had heard every word of the conversation.

Once they had left, as quietly as she could she crept out and went down the corridor to the back stairs, but just as she did she could hear someone behind her.

It was Mr Williams.

'Moira, might I have a word?'

'Of course,' Moira said, her face reddening. She was glad it was still dark so he would not see it.

'Perhaps we could go down to the kitchen and have a cup of tea?'

'Yes,' she said, half terrified.

Suddenly it was all too much for Moira. It was one

thing witnessing the death of Mrs Griffith in such a horrific way but now she had stumbled on this. She had no idea what exactly Rosemary had done but it didn't sound good. She had no idea what it was called not to report such a crime, but she knew it was illegal.

'Go into the kitchen, Moira, and put on the kettle. I will be with you in a few minutes.'

Moira wished she could unhear what she had heard.

She put the kettle on the stove and lit some candles. Her hand was shaking so much she could hardly light them. She had no desire to talk to Mr Williams on his own.

Rosemary walked in. Moira felt faint. Even in the candlelight she could see how shaken up she was.

'Moira … Harry told me that you overheard us talking.'

'I was just looking for Chocolate Bear and I had searched everywhere for him. I thought it might comfort her. I noticed that he was missing earlier. Then when I heard someone come in, I thought that I might get in trouble as I had no right to be in such a private room.'

'You're not in any trouble, Moira. You are indeed a kind person who was thinking of the child. However, you did hear us talk.'

'Yes.'

'I beg you not to tell anyone what you heard.' Rosemary began to cry.

'I wish I had not heard it, believe me, but I did. I know you did something. Probably very bad … but I'm not sure?'

'I beg you, please forget what you heard!'

'I live in a small place. There is going to be enough about the goings-on at Lenashee already, enough to bring the gardaí to my door. I wish … I wish I could run away. They will want to know who was in the house – am I supposed to lie about that too?'

'Well, maybe you can, Moira,' came a male voice.

Harry had arrived.

'What do you mean?'

'Run away.'

'I have nowhere else to go. I was thinking I might go to Vonnie – she said that I might be able to stay with her for a night or two. I can't face my mother with all this. You don't know her – she will keep at me. She will know I am hiding something.'

'Moira, let this be your chance – the one that you have waited for,' Harry said.

'What one?'

'France! That's where you want to go, isn't it? To train there. I will make sure you get there and get trained.'

Moira was astonished. She didn't know if he was serious. 'Why would you do that?'

'I will see that you get to go. I will make sure you get a place at the best school, but you must never utter a word of what you saw or heard here tonight, is that clear?'

'I can't think anymore!' Moira cried.

'Please, Moira, do it for me,' Rosemary said, weeping. 'I beg you!'

Moira could see the terrible fear in her face. She had seen fear in Mrs Griffith's face before she died. A terrible fear that she knew she could never forget. But she was helpless to try to save her. But here she could. It was like some dice had been rolled again. Could she lie? Could she go against everything that she ever knew? She was so full of fear but something else was there too – a burning desire to get away from here, from Druid, from her mother and the life that was being laid out for her. If she stayed, she would never hear the end of it when her mother found out that the gardaí were up at Lenashee. Her mother would be

270

worse than the gardaí and she would assume all sorts of things had happened.

'I don't know!' Moira cried.

'Please, Moira – think about it!' Rosemary sobbed.

Moira knew she was crossing a line that she could never uncross, if she agreed to this. Her agreement to keep quiet and agree to all their plans would seal her own fate. But the alternative of going against them and remaining in Druid with her mother was hard to contemplate. The idea of going to France to train was something she had dreamed about but at what cost? What lies?

But, as she looked at Rosemary, she knew she wouldn't throw her to the wolves. She just prayed that their plan worked, and it saved some of the pain for the little girl.

'Alright,' she whispered.

Rosemary hugged her. 'Thank you, Moira, I will never forget you for doing this.'

CHAPTER 30

It was almost dawn when Moira heard Julia screaming. She ran up the stairs just as Desmond was coming out of the room where his dead wife lay. Moira was taken aback by the haunted and aged look on his face, his body hunched like that of a man much older than his years. How could someone change in so few hours, she wondered. They both went towards the door just as Ida came out of her bedroom and put her hands up to them to halt them in their tracks.

'Desmond, let me handle this,' she ordered. 'Moira, you remain outside the door. I will call you in to her in a minute. Remember now – it was a dream, a terrible dream.'

Desmond turned around, defeated and lost, and went back to his dead wife. Moira stood outside, and she could hear Ida speaking to the child, telling her that she had a nightmare.

'My mommy had a knife and then she fell into the flames!' Julia cried.

'Nonsense, pet, your mother is gone back to Dublin. You just had a bad dream.'

'No! No! It was not a dream! Where is my mommy?' Julia cried.

'Of course it was a dream, pet. *Moira, come inside, please!*' Ida called out to the hall where she was standing.

Moira stepped inside. Going to the bed, she sat down beside Julia. The child instantly put her arms around her, her little hands warm, trusting against her cheek.

'You saw her in the big fire!' Julia cried.

Moira took a deep breath, trying to steady her voice. Julia clung to her and she inhaled the aroma of roses from her hair and smoothed her curls down, making soothing sounds.

'Mama, Mama! I want my mama!'

'Hush, love, hush, it will be alright,' Moira whispered into her ear, praying that she had the strength not to break down herself and begging God's forgiveness for the lies that she was about to tell the child.

'Moira, can you tell Julia that she just had a terrible dream? She seems to think something awful happened last night,' Ida said, giving her a warning look.

Moira could feel her legs going to jelly. She pulled Julia from her embrace. Big fat tears filled the child's eyes, her bottom lip was quivering and her little body almost convulsing in shock.

'Julia, you just had a terrible dream, that's all. Everything is alright.' Moira's heart was breaking for the child.

'*But it really happened!*' Julia screamed.

'Nightmares are like that, pet. But that's all it was, a bad dream,' Moira said, trying to fight the tears herself. She pulled Julia close, hugging her tightly as the child wept and wept until finally exhaustion took over and the child's cries turned to a soft whimper. Slowly Moira lowered her back against the pillow and pulled the blankets tightly around her. Julia's eyes were closing. She had exhausted herself. Moira continued to caress her head to soothe her.

Ida came over to them, the aroma of Chanel Number 5 and cigarette smoke invading the air.

'Now, Julia, when you have another sleep everything will be better again. You are very tired, that's all. Close your eyes and we will stay with you until you sleep and then, when you awake, we are going back up to Dublin and I am going to buy you a beautiful doll! Okay?'

'I'm afraid. I want to see my mama. I saw a big fire and heard a big scream.'

'It was just a dream,' Moira reassured her.

'What if the dream comes back?' she asked, her blue eyes full of tears.

'Nonsense, you will have a pleasant dream this time. What are you going to call this doll?' Ida asked brightly.

'I don't know …'

'You can call her anything you like. Now back to sleep and then we will go back to Dublin and get that doll and go for tea in the Shelbourne.'

'Why did Mama leave?'

'She had to get some medicine,' Ida said. 'Now you are not to worry about anything.'

'But when can I see her?'

'Soon, very soon,' Ida replied.

Moira was shocked at how the child seemed to believe it. Soon she was asleep again.

'She has taken the bait. Now all we have to do is reassure her,' Ida said.

'But what will we tell her about her mother?'

'Leave that to me – for now all she needs to know is that it was a dream. She is leaving here with me as soon as we can.'

Mr Berne arrived, after cutting through the fallen trees, and nothing of the night's events was told to him.

Moira could hear Mr Williams talking to Harry outside the back door.

''Tis a sad day that the big oak has fallen. I will have it sawn up,' Mr Berne said.

'Great, and I need to find a phone as quickly as possible. I have some urgent business that needs attending to,' Harry said.

Moira noted that there was no mention of the fact that Mrs Griffith was lying dead upstairs.

'Very well, Mr Williams. I can drive you and at least if we come to a fallen tree we can try move it. It might not be as bad further on. Maybe Ennis. You can at least send a telegram.'

'Yes, I can. Oh, another thing. I have had second thoughts about the house, I'm afraid. I am postponing my plans about the renovations. I am leaving it as it is. But I won't be able to get back down for a while, so I plan to lock it up and bring the horses and dogs back to a little place that I have in Wicklow. Don't worry, I will look after you and Mrs Berne financially and of course you will remain in the lodge.'

Moira was busy making tea, but she noticed that Mr Berne looked almost relieved.

'Very well, Mr Williams. Whatever you decide.'

As soon as the roads were safe enough, Ida left, taking Julia with her to Dublin. Mr Berne and Mr Williams went in front to make sure the roads were clear. If they were, they would let her continue.

At eleven o'clock Harry arrived back.

'Ida has gone on with Julia. Poor little thing looks as white as a fairy.'

'I'll never forget her little face,' Moira said.

'I managed to get through to whom I needed to. The plans are set. We leave later tonight.'

At four o'clock a black van arrived. Mr Berne had gone on a message for Mr Williams. Moira was in the kitchen with Rosemary. Harry had told them to stay there.

Half an hour later he arrived in and told them that the body of Mrs Griffith was taken away and Desmond had also left in his car. Moira scrubbed the room where she had laid and knelt and said a decade of the Rosary for her soul.

She was making a cup of tea later that evening when Rosemary turned on the radio. The news was on. The newscaster Charles Mitchell said that the Taoiseach Jack Lynch had sent condolences to the Griffith family on the sudden passing of Mrs Florence Griffith. He added that Mrs Florence Griffith, the late wife of Desmond Griffith, had become suddenly unwell in her home in Dublin and had died on route from her home to the hospital.

Moira blessed herself and said another prayer. It had been done. There was no going back now.

Rosemary remained with her at the house. Ida knew nothing of the turn of events regarding Rosemary and believed that Rosemary had decided to stay and help Moira to lock up the house and would travel back with Harry later.

As seven o'clock Moira made what she knew would be her last trip to her home. The Mission was still on and most of the parishioners including her parents were in the church. She took a battered suitcase down from a press in the hall and threw her few clothes into it and her precious cookery books. She tidied her bedroom and left nothing out of place. Her mother wouldn't notice that she had taken anything at first glance. As she was putting her case in the boot, she looked back at the house. She tried to think of some happy memories, but there was always a sense of control within the walls of the house – a feeling that dampened even the joyous moments. She thought of her grandmother who had given her such a love of cooking and knew that she was with her now. She closed the door and, awash with emotion, she got back into her car and drove back to Lenashee.

At eleven o'clock they locked up the house and Harry drove off, Moira driving behind him with Rosemary in the car with her. As she drove along the avenue Moira looked out into the darkness and thought of the young bride that had drowned herself and of Florence Griffith who had lost her life in Lenashee. Was there something in the house, that was almost evil, that had driven these women to their deaths? She got out of the car to check the boot and looked back down the drive. The trees were fully leaved now and there was a hint of jasmine in the air. She knew that whatever happened from now on, this house would remain in her memory for the rest of her life.

She parked the car discreetly just outside of the town of Ennis. It would be a day or two before it was found. She popped a letter to her mother and father in a post box saying that she was leaving. Then with Harry and Rosemary she travelled to Dublin. They didn't risk going back to Rosemary's flat in case the gardaí were looking for her in connection with the events of her missing uncle.

They would stay there for one night in a flat in Dublin belonging to Harry and then take a flight to London the following morning. But first they had to carry out the next part of the plan. Moira watched the city lights that added to the feeling of being almost in a dream. Had she just run away? Had she really conspired to lie about the death of Mrs Griffith? They drove out of the city for a few miles and she could see the sea again.

'This is Howth, Moira,' Harry told her.

They were all quiet, full of their own thoughts.

Then Harry parked the car and Moira got out. Under the cover of darkness, she put a coat, hat, and shoes with an old library book with Rosemary Purcell's name on it, discreetly in a little pile on the pier, making sure that no one saw her. Then she walked back to the car and they drove to the flat that Harry had on North Wall with a For Sale sign on it. But Harry had the keys. He let them in and lit a fire. He had told Moira to bring some food from the kitchen of Lenashee and she laid out some sandwiches, tea and milk. Rosemary ate nothing – Moira could see a terrible fear had gripped her. After Harry left, Rosemary lay down and Moira covered her with a blanket.

'I'm afraid, Moira.'

'I know.'

'What I did ...'

'You don't have to tell me ... it's probably better that you don't.'

'My sister... I needed to protect her.'

'I know.'

'I'm in love with Harry.'

'Is he with you too?'

'I think so.'

'I see.'

'Do you think I am a terrible person?'

'No.'

'I'm so sorry, Moira.'

'I hope the child will be alright.'

'I know. The poor thing,' Rosemary whispered.

Moira held her hand and squeezed it.

'Get some rest if you can,' Moira said softly.

A man in a dark suit and a strong Dublin accent knocked

on the door at six the next morning and told them that Harry had sent him. He handed them flight tickets, documents for travel and money. They left with him for the airport.

Moira bought a newspaper while they waited. She had never been on a plane before and either had Rosemary. She opened the newspaper and there looking at her was a portrait photograph of Florence Griffith. She read the short article. Moira thought she looked utterly beautiful. Like the film star Maureen O'Hara.

Sadness is felt amongst Dublin's elite and political society today at the news of the passing of Florence Griffith, wife of Desmond Griffith, son of the former Minister Charlie Griffith. It is confirmed that she died from a bleed to the brain on route to hospital from her home where she had complained of a bad headache only an hour earlier. Her sudden passing has left the family in shock and grief at the loss of the young mother of two. She will be privately waked at home in a closed casket. Funeral Mass will be in Donnybrook and her remains interred at Glasnevin Cemetery. The Taoiseach and his wife will be in attendance and the funeral Mass will be celebrated by the Primate of Ireland and Archbishop of Dublin, John Charles McQuaid.

Harry's plan had worked. He had connections in all walks of life who could do him favours. As the plane soared into the sky for London, Moira held her breath. As she crossed the Irish Sea, she made a promise to herself never to return. She knew that if she were to cope, she could never look back. She thought of her mother who would damn the day she was ever born, her brothers whom she had never felt close to and then she thought of her father. Although she knew he would miss her terribly, she also believed that he might be relieved that she got away. Then she thought of Druid, the land and the rivers, the smell of hawthorn and the sound of a curlew at dawn. Silent tears poured down her face. Please, God, she thought, give me strength and forgive me for what I have done.

Heathrow was like nothing she had ever witnessed. She had never saw so many people and the first of many fears entered her soul, questioning herself and what she was doing. Here she would part ways with Rosemary. They both thought it better to make their own way now, especially for Rosemary's sake – she needed to disappear.

'I will never forget you, Moira. Never. I hope you have a good life,' Rosemary said, crying.

Moira could hardly see her with the tears. She hugged her back and then they both walked away from each other. Moira was bound for Paris.

Harry was true to his word. He told her that he had arranged everything. He had arranged a place for her to stay, French lessons and managed to get her into the Cordon Blue School of Cooking. She said a silent prayer of thanks but then her excitement was darkened. As she waited at the airport for her flight to Paris, she thought of the last moments at Lenashee and her conversation with Mr Griffith.

She was settling the boot and he was closing the gates of the drive.

'What will you do with the house?' she couldn't help asking.

'I have instructed that it is to be locked up.'

'For how long?'

'For good, Moira. Some houses are not meant to be opened and this is one of them.'

CHAPTER 31

Lenashee 2019

Julia could hear someone, but she had no idea who it was. She could feel herself being lifted and a man's voice telling her that she was okay.

'Where am I?'

'You are alright, love. We have you now,' he reassured her in a calm voice. 'You are in an abandoned house near the town of Druid. But we are taking you to hospital.'

She had no recollection of how she was there or what had happened. She could feel her body convulse and then someone injecting something into her arm … then oblivion. She closed her eyes as they shut the ambulance door.

When she awoke she was in a hospital bed and David was beside her.

'You frightened me so much,' he said hoarsely.

She looked around the room, barely registering that he was there. What had happened? Then flashes of Lenashee came back to her, images of a woman covered in blood, and she began to scream and pulled a line out of her arm. She scratched her face and pulled at her hair, all the time screaming. Again, someone injected something into her arm as she tried helplessly to flee … and again oblivion.

Time had passed again when she awoke. David was again beside her. This time she was calm.

'You have fractured some bones in your back, but they will heal … but you're not well, pet.'

She made no reply.

'They are moving you to the psychiatric hospital, Saint John of God,' he said softly.

She turned her face and closed her eyes. She felt nothing. She was numb.

'I have a private room for you, they will make you better there, Julia. I'm so sorry but you have to go.'

Two days later a porter wheeled her into Saint John of God. It felt familiar. Even though her last stay was many years ago, she had known that she would probably be back. They said her back was badly bruised from the fractures and the pain would ease but she was not here for her back. She knew her mind was broken and might take a lot longer to heal, the worrying part was she was not sure if she cared.

The days passed into weeks and she began to improve, every day a little stronger. Therapy and medication working to heal her mind. There were dark days behind those walls for her where she felt haunted by Lenashee. In her dreams it was calling her back and she cried out as it seemed to have developed long invisible arms that were reaching across land and sea to find her and bring her back to the house, the lake and the unknown happenings of the house. She dreamed of a woman with a battered face locked in a tomb alone in the woods. Her thoughts had become as mangled as the shrubs and plants that had become wild and intertwined from neglect at Lenashee. It was whispering at her, taunting her, and silently calling her back. She begged for more medication to make it stop. Eventually the whispering fell silent.

Two months to the day she had arrived David came to take her home. At first when the doctor suggested that she leave, she had not wanted to. How could she go back to her life, as if it had all never happened?

During her stay she had refused to talk of Lenashee or Druid or Rosemary Purcell. Her medication numbed it now. Frozen it all in time. But it had left her broken – almost dead inside. She had no desire to return to her life. She had grown accustomed to the routine of the hospital, being back in the world frightened her. On the journey home she had tried not to look at the colours that greeted her. Summer had become autumn, a beautiful autumn. Normally she would marvel at the colours but now it was as if her senses wanted to shut down. She did not want to see beauty, it seemed painful somehow to see it. Witness it.

The days passed. Slowly she began to feel some semblance of normality and began to do daily tasks. David had removed everything about Lenashee, all the cuttings from the paper were gone. He had even put away her laptop and phone and she spent her day reading, pottering, sleeping and walking. For David's sake she tried to rise above the desolate feelings that seemed to walk beside her now.

She watched him now, walking in from his studio, deep concern on his face. His easy way of life seemed to have deserted him for now. He was constantly watching her, constantly worried. He walked in and smiled at her, but she knew something was wrong.

He hit the button on the kettle and allowed it to boil.

'Is everything okay?' she asked.

'That was Joseph on the phone.'

'Oh!'

She had not visited her father since she had been hospitalised. She couldn't imagine how he must be now, how he was even alive. The doctor had told them that even with terminal cancer it could linger. Joseph had arrived at the hospital to see her, but it was too much, she was not ready. She had barely spoken to him. Since then, it was David who had kept in touch with him about her father. She knew that he was nearing the end.

'Yes. I'm afraid he's very weak. I don't think it will be long now. You don't have to go up if you are not up to it... but Joseph wanted you to know.'

Her mind was fragile but her beloved father was slipping away.

'No. I want to go. I want to see him,' she whispered.

'Are you sure that you are up to it, emotionally?'

'I have to go, David. I need to say goodbye.'

They got ready and were up in a couple of hours. Joseph was with him when they arrived, and Maggie greeted them, giving Julia a hug and making her and David tea. Julia cold see the strain on Maggie's face, her round soft face with her grey hair cut short. She was touching seventy and had run the house for her father for over thirty years, raising her own family at the same time. Julia knew that Maggie would be devasted at the loss of her father.

'How is he, Maggie?' David asked.

'He's unconscious now since yesterday. But he looks very peaceful,' she reassured them.

Joseph arrived down and hugged Julia. They both cried, glad to have each other. He went back up with her and led her into their father's bedroom.

Julia had to agree with Maggie. He did look peaceful. She kissed his forehead. Then she picked up the framed photograph of her mother and kissed it too.

By nightfall he slipped away peacefully. His secrets would go with him. Questions left unanswered, stories left unfinished. Secrets forever secrets. It was over.

CHAPTER 32

It was a week before Christmas Eve and Julia was beginning to get back to a little bit of work. Some days were still dark for her, very dark, but she fought it as best she could. Pushing herself to get outside every day, eat well, do mediation and thankfully the new meds were kicking in. She had even begun work on a new work project and was expecting a call from her editor about it. David was in his studio and she had decided to try to cook dinner. A vegetable ragu. She was just putting it on the hob when her phone rang with a number that she didn't recognise. It was an English number. She thought of not answering it. It was possibly a wrong number. She never gave her private number to anyone. Then on impulse she answered it.

'Hi.'

'Is this Julia Griffith?' said a very English-accented man.

'Yes, who is this?'

David arrived in.

'My name is Rupert Andrews. I am a good friend of Moira Fitzpatrick, the food writer. You rang our offices to try to get in touch with her and you left your number a few months ago.'

'I ...' Her heart was beating. She couldn't go back there. For David's sake as well as her own. She had to leave the house behind her now.

'Miss Fitzpatrick says she would really like to talk to you. She said it's important. She will fly out from Paris in a few days if you can meet her.'

'Oh! I don't think so.'

'I stress that Miss Fitzpatrick feels it is very important that you meet her.'

'I see ... Well, maybe for short time.'

'Is there somewhere that you might feel comfortable talking to her? I think she will meet you anywhere.'

'Yes, alright, I'll give you the address.'

'Who is it?' David asked, concerned.

'Can you hold the line for a moment, please.'

'Julia, who is it?' David asked.

'It's the chef that was in Lenashee. She wants to talk to me – is coming over especially from Paris.'

'I don't think that's a good idea. You know how sick you have been.'

'I know but I have to talk to her, I have not known something all my life – something that I cannot explain. I believe she has the answers. I don't know why, it's a gut feeling but I have to talk to her.'

CHAPTER 33

As Moira boarded her flight to Dublin her thoughts travelled back to when she had first arrived in Paris. Up until then she had never left Ireland and had rarely left Clare.

How strange and foreign Paris had been for her – the sky, the scents, the history, and the sounds. Paris had made her feel very much the intruder. She had left a land that she was so familiar with for one where everything was new. Pure panic had almost overwhelmed her that first day as she had first taken a seat on the smoke-filled Metro that would carry her into the centre of Paris.

Before they had left Dublin, Rosemary had taken some clothes from her own suitcase and given them to Moira to wear in Paris – a black cashmere jumper, a pale-blue Mary Quant miniskirt, a white silk blouse and a new black cigarette pants that was in her case not even worn. Although Rosemary was taller than Moira the clothes fit her with a little adjustment and with her hair cut and styled by Rosemary, her eyebrows darkened, and a light make-up applied, she began her transformation.

'When in Paris, one must dress like them,' Rosemary had told her that last evening that they had spent together.

She had discarded her brown skirt and faded white blouse and worn the trousers and blouse on the plane. Their shoe size was the same and Rosemary had given her a pair of black pumps.

Harry had arranged for a woman to look after her for her first two months in Paris. Madame Dupont, a tall thin woman who never seemed to smile, had met her from the plane and brought her on the Metro to the apartment that Harry had arranged. It was basic and clean with a bed, wardrobe, tiny kitchenette, and a dimly lit bathroom. She could hardly believe when Madam Dupont showed her Le Cordon Bleu, on Rue du Champ de Mer, and told her that she would begin there as a student under the renowned director Madame Brassart in one month, to train as a Cordon Blue chef. During the month prior to her commencement, she would have to learn as much French as possible as Madame Brassart would insist that she spoke only French. Madame Dupont gave her an allowance from Harry for the month, showed her where the nearest cheap café was and told her she would be back in the morning to begin her first French lesson. That first evening hunger had won out over fear and she had visited the café and through hand signals managed to order a Java café and a croissant. Biting into her first ever croissant was a memory that she had stored away to keep forever. Her love of all things French was not going away.

The following morning Madame Dupont arrived, and her French lessons began. In the afternoons she wandered Paris, marvelling at the architecture, the people, and losing herself in the labyrinth of ancient streets in search of a cheap café to try out her French and have a modest meal. Once the month was over she had some notion of the French language but was a long way off from being fluent.

Madame Dupont had given her clothes and books that were required for the school.

Madame Brassart had welcomed her to the school in impeccable French. Moira could feel herself shake as this petite woman with the palest of skin and piercing blue eyes showed her around and introduced her to the professor in charge. She was informed that 'her sponsor' had also paid for her to eat at the school. Harry's name was never mentioned and all she knew was that her fees were taken care of. There were people from all over the world training there so for the first time since arriving in Paris she did not feel alone. There was a young woman from the States called Madison who was taking the course with her and they became firm friends. Madame Brassart had made it known from the start how strict the school was going to be and how they expected one-hundred-percent commitment. She had paid a price to fulfil her dream, she had sworn secrecy at Lenashee for better or worse.

Slowly she began to relax and relish being in Paris. She fell into its rhythm and became part of it instead of looking in. She became comfortable sitting in a café and walking along the streets feeling something like belonging – inhaling the scent of baking from a boulangerie and sitting alone at a street café watching the sun go down. Slowly she fell completely in love with the City of Light.

She had thrown herself into her new life and vowed to never look back. She had excelled at the school and her career had begun. Once her education stopped so did her allowance and she did not hear from Harry or Madame Dupont again. Her family had never looked for her and she had never contacted them. Her note had told them that she was leaving and was not returning. It had been accepted. It would be harder to disappear today, she knew, but then it was relatively easy. Eventually her life in Ireland seemed like it had almost happened to someone else. Her secrets had remained silent.

But things changed after she had received the request from Julia to talk to her and she knew that she would have to confront the past. She had confided some of the story to Rupert. If he was shocked, he had hidden it well and held her hand and asked her how he could help.

She was glad he was with her now as they crossed the sea to Ireland. He had booked them into the Shelbourne Hotel for the night and then they would go to see Julia.

As they stepped from the plane and then took a taxi to the centre of Dublin, Moira could barely breathe. It was as if the ghost of her earlier self was with her pointing out how different everything was. She may have left Ireland in the swinging sixties but the Ireland of then was far from swinging under the weight of the Almighty Church and State.

They walked into the elegant reception of the Shelbourne and Rupert registered.

'Moira, my dear, shall I book dinner?' Rupert had interrupted her thoughts.

'I think I might have an early night.'

'Would you like me to send something up to you?' the receptionist asked politely.

Moira was taken aback. It was not as if she hadn't heard the Irish accent recently, she had, but to hear it here, in her home country, directed at her, affected her deeply.

'I'm not very hungry, perhaps some light soup,' she managed to say.

She felt a little shocked at the effect being here was having on her and she said a silent prayer that she was doing the right thing.

After her soup she took a long bath and eventually fell asleep. She was transported as she often was to Clare, Druid and Lenashee and the face of a child that she had never forgotten.

A light snow had fallen while she slept and, as she looked out at the hushed landscape of a white Dublin, she vowed that she would tell the truth today, whatever the outcome.

CHAPTER 34

They had arranged to meet at the house in Howth. Julia had not been there since her father had died. As David drove the car up the drive she noticed that the Christmas roses were in full bloom. The two dogs met them. David had not wanted her to meet with this woman. He had begged her to leave it. But eventually he had relented. The door opened and Joseph greeted them. She was glad to see that he was beginning to get some colour back in his face – the death of their father and his care had taken so much out of him. He was back working as a historian. As she walked into the sitting room, she thought how strange it was that her father was no longer there. She prayed he was at peace. They were early. She felt nervous somehow. Was it always better to know the truth, she wondered? She knew that Moira Fitzpatrick would have answers to her questions. She just hoped she was able for them.

Their car arrived. A very dapper, elegant man stepped out and held the door for Moira Fitzpatrick. Julia watched with curiosity through the living-room window. She was smaller than she had expected and a little frailer. Joseph had gone out to meet them.

When she arrived in Julia studied her. Small in stature and dressed as elegantly as any French dame but when she smiled there was something familiar about it as if she knew that smile. Why did this woman seem to hold the key to so much for her?

'Perhaps I will head out for a walk and leave you to it?' Joseph asked.

'Miss Fitzpatrick would like you to stay too,' Rupert said to him.

'Stay,' Julia said.

'Very well.'

David sat protectively on the corner of the armchair that Julia sat in. They were sitting in the conservatory. Julia thought of the day that she had tried to ask her Aunt Ida about Rosemary and Lenashee and how it had all gone horribly wrong. She watched Rupert with interest. He was so polished and so English. He stood up rather grandly and spoke.

'Thank you for meeting my incredibly good friend Moira. If it is alright, I will take a walk in your beautiful garden now and leave you alone.' With that, he walked out.

Julia had to grin as the two wolfhounds jumped up in glee when they saw him, much to his dismay.

'My wife has been through a lot recently and I don't want her upset,' David warned Moira.

'I need the truth, David – that's all I ask,' Julia whispered. She looked over at Moira. 'I believed that somehow that house and I are connected. It felt so important to me. I became consumed by it. I'm bipolar and have suffered with my mental health since I was nineteen. My husband is rightly concerned. But if there is something about that house that connects me to it, I need to know. Even if it is going to hurt me.'

'What I am about to tell you is difficult and I have no idea if you will be able to handle it,' Moira said worriedly.

'Well, the past has proven that, without the truth, life is difficult too. Please tell me what you know.'

Moira took a deep breath and then she looked out into the garden as if she were reimagining the past. Then, just above a whisper, she began to speak.

'We decided to keep the truth from you to protect you. We weaved a web of lies,' Moira said.

Her voice didn't falter and Julia warmed to her immediately.

Then Moira looked intently at Julia.

'Your mother, from what I heard, loved you deeply. But she became ill after her second child – after you, Joseph.' Moira looked at Joseph who was sitting on an armchair across from Julia.

'She died so many years ago, soon after I was born. I never knew that she was unwell after I was born,' Joseph said.

'I met her a few months after you were born. At Lenashee. I was a cook and had been hired to cook for the family for a week. I was told by the housekeeper that your mother was in a psychiatric hospital for a few weeks before she arrived at the house. Being treated for what they called 'the baby blues'. A private hospital called Saint Margaret's. I'm not sure if it still exists. I'm not sure if you knew even this much.'

'No, I had no idea,' Julia said.

Joseph shook his head too.

'You were never told this?' Moira asked, looking from one of them to the other.

'No. Never,' Julia said.

'Well, she was brought to Lenashee to recuperate.

Joseph, you were as far as I know in the care of a nanny in Dublin but, Julia, you were there – it was there that I met you.'

'I remember,' Julia said. 'I remember something now, and Rosemary – she was there too?'

'Yes, she was and your Aunt Ida and your Uncle Harry. When I first saw your mother, she was very frail and had almost to be carried to her bedroom by your father – to be honest, she looked far too ill to be away in the wilds of the West of Ireland. She was not well at all and refused to eat anything. Unfortunately, we did not realise just how ill she was. I believe now that your mother had severe post-natal depression. But you must remember that this was the sixties in Ireland and such illnesses were less researched. But I am afraid that's not all. I am no expert, as I said, but I have researched it over the years and your mother was extremely unwell. I believe she had something called post-natal psychosis. I am not sure but it's possible it was left undiagnosed. Within those few days your mother lost all reason and now I need to tell you the most difficult part that has haunted my memory and is as clear today as it was then.'

David caught Julia's hand as Moira told them the sorry tale of her mother's death and the cover-up surrounding it. Not leaving out anything. There was silence when she had finished. It was as if everything that they ever knew was suspended for now.

'I dropped the lamp,' Julia said. 'Oh my god, I remember.'

'Yes, but it was just an accident. A terrible accident. When that terrible sound filled the house your mother just seemed to fall,' Moira said, fighting the tears.

'I knew something terrible happened there. I could feel it. Do you think my mother went mad and threw herself off the landing?' Julia whispered.

'Are you telling us that you think there was a presence

there, something that frightened her and made her fall?'
Joseph asked.

'I really don't know. Your uncle was sure it was a tree
falling like the beautiful oak that had fallen and we just
thought the sound came from the house. But whatever it
was your poor mother had lost all reason – she was very
ill and perhaps the sound made her lose the small bit of
balance that she had and sent her to her death.'

'Julia, I remember something,' said Joseph. 'I found
some books of Dad's on that very subject. It was all about
post-partum psychosis. I asked him why he was reading
about it, but he got anxious and didn't really answer me,
but it irked me. My god, our poor mother!'

'Julia? Julia, are you okay?' David asked.

Julia had gone quiet. She stood up and looked out the
window at the garden.

'I dreamed of it. All those nightmares, all those years.
It was because of this.'

'On that night it was decided not to tell you,' Moira
said. 'I am so sorry.'

'But Rosemary, what about her?' Julia asked. 'Did she
commit suicide?'

'Rosemary had her own demons and she needed to
disappear. That's all I am going to say on that. Harry
helped her and I left her shoes and personal stuff on Howth
Pier. She left Ireland the same time that I did. Harry gave
me the money to begin in France. I could never explain any
of this to my mother, so I just left. It was a different time,
and it was quite easy to disappear and begin again.'

'Did you ever see Rosemary again?' Julia asked.

'No. We thought it better and safer to have no contact.
However, I do think that your Uncle Harry and Rosemary
grew close. I read an article on her many years ago from

a London magazine. She said in the article that she had an affair with a married man for thirty years until he died. She had a boutique and had won many awards for it.'

'Do you think the married man was Uncle Harry?' Joseph asked.

'Yes, I do.'

'My father kept asking about her,' Joseph said.

'Yes, I did wonder at this. As far as I know Harry never told your father what really happened to Rosemary. So, your father possibly believed that she did drown on Howth Pier that night. But that's all. There was never a relationship between him and Rosemary. I have told you everything but one of the most important things that I can tell you is that I heard from all of them how much your mother loved you both.'

'Why now? Why decide to fly over her and tell us all this now?' Joseph said.

'I can see why you would ask me that, Joseph, and I wish I had a good enough answer. But ever since Julia rang the office I could not forgive myself for my part in her deception. I have struggled with it all these years and then I came to a decision that I must tell you.'

'Julia? Julia, are you alright?' David asked worriedly.

Julia was looking for something in her bag. She pulled out the photograph of her mother from the leather wallet that she kept it in.

'Joseph, could you get me Dad's magnifying glass, please?' Julia asked.

Joseph looked shaken. He nodded and got up. He arrived back in a few minutes with it. Julia took it from him and examined the photograph. Then her eyes brimmed with tears.

'What is it?'

'It's a hatpin that I found at Lenashee. It's of a peacock.

It's here in the summer hat on my mother. I knew it meant something that day. There is so much to say, so much to digest. But there is something that has shifted for me. All my life I was searching for something. At times it has nearly made me lose my mind. At last I now know what it was.' She touched the photograph and the tears flowed down her face. 'It was simply the truth. I was searching for the truth. I witnessed my mother's death. I was there. I know now why at times I can barely breathe. It's like what happened there was locked away in my mind, but always there to almost choke me. Even though I didn't know why there was a terrible pain crucifying me. I thought it was in my head. Driving me mad at times. Now at least I know why.'

'I'm so sorry, Julia, for my part in this,' Moira said, her voice breaking with emotion. 'If it had been today, she would have got the proper treatment and her life and yours would have been quite different. It was a vastly different Ireland. Please know that you know the truth now.'

'I know it sounds ridiculous, but, Joseph, I feel our mother wanted us to know the truth. I think that's why I found Lenashee. She led me there.'

'But why the cover-up? Why did they go to such lengths to hide it all?' David asked.

'It was Ireland of the sixties. This would have been a huge scandal, mental illness was not understood and certainly not accepted, the family was well connected with the State and the Church and there would have been questions – also it could have looked like they had drugged your mother. To this day I still don't know how your mother got up and went out that night – she was so weak – it was as if there was something unexplainable in the house. Something that frightened her so much that it gave her the strength to get out in that storm.'

'You mentioned the Church? Why?' Joseph asked.

'The Archbishop of Dublin – John Charles McQuaid was a close friend of the family. In those times he was like the King of Ireland, and he made sure that it was a pure country with no scandal.'

'Do you think he knew of what happened?'

'After everything I have heard of the Church in Ireland nothing would surprise me, but I know that your Uncle Harry and your Aunt Ida were close friends of the bishop. Ida was the queen of the social diaries, everyone knew the Griffiths, your mother's name would have made headline news if the truth was out and in ways your aunt thought she was protecting you, Julia.'

'She was also protecting her own name and place in society it seems,' David replied dryly.

'But surely the doctor in the hospital could see how sick our mother was?' Joseph asked.

'As I said I have studied this. It was possibly diagnosed as a very serious case of postpartum depression but not postpartum psychosis which is extremely severe with a variety of symptoms including hallucinations and violent or suicidal thoughts. She deteriorated rapidly once she got to Lenashee.'

'She had lost her mind,' Julia whispered.

'Yes, I really do believe she had, Julia,' Moira said.

'Do you believe there was something in the house that drove her to it? When I was there at Lenashee, as beautiful as it is, it was as if there was something about it, something sinister … was there something there that literally shoved her over the edge, to her death?

'I think that's why your uncle ordered it to be locked up. But I think your mother was just unwell,' Moira said gently.

'Did you know that a young woman drowned herself in the lake hundreds of years ago?'

'Yes, local folklore had it that she went mad. I saw her portrait and she was very beautiful. Her portrait was damaged during the storm which at the time seemed like a premonition to me. I told you that your mother had a shroud on her when she died and she must have taken it from the room where the portraits were hanging.'

'Yes, I saw the portrait and I found a silver cross with some old photographs – did my mother own it?'

'When she died – all she had on was the shroud and the cross and chain. Your father must have taken it off later. There was something strange about that room. It has haunted me and especially the face of the young woman in the portrait.'

'The poor woman, she is buried alone in the woods,' Julia said almost to herself. 'Never to escape.'

'Julia, are you alright?' David asked.

'Yes, yes, I am. Thankfully I am.'

Later that day. Julia visited the graveyard where her mother was buried beside her father. She wept as she left a bunch of roses on the grave. It was a calm day and despite the cold a winter sun was shining down.

'Sleep peacefully now, my beautiful mother whom I loved, and know how sorry I am that you suffered so much. Thank you for guiding me to Lenashee and allowing me to know the truth.' She wept.

But, as she walked away, she felt a sudden lightness. She would not be haunted by what happened all those years ago anymore. Moira was right. Dear brave Moira who had travelled to tell her the truth. She looked over at David who was standing by the car. He smiled at her and she smiled back. She would never visit Lenashee again.

She thought of the house that had consumed her all these months. Now she knew it had, unknown to her, consumed her all her life. She thought of the light from the dome, the grand staircase and the lake, the library room, and the lonely tomb deep in the wood. It was over now, and it could no longer haunt her. Thanks to Moira, she could begin again and leave the memories of the lake house at Lenashee locked forever behind those rusted iron gates.

THE END

Now that you're hooked why not try

THE SECRET OF EVELINE HOUSE

also published by Poolbeg.com

Here's a sneak preview of Chapter One.

THE SECRET OF EVELINE HOUSE

CHAPTER 1

New Year's Eve 1949

Draheen, Ireland

Violet Ward's elegant frame, sheathed in a jade-green silk dress, shimmered with tiny glass beads as she walked swiftly from room to room in her home, Eveline House. Her dark hair was pinned up in a tight chignon, her high cheekbones enhanced with just a touch of colour, her lips a ruby-red set against alabaster skin, a string of pearls around her delicate neck.

She looked behind the red-velvet chaise longue in the drawing room for her daughter Sylvia, checking to see if the little girl had crouched there as she often did. Sometimes Sylvia would take her dolls and create a perfect little world there or behind the shelter of the heavy gold-velvet drapes.

She hoped that Sylvia's sensitive little ears had not overheard Betsy Kerrigan, their housekeeper, whispering to her earlier, relaying the latest vicious gossip that she had overheard at Miss Doheny's grocery store that day.

Betsy had been putting the bag of sugar she had just purchased into her bicycle basket when Nelly Cooke rushed into the shop, leaving the door ajar. Nelly had just come from a parochial meeting of the 'church ladies' of

Draheen and was almost shouting across the counter in excitement as she delivered her latest gossip. Betsy had overheard every vindictive word against her employer.

'Nelly Cooke said that you were evil and that the Devil was surely in you, to go and write what you have written. She said that the bishop himself would not be able to absolve you of your sins. Miss Doheny said that you were possibly cursed. Nelly Cooke then said that she had warned the women at the meeting to keep their young people away from you for fear of the Devil getting into them.' Betsy shook her head in disgust. 'Such a group of auld hypocrites! There they are at the church every morning, scrubbing the altar until it shines, making sure the flowers are not allowed to even *think* of wilting, and not a Christian bone in their bodies! I am so sorry, Mrs Ward, but I felt I had better let you know so you can be on your guard. That Nelly Cooke is nothing but an auld sleeveen! Oh, an awful sleeveen of a woman!' Betsy put her hands on her hips as if she was ready to thrash the lot of them for saying a word against her employer. 'My mother always said that there was more religion in a stick of wood than in the whole body of Nelly Cooke. Of course, Agnes the Cat is the ringleader of the lot of them and her tongue is pure evil.'

Agnes the Cat lived alone in a small house at the bottom of the town and was known to have at least thirty cats in the house with her.

Violet had felt sickened as she listened to Betsy. Her first play, *Unholy Love*, certainly flew in the face of Irish Catholic morality. She had expected hostility from the people of Draheen but she had never expected such vitriolic attacks.

Violet had known how the townspeople felt about her from her earliest days in Draheen. A few days after their arrival she had met Miss Doheny on the road outside Eveline

House. A tall rake of a woman with skin so thin it was almost transparent, skinny purple lips and hair secured in a tight grey bun, Miss Doheny had not held back. She had told her in vivid detail how Father Cummins had announced from the pulpit that a notorious playwright and her family were taking up residence in Eveline House. He had informed them in no uncertain terms that her first play, which had been put on in London, was unchristian in every way. He said that Draheen was a good Catholic town and it needed no scandal. Miss Doheny had not given Violet time to respond to this but had jumped on her bicycle and cycled off.

Later, of course, Violet had heard in further detail about the priest's rant from Betsy, after the housekeeper had come to work at Eveline House.

Betsy would never forget it till her dying day.

'*You will be cursed to damnation if you even talk about this play or to this woman who has penned such filth!*' he had roared. '*I believe an illegal copy of this ungodly script has found its way to our town. I forbid any of my parishioners to have anything to do with it – or the writer of it, I might add. If you do, you should never enter this church again. In fact, I forbid you to!*'

Violet knew that it was very unlikely anyone in Draheen would ever see a performance of the play and, even if there was an illegal copy of the script in the town, most of the townspeople would be too afraid to look at it. The play was, of course, banned in Ireland by the severe censorship laws. Obviously, Father Cummins himself had got his hands on a copy as he seemed to be such an expert on it.

It turned out that indeed an illegal copy of the script had somehow found its way to the town. A love story between a priest and a young woman, the dogeared script was literally pulled apart as a group of girls tried to read separate pieces at the same time and then swap them over. Father Cummins was alerted by one of their mothers. The pages of the play were gathered together and delivered into the safe hands of the priest who promised to pray for the souls of those who had dared to read it. Betsy was a horrified witness when he threw the torn sheets down in the street and stamped on them like a child in a temper tantrum.

Things appeared to quieten down a little as time passed and, when a neighbour who had lived down the road from Eveline died, Henry persuaded Violet to attend the Requiem Mass.

They took Sylvia with them. They set out, Violet wearing her fur stole of steel grey over a stylish burgundy suit, with her hair pinned up under a black half-hat and her chin held high, Henry dressed impeccably in a pinstripe suit, tie and navy Crombie coat, and Sylvia all in blue.

Violet had gone to Mass on rare occasions in London but stepping into a church in Ireland was almost overpowering. The aroma of the lingering incense and the stillness that permeated the air triggered deep emotion in her. Whatever her belief, Catholicism was in her bones. There was no removing herself from it. In the same way, Ireland was part of her consciousness. In London, when she slept, she had dreamt of Ireland, a dark brooding landscape that had captured her soul.

But her emotional response to being in the church was soon swept away.

That morning, the priest was not concerned about praying for the deceased – it was the presence of Violet Ward that ignited his sermon.

'We have a darkness in our midst! Mrs Ward forgot her religion when she was writing such filth. She is a shame to Ireland, a shame to the Church and its teachings. The Devil found her on the streets of London!' Then he shouted from the pulpit as all the parishioners stared at Violet with their mouths open. '*Well, not here! Not here! Not in my parish!*'

Violet wrapped her fur stole tightly around her. Protectively she put her arm around Sylvia to shield her from the priest's abuse. Sylvia had started to tremble. Violet wanted to get up and run as far away as possible, but she was frozen to the spot.

Henry was sitting beside her and she could feel the anger building in him at the priest's outburst. He stood up to his six feet and walked purposefully towards the pulpit.

The congregation held their breath. They had never seen the like of it before. Nobody ever confronted Father Cummins like that. He expected a huge level of respect and if one of the parishioners happened to be on the road when he drove his shiny Morris Minor at speed down the town, well, they simply jumped out of the way. He was the priest after all. Now, here was Henry Ward walking threateningly up to him as if he was just anyone and not the parish priest of Draheen!

When Henry reached the pulpit, he stood and stared up at the priest.

'You should be ashamed of yourself, shouting at my wife as you just did!' he spat at him. '*How dare you? I demand an apology!*'

The priest's face became purple and his eyes bulged.

The congregation were wide-eyed and were afraid to blink, expecting him to explode into tiny bits.

'*Get out! Get out!*' he shouted, spit spraying from his mouth. '*You have no place in this House of God! Let the fires of Hell judge you and your kind! Get out!'*

Henry Ward looked in disgust at him, then he turned to the congregation.

'You are as bad as him, if you allow this. Have you no shame?'

Then he walked back down and put his hand out to Violet and the other to Sylvia. They rose and took his hands and, as they walked silently down the aisle, every eye was on them.

A few weeks after the church episode Father Cummins had a heart attack and died. Betsy told Violet that he was resting after an enormous dinner of roast lamb with all the trimmings when his eyes bulged, and it was as if his heart exploded and drove him six feet under.

There were many who blamed Violet for his death – not Henry, even though he was the one who confronted the priest, but her – and the gossips eagerly went on the attack. There were even whispers that she had cursed him.

The young curate Father Quill took Father Cummins' place. Father Quill was a tall handsome man with a gentle air about him. Much to the outrage of his flock, he befriended the Wards and began to visit Eveline House quite often. He told Violet over the odd glass of sherry that he was sorry Ireland had closed the door to her theatrical achievements and apologised for the treatment she and her family had received from Father Cummins.

But the Wards never ventured into the church again.

Ireland had indeed shut Violet out. She had expected it though. So many books and plays were banned. The census was severe and anything that was not about horses or the 1916 Rising seemed to be scrutinised and banned from penetrating Ireland's pure shores. If it gave as much as a hint of promiscuity, adultery, homosexuality or contraception it was banned. She was aware that her second play *The Lightship* fell foul of these laws, so her future in Draheen promised to be even rockier than the present.

Seeing Violet become more and more disturbed by the situation, Betsy tried to reassure her. She told her not to worry as most of the townspeople were just curious about her, and that possibly the women were hostile because the men had never seen anyone as elegant as her and were fascinated by her.

'I heard Timmy Moore describe you as having the looks and allure of Vivien Leigh,' she said with a giggle. 'His wife almost gave him a wallop right there in Miss Doheny's shop. Miss Doheny had to beg her to calm herself and told Timmy Moore to go to Confession for having such thoughts!'

Violet had laughed but she increasingly had huge misgivings about their return to Ireland.

Also available on poolbeg.com

KILBRIDE HOUSE

SHEILA FORSEY

Kilbride House is set on the mystical Dingle
Peninsula. Victoria Goulding, a Protestant, falls in love with
Canice Meagher, born on the Blasket Islands
and a Roman Catholic. To be together they must elope.
Before their escape, the hand of fate plays its cards
and changes their lives irrevocably.

Sixty-three years later, in the leafy suburbs of New York,
Edith Goulding, Victoria's sister, has died. Edith left Ireland
in the winter of 1955 all those years ago, never to return.
In her will she has insisted that her daughter Catherine
and granddaughter Lainey visit Kilbride.

Kilbride House, despite all its grandeur, holds shocking
memories within its walls – memories that have slipped
through the cracks of time. As the ghosts awaken the lies
begin to unravel, and everything is altered. The past
cannot remain untold.

**A STORY OF ENDURING LOVE, SIBLING LOYALTY
AND A SECRET PACT THAT LASTS A LIFETIME**

ISBN 978-178199-773-4